ESCAPE THE DEEP

ESCAPE THE DEEP

THE HEINOUS CRIMES OF SARA SLICK™ BOOK 1

ST BRANTON   CM RAYMOND   LE BARBANT

DISRUPTIVE IMAGINATION

LMBPN Publishing
PMB 196, 2540 South Maryland Pkwy
Las Vegas, NV 89109

First US edition, June, 2020
ebook ISBN: 978-1-64202-972-7
Print ISBN: 978-1-64202-973-4

THE ESCAPE THE DEEP TEAM

Thanks to our Beta Readers
John Ashmore, Larry Omans, Kelly O'Donnell, Robert
Brooks, Mary Morris, Rachel Beckford

Thanks to our JIT Readers

Dave Hicks
Micky Cocker
Peter Manis
Deb Mader
Paul Westman
Angel LaVey

Editor

SkyHunter Editing Team

PROLOGUE

"The shipment is on track. Everything is unfolding according to plan," a heavily cloaked figure whispered as Aldrich hurried to catch up in the dark passage.

"Good to hear." Aldrich hesitated, hoping to control the nervousness in his voice. "Has anything been done about the…leak?"

"I told you there is no leak. No one knows what we're doing or what we have planned," Hobbes insisted.

Aldrich tried to let that sink in while picking up his pace to catch up again.

"It's not that I don't trust you," he replied while ducking to avoid a rock formation that hung low from the ceiling. "I know this plan is—"

"This *plan* is impeccable," Hobbes shot back. "I have thought through every detail."

"I know you've thought this through. But what if someone else has uncovered the details as well?"

Dark eyes cut through the space between them.

"What reason do you have to suspect that?" Hobbes asked.

"I hear…"

Halfway through Aldrich's answer, a sound in an off-shooting corridor stopped him. Hobbes pressed a finger across pursed lips and sent him a glare heavy with warning. The international sign for *shut the hell up before we both die.*

"I told you," Aldrich breathed, pointing with one finger toward the sound, although in the darkness neither of them could see its origin.

"Perhaps we should finish this in private," Hobbes muttered.

They hurried along the passage and around a corner. It seemed to lead to a dead-end, but Hobbes uttered a spell and melted the wall with a brush of one hand along its length. The liquefied stone flowed in front of them to create a set of steps leading down into a hidden portion of the lair.

The staircase disappeared as soon as they stepped from it, replaced by a solid wall behind them. Hobbes flicked his hand to light torches on the wall, and they took seats at a scarred and battered butcher block table in the center of the room.

"Someone was there," Aldrich said. "They were listening."

"It's fine. I doubt they heard anything, and no one can access this chamber. You need to stop worrying. As I said, the shipment will be arriving exactly according to schedule. This is all going to work out perfectly," Hobbes assured him.

"If someone has figured out what we're doing and reports us…"

"That won't happen. No one knows what we're planning. And even if they do, I found the perfect scapegoat. Any blame will fall on them," Hobbes told him with an evil smile.

"Who?" Aldrich asked.

"A human."

CHAPTER ONE

I deleted the sentence for the tenth time and rewrote it. Squinting at the computer screen, I read the new words and tried to decide if I liked them. After jumbling the thought around so many times, it was starting to blur, and I wasn't entirely sure it made sense anymore. But it had to be perfect.

My small TV blared in the background. Dad always scolded me for doing homework with the tube on, but garbage television provided the perfect background noise. I looked up from my computer. It was a new show, one my sisters were going wild for—a teen romance called *Vampire Diaries*. I couldn't help but laugh.

Who the hell cares about vampires anymore?

I sighed, then turned back to my work. This lit analysis paper made up twenty percent of my term grade, and I needed to pull off an A. Going to the college I wanted meant locking down a high GPA and getting a scholarship. The flickering cursor of judgment reminded me that the sentence eluding me was only the middle of the third paragraph, and I had five pages to go.

Fortunately, it was my last assignment of the night. The rest of my homework sat finished on the corner of my desk, and when I completed the paper, I fully intended to land face-first in my bed and stay there for as long as possible. Which probably meant until right after sunrise when one of my little siblings would rush me, needing something.

I didn't mind. Some extra sleep would be nice, but sometimes the morning rush scored me some warm toddler-style snuggles. Keeping them happy during the day and seeing my overworked father smile when he saw us made it worth it. I knew it was what my mother would have wanted.

My phone buzzed on the desk beside my computer. I picked it up to glance at the screen. A text from my best friend Ally stared back at me.

"Come outside."

"Now?"

It was well after midnight, but the squeal of tires coming around the corner didn't leave much time for consideration. Pushing the curtain to the side, I peered out at the street. Ally overshot the house, hopped the curb, and smashed through a sign in the neighbor's yard.

"Well, shit," I mumbled.

She threw her hand-me-down station wagon into reverse. It churned a few times like it was struggling for breath before reluctantly getting into gear.

It turned out there was no smooth way to back off a corrugated plastic sign.

I lifted the window and scrambled out onto the low, flat roof of the porch. By the time I wriggled down the huge oak to the side of the house, the station wagon was rocking back and forth across the grass. Ally leaned out her window, and I waved to get her attention.

"Ally! What the hell?" I hissed as the scraping sounds of plastic on metal from under the car started to resemble the screams of a cat caught in a blender.

"Just a little mishap. Apologize to the sign for me."

"Are you drunk?" I asked when she finally gave up and stopped moving the car.

Her dark, almond-shaped eyes slid over to glare at me.

"I am *not* drunk. If anything, the car's the drunk one," she said angrily.

"Ally…"

"I'm not! The only alcohol I consumed tonight was completely by accident. Blame it on Sam… Peter… Jose? That guy. You know, that guy in biology who has a crush on me. He was there," she said with a dismissive flip of one hand.

"Richard," I told her flatly.

"That's the one. He popped up during my favorite song and we danced for a while. He kissed me, and he tasted like tequila. But, honestly, that shouldn't count. It's part of my culture," she insisted, her voice deepening with wayward meaning.

"You grew up in North Carolina, Ally. No amount of pretending you have a spiritual connection to tequila or introducing yourself as Alejandra is going to change that," I told her.

The name was always much more dramatic when she

introduced herself than I could ever make it. It sounded like she added at least five extra 'a's and rolled her tongue over her 'r' for an eternity.

Her parents had left Puerto Rico before she was born, and Ally had never forgiven them for it. She spent most days trying to wring out every last bit of her heritage in an attempt to convince people that her in-the-womb time in the territory should make her a star of the Puerto Rican Pride parades.

"I find that very offensive, Slick."

Slick. That was Ally's nickname for me.

Which I guess did sound cooler than Sara Slickerman.

Almost anything sounded better than Sara Slickerman.

"It's not my fault you're a lightning rod for shady dudes," I pointed out.

"You should be careful, or I won't give you your treat," she warned.

"What treat?"

Ally's eyes lit up, and she grinned as she leaned back to pull something out of her backseat.

"I felt bad you weren't able to come out with us tonight, so I brought you…" she gave a dramatic pause, then shot her hand through the open window to present a folded white bag. "Tacos!"

Be still, my heart. Tacos. God's most perfect food.

I snatched the bag and opened it to breathe in a lungful of that delicious smell, then sighed.

"Thank you."

"Don't drip them on your computer. In fact, don't eat them near your computer. Just stop doing any homework at all."

"I have to," I shot back.

"It's Friday!"

"And Dad's working, so I have to take care of my sisters all weekend. Tonight is the only chance I'm going to get to focus on my work," I argued. She gave me a withering look, and I passed back a sigh of resignation. "But I'll take a break to enjoy my tacos."

"Good. You need to give yourself a break now and then. All right. I have to get home. I'm already late for curfew."

I leaned through the window to hug her. "Drive carefully. Call me tomorrow if you aren't grounded."

"Pry the sign out from under the car for me. And if you have a chance, apologize to your neighbor."

I rolled my eyes and laughed.

"Not the first time you've jumped the curb, Ally. Probably won't be the last. You should work on that, by the way."

"Duly noted."

It wasn't, and she wouldn't. Chances were, the next time she came to see me, the curve in the road would still somehow take her by surprise and she would end up half in a yard. Hopefully less so than tonight, but we'd see.

I finally succeeded in yanking the sign out and saw what I'd been battling. Holding it up so Ally could see it through the windshield, I pointed at the words.

"Next year," I called, "when you're old enough to vote, promise me you won't leave election signs up in your yard for months after."

She stuck her head out the window.

"Only if you promise me that in three years when you're old enough to vote, you won't get all militantly political on me. I'm not wearing any buttons," she said firmly.

I looked down at the sign in my hand.

"You hear that, Obama? She doesn't want to wear any buttons," I muttered.

After shoving the slightly warped metal stakes back into the ground, I waved at Ally. The yard was surprisingly unfazed by her terrible driving. Mr. Morgan next door probably wouldn't even notice.

I headed back toward the house and made my way around to the side. Climbing down from my window was an effort to not wake up my sisters, but I preferred to go in through an actual door.

Shimmying up the tree would be a chore. And I had tacos!

I went around the side to the door leading into what was once a garage, and now had become a room where my dad's workout equipment collected dust. The single bulb over the door created a pale pool of light that stretched a few feet on either side into the yard.

Movement in the corner of my eye caught my attention. A massive dog lurked in the shadows that fell across the lawn. My body tightened as I braced myself for what I figured was the inevitable attack. That would be my luck.

Go through all this to not disrupt the entire household only to get torn to shreds by some wild animal. Odds were, my body would end up scattered across the lawn next to the jacked-up Obama sign.

Perfect. Mr. Morgan would *not* be okay with that.

The giant dog and I stared at each other for a few

seconds as I reached back to search the door for the knob. When I glanced back, the beast was gone.

Although I couldn't see it, I could still feel the massive dog staring at me as I slipped inside. I weaved through the hunkering shapes of a treadmill, elliptical, and something that could be a torture rack but Dad called a weight bench.

I hurried up the back stairs to the second floor, but I'd only gotten a few steps toward my bedroom when I stopped. A disturbing sound from downstairs made my heart jump. I listened and heard it again. Someone shouted angrily, and a deep thud shook the walls. One by one, doors opened on either side of the hall and the little heads of my four younger siblings poked out. Sleepy eyes stared curiously at the landing. I touched my finger to my lips.

"Shh. It's okay. Go back to bed," I whispered.

"What's wrong?" Mia mumbled.

"Nothing. Go back in your room," I insisted.

The little heads disappeared behind their bedroom doors, and I drew a breath. After setting the bag of tacos aside on a small table in the hall, I made my way downstairs. Whatever was happening down there, I didn't want the little ones involved.

It was only the five of us and Dad since our mother died. He did the best he could with us, but long hours and extra shifts to make ends meet meant it was often me taking care of the house and them. It gave me a strong need to protect them.

I deftly skipped the steps I knew would creak. If something serious was going on, I didn't want to bring attention to myself.

The commotion was coming from the living room. I

eased myself up to the end of the hallway, then peeked around the corner while keeping most of my body out of sight.

Dad was sitting in his recliner, but there was nothing relaxed about his posture. His hands clenched on the arms of the chair as he leaned back, his eyes wide as he stared up at the hulking man bent over him. The stranger's hand was balled in Dad's shirt.

"Confess. We already know you did it. We have all the evidence. Just tell us the truth," the man growled.

My dad didn't answer, and another man stepped forward.

"You're making this harder on yourself. Stop wasting our time and give us what we need to know. It will all go easier on you if you come clean," he said through gritted teeth.

"I didn't do *anything*," my father insisted, fear trembling in his voice.

I fought the urge to scream as the second man smashed his hand across the side of my father's head and leaned closer.

"We can bring you where you won't have any choice but to answer our questions. Or...you could cooperate here and now," he said like he was offering a good deal.

They sounded like cops, but they looked like detectives from one of my dad's old black-and-white movies, complete with bowler hats and sunglasses. I couldn't understand why they were there. There was nothing my father could have done to justify that treatment. Another crack across his face made me shudder, and terror shot through me.

They couldn't take him away. He was all my siblings and I had, and if they took him, who would care for them? I was only fifteen. No one would let me be responsible for four kids. I was trudging through my term paper, and advanced algebra was a freaking mystery. I couldn't be a single parent. I couldn't even drive.

"Taking him will do nothing," the first man said. He looked back at Dad. "If he doesn't confess, we'll kill him right here."

The words alone were enough to flip my world upside down. An instant later, confusion tangled with the fear when he raised a sword above his head.

Now, I didn't know much about law enforcement, but I had seen enough TV to assume swords weren't standard practice. Especially swords that looked like they were carved from ice.

"Any last words?" the large man with the blade asked.

At that moment, all my fear and confusion disappeared. I had to act.

"It was me," I blurted as I burst into the room.

I had no idea what I was confessing to, but it didn't matter. I would say anything to stop them from hurting my father any more than they already had. Worst-case scenario, I'd spend the night in jail before this all got sorted out.

Maybe I'd get a good mugshot out of it. This could give me my fifteen minutes of fame at school.

"Sara, what are you doing?" Dad asked.

He tried to get up from the chair, but one of the men shoved him back down. The other stepped toward me.

"It can't be you. You're only a child," the man spat.

That wasn't an encouraging reaction.

"I look young for my age. And I definitely did it. I'm the one you want, not him," I insisted.

"There it is," a third said. "She confessed. We did our job. Let the Guild figure the rest out."

That brought some of my confusion back. The only Guild I knew of was the awkward Sewing Guild at school that Martha Hubert ran. Somehow, I didn't think they were into roughing people up and dragging them in for unknown crimes.

He moved toward me, and before I could react, something bound my wrists together so tight it felt like it was cutting into my skin. His sunglasses slipped down on his face, and it looked like his eyes were glowing red.

"Sara Slickerman, for your heinous crimes against The Far, you've been sentenced to ten lifetimes in The Deep."

I didn't have time to try to process the jumble of nonsense before the man wielding the sword stepped closer. He pulled an ornate, glowing key out of the pocket of his long coat.

He shoved the key forward into nothingness and a section of the room swung toward me as if it were two-dimensional, opening like a door into a dark swirl. I took one final look at my father's tear-filled eyes before the men grabbed me and shoved me through the gap in reality, into the darkness beyond.

Fuck fame. I wanted to know where the hell I was going.

CHAPTER TWO

They pressed the back of my head down, forcing me to look at the floor as the red-eyed man led me roughly down a narrow corridor. My mind raced, trying to make sense of the senseless. When we entered a dank, cold hall, I could finally see more of my surroundings.

One of the men wrenched open a door, and the screeching, grinding sound of rusted metal against rusted metal sent a shiver through my spine. He tossed me onto a damp stone floor and reality sank in.

I was *so* not getting my paper done on time.

My hip hit the floor hard, but I tried to scramble through the pain toward the door before it closed. The men slammed it shut in my face, and I collapsed, the sound of their laughter radiating around me. Sitting and pulling my knees up to my chest, I noticed a sliver of light slashing across the floor. I followed it to a small window high on the stone wall. There was something wrong with the sky outside.

I crawled forward, staring through the bars as I tried to

figure out what was off. It took several seconds for me to realize there were no stars. It wasn't like when it was cloudy, and the sky was nothing but blank black and gray. They simply weren't there at all. In their place were several small moons scattered across the dark expanse.

A sudden voice at the door startled me into heart palpitations. Whipping around with exactly zero semblance of having my shit together, I glared through the dim light of the cell.

"What did you say?" I tried not to let my voice tremble.

"I said, welcome to The Deep."

I did not get the warm and fuzzies from that welcome.

"Who are you?"

"I am Beccaria the Eighty-Second, Warden of this prison."

"Oh, thank goodness. Someone in charge." I stood and rushed up to him. "Listen. This is all a big mistake."

"What is?"

I gestured around myself frantically.

"This. All this. Me being here. It's kind of a funny story. Well, maybe not funny. Anyway, I shouldn't be here. Wherever the hell *here* is. I didn't do anything wrong. I was at home, being a responsible student, doing my homework. Then my best friend and her terrible-driving-self came to bring me some tacos. I went back inside and…"

"Stop."

His voice was harsh and intense, immediately cutting off my words.

"What?"

"I don't want to hear it. The very sound of your voice makes me sick," he said bitterly.

"I don't understand."

My stomach had sunk so far that if it went any lower, it was going to have to split in half so it could start sliding its way down my legs.

"We've never had a *Nearsider* here before," Beccaria muttered.

"A what?"

I didn't understand what he'd called me. I didn't wear glasses. That vision chart had no secrets from me.

"I've heard about your crimes against my people, and they disgust me. If I weren't so honorable, I would kill you right here, right now. But the *Pax Philosophia* would not allow it. I'm not too concerned, though. As it is, I highly doubt you will last the hour. You'll get what you deserve. One way or another, justice is always served in The Deep," he warned.

Without another word, he turned and walked away.

"What do you mean?" I shouted after him, smashing myself against the door and grabbing the bars. "Am I getting bailed out? Do I get a lawyer? What the hell is a Nearsider?"

There was no response. I had been abandoned in a dungeon in a world with at least a dozen tiny moons. And I was wearing my damn pajamas. I had never felt so alone.

Something stirred in an unseen corner of the room. My heart jumped. Maybe I'd rather be alone. A few seconds later, another rustling sound made my body shake.

"Hello?" I tried to make my voice sound as confident as possible, but knew it was squeaking.

"What is it?" a voice said.

"Beccaria said she's a Nearsider," another murmured.

"Do all Nearfolk look that strange? It's been so long since I saw one," another added.

"Who's there?" I asked. "Where are you?"

"Oh, she can't see us," the first voice taunted. "I wonder what she's thinking."

I hoped those voices were human. There it was—a sentence I would never have imagined thinking, but the only one that came to mind.

"Maybe if we break her head open and suck out what's inside, we'll know what she's thinking," one of the voices hissed.

Well, shit. Human or not, I didn't like that idea.

"You can have what's in her head, but I get the rest."

"What do you think she tastes like?" the first asked.

"She's kind of spindly. I don't think she's going to be very satisfying."

"Maybe we don't have to eat her. We could keep her as a pet," another suggested.

It was a new voice, and it wasn't any more encouraging than the others. A dark shadow stretched into the faint patch of light glowing from the window on the floor in front of me. It grew larger as a heavy footstep shook me to my bones.

A massive woman stepped into view, easily nine feet tall. I recoiled from her monstrous size and grey-tinged skin. She moved one leg to the side and a slimy-looking creature skittered between her feet and onto his hands and knees in front of me. I couldn't help but think he looked like an overripe Yoda.

Holy living booger. Had she been here the whole time? How did I miss either of them?

The smaller creature sniffed in my direction, then crawled back toward the giantess and latched onto her leg.

"The Nearling looks scared," the third voice said.

No shit. The Nearling *was* scared.

The giantess's eyes glanced upward briefly as she made a confirming sound. That couldn't be good. Nothing that was waiting above the head of a giant woman in a dungeon could possibly make a situation better.

A fuzzy white leg appeared beside her head. It stretched out, its pointed tip finding a spot a couple of feet ahead of her, then a second leg appeared. Then a third.

Nope. Not good.

My stomach turned and glowing red dots flashed in front of my eyes. If the inside of a s'more and a spider had a baby, and that baby had a shriveled old lady head, this was what it would look like.

The hell-marshmallow crept forward, then dropped from the ceiling right in front of me. I screamed, unashamed of the sound. These nightmarish creatures were coming at me like I was a vending machine at a Phish concert.

I was way past the need for composure. One fuzzy white leg reached toward me and something snapped inside my brain. A red-hot temper flared up inside me, and somewhere in my mind I decided I'd rather not go out like a punk.

If they wanted my apparently tasty brains and the three paragraphs of a term paper still in there, they were going to have to fight for them. A distinctly inelegant flail was all I could do to fight back. It showed absolutely no skill, but it was enough to stop the creature's approach. It started toward me again with the giantess and a goblin in tow.

I lashed out again, determined not to make this easy for them. A kick landed on the goblin's leg and he scurried back to safety. A momentary victory emboldened me, and I began swinging wildly at them.

No matter how hard I fought, they kept coming. I was literally against the wall now, the three of them closing in on me, laughing as they approached. This was it. I was only some girl who got plopped down into a world of monsters and promptly got eaten.

The end.

What a shitty fairy tale.

The crawling cream filling made a growling sound and launched toward me. The huge dog flashed back into my mind. For the second time that night, I tried to imagine what it was going to feel like to be eaten and braced myself for it. Before I could get torn to pieces, a bright light flashed in front of me. Maybe it had killed me with some sort of instant shock, and Heaven had already taken me.

It was a pleasant theory for the split second before I realized I still could hear the creatures hissing and snarling. When my eyes adjusted to the shock, a new figure had appeared in the cell. He took a sharp step forward, and the creatures scattered back into the darkness. His hand, lifted high above his head, held a switchblade.

Not exactly a sword carved from ice, but it seemed to do the trick.

Pale-blue eyes shone out of the old man's bearded face that turned to me. They held concern for a split second before it shifted to surprise. He snapped the switchblade closed and it made a sound that told me he hadn't purchased that particular weapon at a camping store.

"Thanks," I said.

He took a step toward me and his eyes widened even further. They glowed a gentle blue.

"Are you human?"

There it was again. People going around questioning my humanness. I was not appreciating that. There had been a few times when the automatic sinks in public bathrooms hadn't turned on no matter how much I waved my hands around in front of the sensor, and I briefly and privately entertained the thought that I might not *actually* be real. But others sharing that possibility and vocalizing it all over the place was downright offensive.

"Yes?"

The answer seemed to have much more impact than I expected it to, and the old man's eyes darted around the dark cell almost frantically.

His hand reached out and wrapped around my arm, pulling me in closer to him.

"Come with me. I'll keep you safe."

CHAPTER THREE

Ten years later...

"No matter what happens, this is my last night in this filthy cell," I muttered.

Sometimes when I sat on the cold floor with my back against the wall, I pretended I was back home sitting in my father's recliner. It gave me a little comfort in the grimy, brutal prison where I'd been held captive for a decade.

When I arrived in The Deep, I was a child.

My understanding of the world around me was so stunted. Not just because I'd only been in it for fifteen years, but because my awareness was so narrow. I was like a duck floating around in a peaceful pond thinking that was all that existed. That poor duck didn't know shit about the scaly monster slithering around beneath it.

Now, at twenty-five, I knew about the chaos that existed below the surface. Monsters, magic, mythical realms.

The night Solon saved me, my first night in prison, he started teaching me. I learned there used to be two dimensions, The Near and The Far. I learned about Pan'Rhea, the ancient cataclysm that smashed our realms together, unleashing all manner of bizarre creatures upon the human world. Creatures that lived in secret, right alongside humans.

He taught me a lot.

It wasn't so much nurturing mentorship as shoving as much information and as many skills into my head as he could as fast as possible so I'd live from moment to moment. Keeping me alive in The Deep was about understanding the ways of The Far and using them. But that didn't keep me from thinking about home and the life I had left behind.

That night I was preoccupied with thoughts of Solon. The old man's switchblade rolled back and forth between my fingers like it was waiting for me to open it. I hoped he taught me how to use it well enough before he died.

I put the blade back in one of the hidden folds of my tattered uniform and pulled out a locket. A rune. One of the first gifts Solon had given me. I opened it, and in lieu of a picture, a faint blue light glowed in the darkness.

"Did you know it took him three days to explain to me why they kept calling me a Nearling? I was a little thick, but he never gave up on me." I launched into the story like it was penance for the less-than-respectful thought about Solon.

"He promised to be my protector. Started training me. It's like he knew he was running out of time. I guess being older than dirt will give you that kind of awareness. It was a damn good thing he still had ten years in him."

Splinter gave me the kind of withering look children give their parents when the old folks started waxing poetic with the same *when I was young* story they'd told a million times before. At least, that's what the look felt like.

It was hard to tell with a rat.

Well, not technically a rat. But it was the closest comparison I could come up with.

Splinter was my only companion now that Solon was gone, and he had heard every story I had to tell, multiple times each.

If he started talking at any point, he'd be able to host a master class on my life before being dragged out of The Near and tossed into the bloody confines of The Deep. One whole module could be devoted to theories on the egregious crimes for which I had confessed. And didn't commit, if you needed the reminder.

Talking to Splinter kept my mind occupied and stopped me from losing my ever-freaking-loving sanity. There were definitely times when that was a little touch and go. It was hard not to start slipping away when I thought about everything I was missing in adult life on the outside. My family. Friends. College. Boyfriends. A career. Tacos. I'd missed out on so many tacos.

Splinter made it easier. He sat in his favorite spot on my thigh, nibbling on some crumb he had managed to find somewhere. Sometimes I wondered what type of furniture he pretended I was when he was sitting there. Maybe I was his recliner. Perhaps a nice chaise lounge. I could even pull off an ottoman. He deserved a really nice whatever I was.

It had taken a few weeks for us to come to terms with each other in the beginning. The little dungeon hole I'd been thrown into turned out to be a holding cell. The guards moved me to a new room that managed to be colder, slimier, and darker than the first. There was one silver lining.

After Solon saved me from them, I never had to see the giantess, goblin, and rice-creepy treat again.

But then I was mostly alone. Solitary.

Solon came and went, as wizards are wont to do, leaving me with long, hollow stretches between lessons. I quickly learned that was part of the torture of The Deep. Even the occasional meal that showed up in my cell wasn't brought by a living creature. It would materialize at irregular intervals, then disappear. Eventually they caught on to me counting the stones of my cell for entertainment and an enchantment wiped them away, replacing them with a smooth, empty surface.

Bastards.

In those days, the only other living beings I saw were the guards. Suffice it to say we didn't become best friends. Torture embellished with the occasional detail about my crimes isn't exactly a charming backdrop for bonding.

Then Splinter showed up. He scuttled through the bars of the door like his tail was on fire and curled up in the corner. We were not immediate fans of each other. We gradually got used to sharing the space, then I started talking to him. He didn't provide me any extra details about The Deep, but he was a damn good listener.

Eventually, I received The Deep's version of an increase in privileges. My reward for survival of my initial isolation was that sometimes I got to leave my cell and go to the dingy lunchroom to eat with the other prisoners. Splinter would curl up in the pocket of my uniform and come with me. He decided we were friends before I did, but I didn't have the heart to argue with the little critter.

The other prisoners heard the rumors about me and ranked me about four steps lower in the hierarchy than the molded, leftover food splatter on the floor, so I appreciated Splinter's companionship.

One of his little arms stretched out, showing off the flap of skin that connected his wrist to his ankle to turn him into a glider. Those flaps along with fur that made him look like an abandoned toilet brush, his bug eyes, and a long thin tail concocted a Franken-creature that seriously freaked out the other prisoners when they glimpsed him.

Their dirty, raggedy selves even had the gall to mutter that Splinter was ugly. I frequently reassured him he was adorable. He was most *certainly* ugly, but in an adorable kind of way.

"His switchblade, my runes, and the lessons he taught me are all I have left of him. I'm going to make sure everything Solon put into me wasn't in vain," I told my little friend.

Splinter's bristle hairs stood on end, increasing his toilet brush chic appearance, and his big green eyes darted around frantically. Apparently, my soliloquy didn't impress him. He bounced around on my thigh, then ran into the shadows. Him getting skittish like that could only mean one thing.

Showtime.

Footsteps and muffled voices came toward my cell. I

closed the locket and placed it around my neck. Power left the rune, flooding my body as I rose to my feet. I didn't want to be sitting when they arrived.

Like I said, one way or another, this would be my last night here.

CHAPTER FOUR

"Well, well, well, if it isn't little Sara Slick..."

Ten years in this dungeon, and the nickname was the only thing left of me from my life in The Near. I was practically a legend in this place.

The goblin's voice slithered through the bars, without fear that the guards would overhear. They didn't care what happened inside The Deep. But I knew why these assholes were here. There wasn't any doubt they'd be coming that night.

"I have to say, ten years was a pretty good run," another voice said. This one was deeper, probably an ogre of some variety or another. "We tried to put together a pool to bet on how long you would make it, but no one would place their money on anything more than the first night. I guess you proved us wrong. But a lucky streak can't last forever."

In the Big Book of Nasty Far Creatures I'd been compiling in my head for ten years, ogres ranked among my very least favorite. Right below goblins. Big, brutish, and dumb as toast, what they lacked in charm they made up for in horrible smell and ego-driven displays of machismo.

They were like overgrown frat boys with poor hygiene and delusions of grandeur.

He paused. He wanted me to beg. The cruelty in their eyes told me they already had plans for me. They were there to take revenge and were ready to bring my sentence to a close.

"Don't you have anything to say for yourself?" the goblin demanded.

He was clearly the leader of the posse.

"Um. Let's see..." I tilted my head as I pretended to think. "My name is Sara. I like long walks on the beach and sharing tacos by candlelight. My favorite show is that one with the show choir. Embarrassing, I know..."

The ogre hissed, obviously offended.

"How dare you? Little piece of Near filth. You know what you did. Your insolence knows no bounds. Explain yourself."

This particular *insolence* was sticking my foot out in the lunch line and tripping their boss, a pig-looking creature on two legs. It was a memory I would cherish for a long time.

"How about no, and fuck off? That work for you?" I snapped.

"Maybe if you showed some remorse," the goblin said, "we would have killed you fast. But because you insist on being defiant, we'll make sure your torture is slow and your death even slower."

He cackled as he stepped aside, letting the ogre get

closer. A second later, the sound of rusty hinges greeted my ears as they opened the door.

Check. Step one complete.

"You could have at least called ahead. I'd have put on a pot of tea," I said.

As my cell swung open, I saw four of the ugliest creatures to have ever assembled in the history of ever. Their stink wafted into my room, and I figured even if they managed to gouge out my eyes during the fight, I could still use my sense of smell to find their nasty asses. Bonus.

"We're feeling generous tonight," the goblin said. "So I'm going to give you one more chance to show how sorry you are and beg for mercy."

"Not happening."

The goblin wasted no more time. He rushed me, wrapping leathery arms around my neck and lifting me off the ground. Goblins weren't large creatures, but I'd learned over the years not to judge any of the beings within the prison by their size.

The sheer overwhelming power of his crushing grip held me immobile against the wall, and I felt myself slipping into unconsciousness as he pushed against my windpipe. All four of his eyes gleamed with cruel pleasure.

The plan was *not* going well.

The ogre entered next, and I felt Splinter run up the back of my leg and around my waist. Normally a bit of a coward, Splinter knew full well what was at stake. He leapt past the goblin and latched onto the ogre, sinking his pointy teeth into its giant knobby nose. The grip on my neck lessened as the goblin got distracted. Just like that, the tide had turned in my favor.

This was my chance.

I drew on the power of the locket and kicked my captor. The magic of the rune combining with my muscles meant my foot could have broken through cinder blocks. The goblin took the full force of the kick in whatever soft parts his kind had. He folded like an accordion, a soft wheeze escaping his lips.

The ogre was still flailing and grabbing at Splinter clinging to his face, so I rushed past him. The third member of these self-appointed executioners, a thin pale wight, stood right inside the door. I leapt forward, aiming as high as I could, and only reached his chest. The blow sent him stumbling back a few steps.

The last dipshit, another goblin, was coming in when the wight barreled into the door and slammed the metal shut on the goblin's hand. The distinct snap of bones breaking echoed through the cell, and the goblin cried out in pain. That hadn't been my plan, but I was never one to turn down a blessing in my favor.

"Thanks for giving me a *hand* with that door. Wouldn't want to air condition the whole neighborhood," I said.

I grabbed the wight's head and slammed it backward twice, smashing it into the metal bars of my cell and knocking him out. Splinter scurried up my shoulder, and I felt him tugging at me to turn around. I ducked barely in time to dodge the ogre's hands. His bloody face helped the urgency.

Charging forward, I led with my shoulder and tackled him against the cold bricks of the wall. A piece of stone lay within reach and I grabbed it, then slammed it against the ogre's body and head until the brute stopped moving. My muscles were getting tired and my vision started to spin. The locket around my neck weakened with each hit. That was the downside of relying on magical runes. Each had their limits. I needed to bring this shit to a close before the locket left me with nothing but my unaided human capabilities.

The goblin with the bloody hand and broken fingers made his way in after shoving the body of the unconscious wight aside. Time for the big finale.

"This was fun, but I really have to be going." I surveyed the gore and broken stone around me. Solon would be proud.

But it wasn't quite over, not yet.

Goblin number one, the spokesperson for this gang, had finally found his wind again. With a flick of my wrist, I pulled out the switchblade and let it fly. The beautifully crafted weapon caught the goblin in his shoulder and he reared back. I reached into what amounted to a pocket in the rags of my uniform and took out a sharp triangular rune. These were only good for one use, but that was all I needed.

Thanks to many long nights of target practice with Solon, my aim was perfect. One point of the triangle hit the distracted goblin right at the base of his neck. He dropped to the floor as the magic from the carved stone dissolved his control over his body. His limbs twitched with the shocks that buzzed through him from the point of impact.

I walked forward and pressed my foot against his throat. He didn't look so powerful now as I ground my heel into him like I was putting out a cigarette he had swallowed.

His hands clawed at my leg, and he thrashed, obviously shocked by the turn of events. I leaned down toward him.

"Move again, and I'll kill you." His four eyes widened, and a grin turned up the corners of my lips. "I've always wanted to say that to one of you. I'm not going to kill you. But I do need a little something, so your cooperation would be much appreciated."

"Go to hell," he croaked out past the pressure of my foot.

"Step two of my master plan. You showing up here tonight was no accident. After ten years in this hellhole, you think I'd suddenly decided to trip Captain Pig Face in front of everyone? Give me some credit. Embarrassing him was the simplest way to get some alone time with you."

I reached into my pocket and pulled out the palm-sized rune I'd been protecting for many long months leading up until now. It took nearly ten years for Solon to weave the intricate circle of my hair into something useful, and it was nearly complete.

The rune around my neck would be depleted soon, but this one would be much stronger.

It only needed one more ingredient.

"You know the old saying 'Roses are red, like blood on a spear. Making a Rune needs something from The Far and from The Near'? No? Don't know that one? Guess Solon made it up."

"Solon was a traitor to his kind and a piece of shit," the goblin spat. "He deserved to die in this place."

I ground my foot harder into his throat.

"See, it's funny to hear you say that when you're the one on the floor pinned down by me, his protégé. I'd hold still if I were you. This will hurt."

I yanked Solon's switchblade out of his shoulder. It glinted in the light coming through my small window as I plunged it into the goblin's eye socket. His eyeball popped out with surprising ease, and to his credit, he smothered his screams. My foot on his throat might have helped. One slimy hand pressed over the bleeding void.

"Relax. You have three more."

The eye was small and hard, and I tucked it into place within the rune. The final piece to complete the magic.

I felt it hum to life.

"What the hell do you need that for?" he shrieked.

"Step three. Escape. Clean the place up before you leave."

I smashed my foot into his head and knocked him unconscious, gathered Splinter, and took off through the open cell.

There was no time to lose.

The world was at stake.

CHAPTER FIVE

Maybe not the *world*, world. But the urgency behind my escape was fueled by learning *my* world was at stake. At the very least.

Getting that tidbit of information wasn't easy. The only news I could get about the outside world came when new prisoners were shipped in. Of course, almost every new prisoner dumped into our midst was a thief or a murderer or a monster on top of being a liar, so anything they said was always suspect.

But there were kernels of truth in what I heard from the often-fuming, frequently foaming new prisoners.

And the strange creature known as Burne was one such figure.

I never learned what species of Farsider he was. He looked like elements of various creatures had been stuck together with some sort of Far super glue. He was much like Splinter in that way. Only not adorable.

But it didn't matter to me what Burne was. All that mattered was what he had to say, and there was a lot of it.

Even before he was in the same room with me, I heard his unchained rantings and they didn't slow down or lower in volume once he was twirling around in the middle of the room like a demented top.

For the next several hours, he ran his mouth about being the one true servant of Hobbes the Twenty-Third and that he wouldn't be in The Deep for long. Then he added that the end was near. It would all be over soon.

Pax Philosophia will be undone!

He repeated the assertion so many times it became background noise. It wasn't a novel thing for new prisoners to come in spouting only vaguely coherent nonsense about the *Pax Philosophia*. The ancient law put into place by the Philosophers Guild was a popular topic of debates, rants, and raves among the prisoners. To say it was a touchy subject was a tremendous understatement. It was meant to bring relative peace to the realms, maintaining balance between The Near and The Far, the humans and the weird.

As good as that sounded, and as much as it should inspire sitting around holding hands and singing *Kumbaya,* not everyone felt the same way. According to Solon, many hated the Guild's control and believed it was dragging down the magical creatures of The Far.

They wanted it abolished. A rogue underground cult called the Harbingers had formed. Led by this mysterious Hobbes character, their sole goal was bringing the *Pax* down. Which would almost definitely lead to a war between The Near and The Far.

So...not great.

A fair percentage of prisoners who ended up tossed

into The Deep claimed to be part of this revolution, but none had ever produced any even slightly reliable information.

Until Burne.

Even with his adamant name-dropping of Hobbes, this new prisoner's rants were run-of-the-mill crazy talk until those disturbing words came out of his mouth.

"The war is beginning, and we will strike the first blow in the Holy City!"

He could have been talking about Jerusalem. Or maybe Rome. But I knew, *knew*, in my gut what he meant. He was talking about Charleston, nicknamed the Holy City because of the abundance of churches.

And it happened to be the city where I was born, raised, and snatched by the Guild.

The words were barely out of Burne's mouth when I cornered him and demanded more information. He spilled, but what poured out once I got him literally up against a wall was mostly a jumble of words loosely linked together into sentences that made no damn sense.

I had gotten very little out of him before the guards decided to break it up. Fortunately for me, by that point I'd already learned how to measure my behavior and not ruffle feathers. Unfortunately for Burne, he hadn't gotten that crash course yet, and the continuation of his screeching rant resulted in his first night in The Deep also being his last.

His murder was brutal, but I was already hardened against it. Watching him die cut deeper because he had, moments before his last breath, revealed to me the only bits of truly valuable information I'd gotten about The

Near since being in prison. Starting with the threat that my hometown was in danger.

The sobering news came along with the location of the Harbinger's hideout and the promise that Hobbes' followers were planning to do something so terrible it would make the world tremble.

That was when I decided to finally make my escape.

Solon and I had planned it from the beginning. But when he died leaving me with his switchblade and a half-finished rune, I hesitated. For weeks I waited, scared to move. I knew I would only have one shot. If I failed, I'd either be killed or thrown into a hole so deep there was no dream of escaping.

Fear of death, or worse, kept me in a holding pattern. I was biding my time, waiting for the perfect opportunity.

Until this Hobbes radical threatened my city. My home. My family.

I immediately put Solon's plan into action.

And his plan brought me *here*, sprinting down a long corridor toward either escape or doom, the fate of my world at stake.

No pressure.

My sprint dead-ended at a thick door with a series of complicated locks. I seriously didn't have time for this shit.

Four creatures coming down to my cell to kill me and not coming back to the rest of the horde with bits of my carcass wouldn't go unnoticed.

I had to escape, tonight. Now.

Dropping to my knees in front of the door, I reached into my pocket and pulled out the implement I'd crafted out of several of Splinter's bristles. It was an as-of-yet untested device, but now was as good a time as any to see if it worked. Poking it into the first lock, I jiggled it around until it caught. One down. The rest of The Deep to go.

There was a reason no one had ever escaped The Deep. It wasn't a prison in the *normal* sense. It was its own dimension. Well, fragment dimension. The physics of it all were still a little fuzzy.

After Pan'Rhea, the great collision between realms that sent all manner of strange into The Near, our world, what remained of the dimension known as The Far split into two. Two splinter realms, different from each other in every way. But Philosophers were never ones to waste a good dimension. They turned one half into a magical utopia, known as The Heights, where the Philosophers Guild made their home.

The other half, the antithesis of The Heights, was The Deep, an inescapable prison world crafted out of night-mares, evil, and probably more than a little spit and bile.

The entire violent dimension existed purely for the purpose of torture and punishment, which meant moving through the building wasn't as easy as simply going through doors and climbing stairs. This place put the Winchester mansion to shame.

Stairs led to nowhere. Passages turned progressively smaller, the walls embedded with glass and sharpened metal to shred anyone trying to run through. Levels of the prison were uneven and irregular, so some were small and low and others wide with towering ceilings. Doors opened to blank walls and pits of blood and bones.

The map Solon once drew before quickly destroying it was still etched in my mind and that part stood out the most. I was not interested in swimming through Corpse Lake.

Keeping part of my awareness focused on the cell behind me so I'd hear if the goblin or one of his men approached from behind, I picked my way through the rest of the locks. It felt like it was taking forever. A sense of doom pressed in on me from every angle, but I pushed away the fear. My hunger for freedom drove me, and I could already taste it.

Finally, the last lock clicked, and I breathed a sigh of relief. I slipped through the door, then paused. Without the key, I couldn't lock the door without reversing the process with my homemade pick. That would take time, time I didn't have. I weighed my options, pulled the door shut and fled down the hall.

If the goblin and his friends woke up, I'd simply kick their asses again.

CHAPTER SIX

There were plenty of places within The Deep I had never visited. But my working knowledge of the prison's layout meant I had a chance. It was a chance Solon knew he didn't have.

No one had ever escaped The Deep. Not even a prisoner as powerful as my teacher could do that. That fact was drilled into my head countless times over the years. But no Nearsider had ever been there, either, which gave me an advantage.

Like the assholes bleeding in my cell, every Farsider underestimated us humans. I was the first human ever sent here, so I figured I might as well be the first to break out. It would save them having to make two honorary plaques someday.

I hadn't gone far down the next hallway when a guard came around the corner. He was easily recognizable as one of the Philosophers—he looked like a run-of-the-mill human, except for the pointy ears. The uppercrust among The Farsiders, these wizards reigned over the prison.

While the goons and ghouls did the dirty work, these bastards kept their hands clean and the place in order. I'd been told they also walked on Earth, mixing in among the sapiens.

Solon was one of the most powerful to ever live. Then he became a prisoner.

I weighed my options and decided to duck into a shadowy corner. The Philosophers were powerful, but they weren't all-knowing. It meant they didn't know I escaped yet. That gave me some wiggle room.

I pulled out my switchblade just in case and wiped the goblin's blood off on my rags as the Philosopher walked by.

It looked like the wizard wouldn't be the wiser. Then I remembered the unlocked door at the end of the hall. Shit. As soon as he saw that, all hell would break loose. I was going to have to go for a more proactive approach.

Without giving myself time to hesitate, I ran toward the guard. He turned and opened his mouth, but whatever spell he planned on frying me with died on his lips as I plunged the blade into his chest. His entire body shuddered before collapsing to the floor.

I turned and ran while going over the map in my mind. I needed to go up several floors and to the center of the building to reach my first goal. But trying to do that through the corridors would take too long. I needed an alternative route.

My eyes scanned the walls and the ceiling until I found the edge of a tiny access door. I used the switchblade to pry it open and slipped inside. Closing the door cast me into utter darkness, but I pulled the locket out from under my shirt and allowed its subtle glow to guide me.

"Welcome to the body chute," I whispered to Splinter.

The Deep was a murderous hellhole, filled with the worst creatures imaginable and built with no regard for their safety or even survival. The weak didn't last long. Hell, the strong rarely lasted long. Inordinately long sentences were more for the drama and mental torture of it than any actual thought the prisoner would see it through.

To manage this swift turnover of residents, the designers of this lovely place provided the guards with an easy way of disposing of bodies. The prisoners knew it only as the body chute. There was really no reason to call it anything else.

For someone as small as me, it doubled as an excellent escape route, despite the fact that it smelled exactly like what it was.

My hand slipped in something I chose not to identify. It was wet and sticky and smelled like old cheese. Splinter wriggled out of my pocket and went ahead of me. I didn't know if he was trying to be helpful, or if he wanted to get through the disgusting passage as fast as he could.

We passed through two floors and I scrambled over something I told myself was a pile of discarded clothes that happened to have a few sticks and some pudding shoved inside. I decided it was time to take my chances out of the chute. The glow of the locket was slowly fading, which meant its power faded with it.

It would recharge, with time. But if I didn't make it out of here before it quit, I would be dead long before it regained full power.

I found a door and kicked it open, then dropped

through it before looking out. Not my smartest move. As soon as I hit the ground, something scooped me up and dangled me in the air.

A familiar face leered up at me.

"Look who it is." He shook me. "The *Nearsider.*"

CHAPTER SEVEN

The gross, gooey candy spider-creature stared up at me. I now knew this was a baalarach, one of a clan of particularly nasty monsters that hid out in old forests and ate unsuspecting hikers. This particular spider was missing half his face and seemed to be down one leg since the first night I saw him.

"Well, if it isn't Itsy Bitsy," I replied. "Long time, no see. But as much as I'd love to hang out and catch up, I really need to go. I have appointments and important meetings to attend. You understand."

"Oh, I understand." Its face contorted into what I could only assume was a smile. "I understand that your wizard friend is dead. So sorry to hear that. Did you know he gave me these lovely scars? The night you first arrived, after our fun was interrupted. He showed up in my cell, murdered my compatriots, and left me half-blind. Guess it was to serve as a warning to the others."

In fact, I didn't know this, but it didn't surprise me.

Solon had skills I could scarcely imagine, and he wielded them ruthlessly to keep me safe.

"That's a shame. You were such a looker before."

"No matter," it hissed. "With him gone, we can pick up right where we left off. I've been craving my snack."

"After ten years, you're still obsessing about eating me? That seems unhealthy. You should consider a chat with Dr. Phil."

Taking a page from Splinter's book, I chomped down on the leg holding me. It tasted like hot garbage, and it was all I could do not to throw up on the spot.

The dig of my teeth wasn't enough to make the spider drop me, but it pissed him off enough to bring me closer to his mouth. I took the opportunity to kick him in the face at the same moment I slashed his leg with my switchblade.

It wasn't graceful. Something about this thing brought out the flail in me. Still, it worked.

I hit the ground and ran, not bothering to glance back. The spider creature was one of the more privileged prisoners, which meant the body chute had dumped me out into what passed as a recreational room but was really a larger version of the cells.

There were no doors in these rooms. Prisoners allowed to use them were transported in. But that didn't mean they were completely secure. A jagged crack along one wall looked like the perfect opportunity. My only opportunity, really, but I was going for optimism. I ran toward the crack and wriggled my body through it.

I was twenty-five, but the less-than-exemplary prison diet meant I had maintained my teenage weight.

Bonus.

I popped out the other side as I heard the baalarach slam into the wall. It reached its spindly legs toward me, but its massive body prevented it from making the journey.

"Send my regards to the rest of the gang," I yelled and ran down the hallway, the baalarach's screams echoing behind me.

One more jaunt through the body chute brought me to an empty corridor. The walls looked solid, but I knew not to be taken in by the deception. I had made it to my destination.

Now it was up to my newest rune.

Taking the thin bundle of hair and magic from my pocket, I held it to my face. The goblin eyeball let me see through it like a looking glass, revealing hidden details that existed throughout The Deep, but had always been concealed from me.

I slowly turned and found the door.

The Warden's private quarters.

Runecraft is a tricky form of magic. It requires intense focus, a powerful will, and two kinds of ingredients. Something from The Near, and something from The Far. While this hell of a dimension was crawling with Farstuff, no human had ever been sent here. Which meant that Nearstuff was in short supply.

A problem I solved by unjustly getting locked in this place. A problem Solon turned into an advantage.

I stepped up to the hidden door and placed the delicate rune on the handle. This was it. The whole plan hinged on this one moment. I skipped knocking and smashed the rune with my switchblade, sending a force louder than a cannon blast echoing through The Deep.

And blowing the door wide open.

A small fire illuminated the room. Plush carpeting welcomed my feet. I had to fight the urge to lie down on it and roll around. Compared to the rest of The Deep, this place was a paradise, but I had no time to enjoy it.

Warden Beccaria sat up groggily, trying to make sense of the sound. He jostled awake quickly enough when I grabbed him by the front of his nightshirt and yanked him out of his covers. The end of his pointed nightcap fell over his face like Rip Van Winkle, and he thrashed around at the end of the bed.

"Knock it off." I gave him a hard shake.

His eyes opened, and he pushed the cap away so he could see.

"Nearscum?" he muttered, his sleep-induced fog almost making the word sound like a term of endearment.

I pressed my switchblade to his throat.

"Give it to me."

I didn't have to specify what I was demanding. He already knew.

"No. No way." He shook his head adamantly.

I pushed my blade deeper as I yanked him closer.

"Now," I growled. "Even a powerful Philosopher like you can bleed."

Relenting, Beccaria reached under his shirt and pulled out a chain. Dangling from the end was the ornate key that had been seared into my memory for ten years. I snatched it from his hand and stuck it forward into the air in front of me like I remembered those men doing the night they ruined my life. The door in reality opened with a click, and I smiled, my chest nearly bursting.

The Warden laughed. "You won't escape for long, not with the entire Guild hunting you down. There's no place for you to hide. By now your friends and family have forgotten you, but every Farsider knows of your crimes and they all despise you for it. Your name fills every one of my kind with righteous anger. They'll give you no quarter, no mercy. You won't last the hour, Sara Slick."

I turned back to him with a wider grin stretching across my face.

"Funny. You said that to me ten years ago. Care to see how long you last among your prisoners?"

I dragged him toward his bedroom door and threw him into the hallway. He looked up at me in horror as I slammed his door shut and overturned an ornate desk in front of it. That should keep him occupied.

Opening my pocket, I glanced in at Splinter. "Time to go, boy."

I took a breath and leapt into the portal. There was a moment of darkness followed by a feeling somewhere between being torn apart and crushed. After an eternity of the universe playing accordion with my body, it finally spit me out. I hit solid ground.

Something cool touched my face, and I realized it was air. Fresh, sweet air without even a hint of goblin piss or body chute. My lungs sucked it in faster than I could exhale, and I felt a touch woozy when a loud sound startled me to my feet.

It was a car whipping past. A car illuminated by the glow of an electric streetlight.

I had made it back.

CHAPTER EIGHT

I jumped to my feet and looked around with almost giddy anticipation, ready to take in the familiar, beloved surroundings again. I had dreamed of this moment for ten years.

Hoping I hadn't landed too far from my mark, I rushed to the edge of the nearby street to get a better idea of where the hell I was. A truck cut me off, and I laughed. Even the exhaust fumes smelled good. I'd take just about anything outside the walls of the magical prison that had stolen the last decade of my life.

After what I had to do to survive the three thousand, six hundred sixty-four days and nights tallied in hash marks on my cell floor, a lungful of soot was heaven. I'd taken my freedom with me when I jumped through that portal. Now that I had it, I was savoring each second of being back on Earth.

Back in The Near.

It stretched out around me, ready for me to soak up

every bit of experience possible. It felt like being in the middle of Wonka's factory, and I wanted to lick every wall.

But the grumbling in my stomach and the wind whipping around the rags of my prison uniform told me the wall-licking would have to wait for at least a little while. My head still spun from the interdimensional trip, and nothing looked even close to familiar. I needed to get my ass off the street. I needed to lay low until I could figure out where I was and what my next steps were.

Before he died, Burne had let slip that his friends on the outside were planning a deal tonight. Something that threatened Charleston and maybe the entire *Pax Philosophia*. I got the general location out of him, but that did nothing for me if I couldn't get there from here, wherever here was.

The key hung heavy in my hand. Solon had told me it would bring me anywhere I wanted to go. But this was the first time I'd ever used it. Maybe I'd done it wrong. Either way, it was a one-time deal. Beccaria wasn't bluffing. The whole Guild would be out to get me, and once they knew I stole the key, they'd be able to trace its use. Opening another door with it would be like firing a flare into a crowded room. This key was a Pan-Relic and contained a precious material only the Philosophers Guild was authorized to use.

As soon as they realized I was missing, I was screwed. Agents of the Guild would immediately start hunting me down, which meant I had to stay a step ahead of them. Several steps, if at all possible.

Especially if I wanted to save the world.

I slipped the chain over my head and hid the key. I needed somewhere to rest and something to eat, but my first priority was finding something to wear. The less attention I drew to myself the better. I was fairly certain it wasn't Halloween, so I couldn't get away with the *Les Misérables* look I had going on. Splinter made a few chittering noises at me from my pocket.

"We'll find a snack, buddy. Don't worry."

Light and muffled music from a bar a short distance down the sidewalk lured me. If I was going to gather the intel I needed, a bar full of people seemed like a fantastic place to start.

Puddles lingering on the pavement from some past storm reflected the neon light that splashed from the door as it swung open. The bar spit out a man who stumbled a few feet down the sidewalk. I watched to make sure he'd rebound rather than end up as one of the puddles.

"Get out of my way, asshole," he mumbled. I stepped aside, and he reached out for a light post. I thought he was bracing himself to hurl, but instead, he swung around the pole like a kid on a playground. To his credit, he let out a cheerful *weeee* as he twirled.

I grabbed his sleeve and let him take another spin around the post so he unraveled from his black leather jacket like a mummy. A cab pulled up to the sidewalk, and I slipped into the jacket as the drunk found his feet and stumbled his way toward the car. I turned back to the bar. Another patron was walking out with a much higher degree of control, and I reached forward to catch the door as he walked past me.

Now that my rags were somewhat covered, I felt slightly more at ease in the human world. The swagger was short-lived. As soon as the smell of fried food washed over me, Splinter gave me an encouraging bite on my thigh. My leg shook a little to dislodge him, and I noticed eyes on me. I could have kept walking.

Instead, I tried to blend in.

There were so many ways I could have blended. So many ways to insert myself back into reality. I chose to dance. My hands dropped to my knees as my hips wiggled.

"This song's my jam," I said with a somewhat unhinged gesture toward the speaker.

It took another ten seconds of blank stares for the music blasting from the speakers to sink in and let me know I had been booty dancing to a truly gut-wrenching country song. My ass had twerked to a stolen pickup truck, at least three ex-girlfriends, and a lost dog.

Perfect.

That had gone smoothly. Fortunately, the looks eventually turned away from me and I scanned the surprisingly dense crowd in the bar.

Tables and stools scattered around the room hosted clusters of people laughing and dancing. They tipped back drinks ranging in shade from the pale brown of straightforward chugging beer to vibrant rainbow hues of cocktails that very well could be nothing more than melted ice pops.

None of them instantly struck me as a masquerading Farsider who might ID me—or give me the intel I needed. Not that I expected to walk into the bar and find a cluster of them hunkering in the corner growling at people or wearing convenient self-declaration t-shirts. I would have to get more creative in needling out the details I needed.

I could do that. But first, there was something important I needed to do, something that had haunted me every one of those three thousand, six hundred sixty-four days I spent in prison.

CHAPTER NINE

The bartender lifted his eyes to me as I dropped onto the one empty stool in front of him. His dirty rag swiped absently back and forth across the prep station in front of him like he didn't know how to function without it. He leaned close to hear me shout over the increasingly rowdy crowd.

A single nod said he got my message as he turned away. A few seconds later, he came back and slid a yellowed piece of paper across the scarred surface of the bar. My hand flattened over it and I pulled it protectively close, my eyes darting across the words on it as fast as they could move.

This couldn't be true.

I read it again, forcing myself to slow down to ensure I didn't miss anything. My head spun. It was all I'd wanted, all I'd longed for when I was in prison, what I'd promised myself if I ever escaped into freedom. And this slip of paper tore it away from me.

My eyes snapped up to the bartender.

"No tacos?"

His eyes narrowed as he shook his head.

"No. We don't serve tacos except on Wednesdays," he told me without the regret and dismay he rightfully should have felt.

"*Wednesdays?* What the hell do you mean you don't serve tacos except on Wednesdays? Who ever heard of Taco Wednesday?" I asked indignantly.

I slid the menu back toward him in disgust.

"We already had an established Tortellini Tuesday," the bartender explained.

I glared at him for a few seconds.

"Well, that sounds delicious," I said bitterly.

"But you still want a taco?"

"Yes," I told him.

"Sorry. Is there something else I can get for you? Beer?"

"Sure."

My body sagged under the weight of the sheer taco disappointment. He grabbed a mug from the rack above his head, performed a masterful pour, and set the frothy drink in front of me.

Bubbles bounced around in the pale brew. Cheap and approachable. Everything you're looking for when you wander into a bar alone at night. I scooped up the mug and took a cautious sip. The flavor that filled my mouth was better than anything I'd ever tasted, and I swigged the rest at a speed about ten degrees to the left of dignified.

"Another one?" the bartender asked as I wiped away the bits of foam clinging to my lips.

The lingering taste of the beer lured me in, and I nodded. While I waited for my drink, I glimpsed the TV above the bar. A cable news show played with the volume turned off, but it was the chyron that caught my attention.

Charleston Congressional Race Grabs National Attention.

It wasn't often I saw my hometown discussed on cable news, but I was about ten years out of date on politics. Maybe things had changed since my last civics class.

The bartender pulled my thoughts from the TV when he returned with a beer and a paper plate.

"You look like you could use this."

It wasn't a taco, but it was almost as seductive. A slice of pizza hung off the sides of the plate, and the smell of pepperoni made me dizzy with desire. I snatched it before it even touched the bar and shoved a massive bite in my mouth. It was incredible.

Washing it down with a swig of the fresh beer he set down beside me nearly put me in a state of delirium. I ripped off a chunk of the crust and subtly slipped it to Splinter. His happy little sounds reminded me I wasn't the only one who was finally free.

"Want to dance?"

I was so swept up in the joy of my pizza and beer that I almost didn't process the question. It took a repeat for me to turn and look at the man standing far too close to my barstool. His shirt was at least two sizes too small.

"Dance?" The closest thing I'd had to a dance partner in a decade was a demon who wanted to rip my arms off and use them for a necktie.

The man laughed and nodded. His teeth looked like he washed them twice daily with bleach.

"Yeah. This is a great tune, don't you think?"

I listened for a few seconds, expecting another cater-wauling country song, but heard a loud girl's voice belting out an almost indecipherable ballad.

"Who is this?"

The man looked at me like he knew I'd popped an eyeball out of a goblin earlier.

"Ariana Grande."

"Who?"

His head tilted to the side.

"Have you been living under a rock?"

Sort of.

"I'm not that big into...current music."

After finishing my beer in one swig, I met eyes with the bartender.

"Another one?" he asked.

I shook my head. Then an idea struck me. Shiny Teeth might be useful after all.

"I'm going to dance, then this fine gentleman's going to pay my tab."

He swept the mug away, and it disappeared into an unseen sink. I already missed it.

"I don't think I've seen you around here before," the man said as we made our way to the dance floor. "Where are you from?"

"Charleston," I told him.

"What are you doing in Summerville?"

My breath caught in my throat. Summerville was only half an hour outside of Charleston. I maintained my composure and let him wrap an arm around my waist. There were at least six ways I could break that arm, but none that worked in rhythm with the music.

"Just…visiting," I answered.

I was relaxing and enjoying the music when something I spotted out of the corner of my eye made my stomach sink.

A troll stood not twenty feet away, his eyes locked on a woman I knew he had plans for. Plans she wouldn't enjoy.

Before taking the blame for my father, I didn't know a lick about The Deep or The Heights, or of the presence of Farsiders among our world. Hell, I didn't even like vampire romances. But some time in The Deep quickly brought me up to speed. It was like knowing people who carry designer bags.

After long enough, you learn to spot the fakes. No matter how hard they try, a doctored-up tote isn't ever going to be the real deal. This man might look like a nice, chiseled specimen of perfectly human bar-goer, but he was no Prada.

Of course, no one else noticed the Farsider. People would like to think a troll plugging himself into a room with a bunch of humans would be obvious. Unfortunately, magic didn't make it that simple.

No one frequenting the bar could hope to see a massive, foul-smelling creature wedged onto one of the barstools and easily steer clear. Likewise, no big empty eyes or tufts of neon hair marked the troll's presence. Farsiders were much more adept at hiding themselves, as Solon had taught me. But I could tell.

I was onto him.

If he wasn't a troll, then I wasn't Sara Effing Slick.

I needed to get the imposter out. As convincing as his human-poser game was, it would all go to hell if something pissed him off. And it wouldn't take much to piss him off. If I didn't get him out before then, he could cause serious damage and take out a staggering number of these people before anyone knew what was going on.

Fighting with a troll couldn't have been a worse move for my plan of laying low, but I couldn't let him hurt these people. I was a fugitive, not a monster.

Giving an apologetic look to my dance partner, I gestured toward where I hoped the bathrooms were, silently communicating that he was on his own. I broke through the rest of the dancing bar-goers and into the other half of the room.

My eyes locked on the tall figure who leaned back against a wall, his ankles crossed like he was channeling the Marlboro Man as he chatted up a visibly swaying, barely clothed woman. Trying to plaster a smile on to cover the plan, I swaggered my way over to the troll in disguise.

"Hey," I said as smoothly as my disgust toward the creature would allow.

The slow turn of his head told me my mad flirting skills hadn't had any effect.

He looked me up and down. "Not interested," he spat.

He didn't bother to even slightly change his posture but simply turned his head away. I was dismissed. Sucked for him. I'd used up all my dancing, flirting, and patience skills. All I had left was getting dirty. Taking a step closer, I leaned toward him.

"Look, you Farfucker, your getup isn't fooling me. We both know you aren't human, so let's make this easy and leave these people alone. There's no reason to get them involved."

The rune around my neck had enough power left to fuel me through another fight. Combined with adrenaline in my veins and pizza in my gut, I could have taken him down right there. But it would be better not to make a scene if I could avoid it.

"Back the fuck off." He scowled. "I don't know who you think you are, but I'm not going anywhere with you."

"Yeah, you are." I reached into my pocket for my switchblade.

CHAPTER TEN

At the sight of my blade, the disguised troll let out a sound that was somewhere between a grunt and a choke, but that I interpreted as a mirthless laugh.

"Just try. I could snap half these people into pieces before you did any damage with that cute little knife of yours. Where did you get that thing, anyway? Does it have a spoon? Maybe lip gloss?"

That was it.

Masquerade as a human to pick up chicks. Fine. Commit some egregious social faux pas. Also fine. Threatening innocent people *and* insulting my switchblade? Too fucking far.

My thumb flicked the blade open.

In one swift movement, I slashed the blade across his face. It wasn't a deep blow, but thick green blood dripped from behind his human mask. Gross. And revealing. The startled troll leaned toward me, and as he did, I kicked his knee. Not an elegant move, but effective. Trolls are a little top-heavy, and his sudden movement paired with the attack on his legs threw him off balance.

He crashed to the floor with a heavy thud.

The humans around us gasped and scattered, some trying to get as far away as they could and others hovering nearby to watch the circus unfold. All they needed was some popcorn.

Dropping on top of him, I flung a smile in the general direction of whoever was watching.

"My brother," I said apologetically. "Doesn't know his limits. Can't hold his mimosas. Don't mind us."

I held the small blade against his neck, pushing it deep enough to let him know I meant business, while pretending to pat the troll's face lovingly.

"Get the hell up and come outside with me willingly, and we can make this easier," I whispered through the gritted teeth of my forced smile.

There were too many inquisitive human eyes on us right then for me to finish this inside the bar. I still needed to get him outside to do the final takedown, and it looked like that would be more challenging than I'd hoped.

All the starry-eyed optimism of getting out of that prison had warped me into thinking this would be *My Evening with the Troll: The Musical.* No chance we would hold hands and skip along merrily as he followed me out of the bar and let me send him back whence he came.

I climbed to my feet and the blade slipped from his neck, giving him time to move. He let out an infuriated roar and pushed himself up surprisingly fast for someone so large. Bloodshot eyes locked on mine. They held promise of a battle he thought would be swift and easy.

My name might be infamous among Farlings, but they would never stop underestimating me. I was only human after all—and a short, starved woman at that. What could little old me do against such a big bad beast?

But this beast didn't know me, didn't know how dirty this human woman was willing to fight. I might not have known everything about The Far, but I knew myself and what the skills Solon taught me made me capable of doing.

He swung a massive fist at my head. It would have knocked me flat on my ass if it made contact, but being considerably smaller gave me the advantage. I ducked it easily and stabbed the soft flesh under his armpit. Then I moved in close to him, throwing my arms around his waist in a fake hug I hoped would conceal my knee plowing directly into his groin.

"I know, Big Brother," I said loudly enough for everyone around us to hear. "Learning you have shriveling dick disease is hard. But I'm sure the doctors will find the right medicine. Let's get you home."

The wheezing sound that escaped him was a few octaves higher than the growl he'd been talking in earlier, and I grabbed the back of his shirt, thinking he might be easier to get outside in his incapacitated state.

"I don't know who you think you are, but you'll regret coming in here. Playtime is over, little girl," the troll snarled.

It was almost immediately obvious I had miscalculated the intensity of the impact as the troll spun out of my grip.

I turned and caught a face full of flying chair, sending me crashing backward into an ancient jukebox. Some fun honky-tonk music popping on would have added atmosphere to the fight, but it moved with me, and I realized it was unplugged. The soundtrack to the fight would have been nice, but I didn't have much time to be disappointed. I reached back, grabbed the cord that snaked along the ground, then shot to my feet.

He lowered his head as he charged me—a primitive battle tactic from the days when trolls wore large horned helmets into battle. That was a piece of information I'd told Solon would never come up. As usual, he was right and I was wrong.

I sidestepped him easily, wrapping the cord in my hand around his neck and lassoing him to the ground. His skin turned a sickly green color, which I knew meant we were running out of time. The human image was cracking and the troll within was leaking through. I needed to get him out of the bar fast.

Pulling tight, I hoped to knock him out, gaining enough control to drag his unconscious carcass out of here, but the troll hadn't given up yet. He pushed himself up to his knees, and the muscles in his neck strained until they snapped the cord.

Shit.

"Stop trying to be a hero," the troll growled.

"Come on," I said. "I see your true colors." As I hoped, the onlookers picked up the song. "Listen to that. We didn't need the jukebox after all."

The big boy was pissed and shoved me like a linebacker trying to break through the defense. My body went soaring, crashing through a door and landing on a sticky tiled floor just beyond. I pulled myself up, brushing my hands on my legs and wondering why they were suddenly wet, when I realized I wasn't alone in the room.

Standing in front of me, his hands still on his zipper, was a very confused, heavily intoxicated man in his early thirties. Gross. Trolls weren't known for their manners, but tossing me into the grimy bar bathroom was just wrong. My new inebriated friend swayed a little as his brow creased, trying to figure out where I had come from. He didn't have a lot of time to think it through, because the troll barreled in after me, and I dove to avoid him.

He crashed into the mirror and dislodged a urinal from its place as his body slid down the wall. Before I had time to react, he grabbed the urinal and ripped it off the wall. Water sprayed everywhere as he flung it spiraling toward the confused patron, narrowly missing his skull.

"Hey…" he said in a tone that suggested that he realized something was offensive about the situation at hand, but he couldn't quite place what it was yet.

I didn't stick around to let him finish his thought. I ran headlong into the troll's stomach, ramming the back of his head into the shattered mirror.

"You have *got* to stop throwing stuff. Keep your hands, feet, and urinals to yourself."

He let out a roar of pain and clubbed my back, but I yanked my knee up and planted it firmly into his gut.

Unfortunately, trolls have quite a sizeable gut. He wheezed for a moment and crumpled, but suddenly exploded forward again, sending us crashing into the stalls. I rolled with the momentum and found myself behind him as he climbed up from the remains of one of the old wooden doors.

I hopped up on his back and wrapped my arms around his throat, hoping to choke him into submission. At first, he thrashed and grabbed at me, but then he resorted to running backward at the wall. After the first bone-crushing smash, I kicked out my legs on the way back and as soon as they were in touch with the concrete I straightened my knees, propelling us both out of the door and back into the main room.

"He feels so much better now," I announced.

The scattered applause reminded me of why drunk people were simultaneously some of my favorite and least favorite people before getting sent to The Deep.

I tumbled off the troll and saw him slumped against the wall, seething with rage. A fluff of pink soap foam he must have collected during his encounter with the sink clung to his hair, taking some of the edge off his intimidation factor. Now he looked like a *real* troll.

A hand touched my wrist, pulling me back, and a man stepped in front of me. It took a few seconds for me to process that it was the bartender who had poured me the heavenly beer to soothe my taco heartache.

"I'll take care of him for you," he said heroically.

Of course. Now he decided to swoop in and help. Not when a chair was flying at my face. Not when I was flopping around on the bathroom floor trying not to let any bare skin touch the tile. But now that I had already done the fight equivalent of loosening the jar lid for him. Outstanding.

"Oh, shit," I muttered under my breath. Ducking around him, I inserted myself between the two men again. "It's fine," I said. "I've got this."

"You leave her alone," the bartender demanded. "Get out of here."

"I've *really* got this. We used to roughhouse like this all the time as kids. I just need to get him home."

"Are you sure?" he asked.

Stretching my face into another smile I hoped would come across as confident and pleasant rather than terrifying, I turned to face the bartender again.

"Absolutely," I told him.

His eyes grew wider than I would have thought the word warranted, and I whipped around to see the troll holding the jukebox over his head.

Shit. Apparently, he thought we did still need it.

The troll took a step forward as he lifted the jukebox higher. All pretense of this being a normal bar fight had officially evaporated. These humans would have a story to tell tomorrow, a story that would reach all the way to the Philosopher's Guild. Which sucked for me. But it also meant that there was no more reason for me to pull my punches.

Shoving the bartender out of the way, I darted to one side, hoping to divert the troll's attention. It worked, and he launched the jukebox in that direction rather than at the crowd. I tried to drop to the ground to roll away, but the corner caught me in the back of the shoulder. Rather than a smooth Bond-esque move to escape the assault, I ended up crashing through a table and narrowly avoided the discography of several generations past crushing my head.

If it wasn't for the strength Solon's locket gave me, a blow like that would have knocked me out of commission. Even with the rune, it hurt like hell.

I looked down at myself. Piss and blood covered my new coat, and I even noticed a chunk of the troll's hair plastered to the leather.

All right. I was ready to wrap this up. It was time to roll credits.

Checking to make sure all the humans were safe, I grabbed the nearest shard of wood and threw it at the troll. It had no chance of hurting him, but it achieved the distraction I'd intended. Time to go all in.

Jumping onto a nearby table, I threw myself through the air at him, spreading myself out like a spider monkey. My foot caught him under the chin as I flipped backward. The force of the blow sent him reeling, and I heard his head crack against the wall.

I landed in a crouch, then dove forward, swiping a pint out of the hand of a confused woman. I quickly downed the drink, as much for badass points as for the beer itself, then smashed the empty glass over the troll's head. That seemed to do the trick, and he slowly went limp.

Part of me wanted to give him another whack for good measure, but I figured that might be overdoing it, considering I was fairly certain at least twenty people had already called the police. There wasn't enough creativity in me to fancy-talk my way out of this if they showed up. I needed to get out of here now.

Scrambling off him, I grabbed the troll by his wrists and started dragging him across the floor. His head smacked into a chair, and I grimaced. Two men in front of me rushed to move a table out of the way and I flashed them a smile.

"Thank you so much. That's sweet of you. I had a lovely evening. Goodnight, everyone. Tip your waiters."

I dragged the troll to the bar door against a backdrop of shocked whispers. A woman caught my eye, and I glanced back at her. She stared at me like she knew me for a fraction of a second, but one of my new fans stepped in front of her to cheer me on, and I lost sight of her.

Pushing away the strange feeling, I yanked the troll through the door and out into the night. I waited for the door to swing closed behind me to roll him off the curb into a puddle. The neon light reflection rippled as the troll sputtered, and I planted a kick in his side to force his face out of the water. No need to add troll drowning to my charges.

"Can I help you get him in a cab?" a man asked as he stepped outside.

My arms flung around the troll in another fake hug. This was awkward family photo circa the 1980s realness, and I hoped it would convince the Samaritan-wannabe for a few more seconds. Sirens rang out in the distance. I blew a stream of air at a chunk of hair that had fallen in front of my eyes. It promptly dropped right back in place.

"You know, I'm good. But thanks so much. Tell the bartender I'll see him Wednesday. Two crunchy and a soft. All the beans. He'll know what it means."

I gave him a finger-wave. That finally seemed to convince him, and he nodded before reluctantly stepping back inside. The troll plopped out of my arms back into the puddle. A soft groan spilled out of him.

Now to figure out what the hell to do with him.

CHAPTER ELEVEN

"What am I supposed to do with you now?" I asked the troll.

He let out a garbled groan, and I nudged him with my toe.

"It was a rhetorical question."

I was in a moral conundrum. A big part of me wanted to just continue with the direction I had already been going during the fight and kill the thing.

If I did it fast enough, no one would notice and I could slip away, letting whoever eventually found him deal with it. But the annoying little Jiminy Cricket part of my brain stopped me. It's not like I hadn't disposed of creatures before, and I'd certainly been there with Solon when he did what he needed to do to make sure we both survived the prison. He could wipe out creeps with the best of them.

But that was in there. In The Deep. Out here, breathing in the earthly air, it didn't feel right to do the exact thing I had been wrongfully accused of. It's not like I had *seen* the troll do anything bad. And Solon told me that there were plenty of decent Farsiders, although he was the only one I'd ever met. This troll didn't seem decent, but did I know enough to off him?

Weighing the ethical pros and cons was wasting time, so I came up with an alternative.

If I tied the troll up in some inconspicuous place, it would ensure he didn't lash out at the humans again, while also keeping him contained. As much effort as went into not making a huge scene in the bar, the truth was it had been a dumpster fire of fairly epic proportions, and that wouldn't slide by.

When something like that happened, there was no way the Guild wouldn't hear about it. They didn't automatically know what was happening or what crimes were committed, but Farsiders were everywhere. And they sure loved to gossip.

The troll stood out to me in the bar, but if I'd taken the time to look around, there probably would have been more. That meant they knew what was going on and would have alerted the Guild. I looked around and spotted an option. The big dented van a few parking spots down was bound to have what I needed.

It didn't take long to pop the lock on the back and open the double doors. Most of the lessons I'd need to carry me through my return to The Near came from Solon, but there were a few that were leftovers from my time before prison. One was that big ugly vans like this always had a tangle of bungees or extension cords in the back. Sometimes both.

Grabbing a couple of each, I rushed back to the troll. He was still sprawled out on the ground and I grabbed his arms again, using the same technique from the bar to drag him a few feet down the sidewalk and into a nearby alley. I made quick work of binding his wrists and ankles, then attached them together to make it even harder for him to escape should he spring back to perkiness anytime soon.

It almost wasn't quickly enough. As I was tying the last of the knots, Splinter started chittering in my pocket. I ducked behind a dumpster as muffled voices announced the arrival of two figures in the alley.

I didn't have to be closer to them to know they were agents dispatched by the Guild. What I could see from my vantage point was reassuring. Well, as reassuring as anything could be considering the situation. The Guild could have sent out some of their more ruthless agents. Instead, I recognized Philosophers Ficino the Third and Rozanov the Ninth, the bumbling buddy cops of The Heights.

I had seen them in action several times in The Deep, from a distance. I'd been lucky enough to stay out of their hair. Not that they were the worst I'd seen. Far from the high-level thinking and astonishing power of some other wizards, these two represented far less of a risk than most. The lack of intellect did nothing for the confidence of these wizards, and they both puffed out their chests as they prepared to handle the issue in front of them.

"Who do you think tied him up?" Ficino asked.

Rozanov glared at him.

"Who cares? This makes it easier on us."

"I don't know. It seems strange to get here all ready to have to take down a rogue troll only to find it already tied up and out like a light."

"The tip the Guild got said the troll was fighting with someone in the bar," Rozanov said. "Probably one of them tied him up.

"That means Nearlings must have seen what happened. We need to take care of that."

"Fights happen in Near bars all the time," Rozanov dismissed.

"Not like this. It was apparently quite the performance."

I couldn't help feeling a little proud about that. It would have been better to get through the fight without causing a ruckus, but the fact that my skills caught the attention of a Farling felt like a compliment. But I couldn't let that soften me.

Not knowing which of the seemingly unassuming onlookers were Farfolk was disconcerting. I'd have to be more careful and aware of my surroundings moving forward. Disguised Farlings couldn't be trusted, and I had to protect myself.

Rozanov kicked the troll's boot.

"Go ahead and call in a crowd control team. They can take care of the Nearsiders in the bar while we get this lump out of the way."

Ficino crossed his hands in an intricate motion. I knew what that meant—a spell designed to call in reinforcements. They'd arrive in a matter of moments, infiltrate the bar, and wipe the memories of everyone there. It was one of the Philosopher Guild's many methods of maintaining secrecy.

I'd seen it happen during my time in The Deep and it was even more horrifying than it sounded. It was possible not to cause too much damage, and those who only had their minds wiped once or twice could usually get by all right. But some Philosophers took joy in chipping away at people by siphoning away their core memories.

Rather than choosing a few minutes or a couple of days they wanted to selectively remove, they'd wipe away huge chunks of time, digging into the base of the person until they started forgetting basic elements of themselves.

The worst were the ones whose memory of The Deep and why they were there was taken away. They'd come out of the memory removal oblivious to what was happening to them. The wizards let them stumble around, terrified, until they figured out what was going on and started to adapt. Then they'd put them through it again. It was *Groundhog Day* from hell.

The two Philosophers stepped up closer to the troll and took turns nudging him with their boots. This turned into repeated kicking before they untied him. Even a pair of trained Philosophers wouldn't fight a troll if they didn't have to.

They'd loosened up his feet and were trying to navigate the complex series of knots that attached his hands when the troll started waking up. At first, he only made a few grumbling sounds. They could as easily have been him thinking he was having a heart-to-heart with his teddy bear. Then the sounds started turning into discernible words.

"Stupid human bitch," he muttered.

It wasn't the most pleasant thing to hear from someone when they first woke up, but it at least verified I hadn't scrambled his brain too much.

"Did he say *human?*" Rozanov asked.

Ficino the Third's eyes widened.

"You don't think he's talking about…" he started, but his voice trailed off.

"What? Sara Slick?" Rozanov scoffed. "No way. She's only some nonsense the Farsiders use to scare kids."

"I don't know, man. The Guild is all up in arms about something tonight. And the boss told us to keep a lookout for a badass human-looking chick."

"The boss doesn't know what she's talking about. Think about it. There's no way some Nearsider did enough to get sent to The Deep. And then escape? Bullshit. No one has ever escaped from The Deep. Especially not some little human woman. She's nothing more than a boogeyman," Rozanov told him.

"But you heard him. He said *human*," Ficino insisted.

"The drunk ass troll doesn't know shit. Let's get this cleaned up."

I had to bite my lip to stop from laughing. The interaction was one of the most amusing things I'd heard in as long as I could remember. These two men were talking about me like I was what lurked in their nightmares and they had to put on a macho front to avoid admitting they were afraid. Of me. Little rag-wearing, glider rat-carrying, taco-loving, goblin eyeball-stealing Sara Slick.

But it also meant that the Guild had alerted their agents to my escape. Ficino and Rozanov might be too dumb to believe it, but that wouldn't hold for long. What I had to do next would be more challenging than I had imagined.

The whole incident with the troll only made it harder for me to stay out of their grasp. The Guild would have everyone out hunting for me, and every step of what I faced would draw more attention to me.

The thought that I could ignore it all went through my mind. Maybe Burne was merely some blitzed out monster. Maybe this Hobbes figure and his death cult didn't really exist. Maybe I could cut my losses and run. It might not last forever, but I could enjoy the time I had free, maybe laying out on the beach eating tacos.

But that dream felt like shit. Tacos or no tacos, escaping from The Deep wasn't only about regaining my freedom. There was no way I'd be able to live with myself if something bad happened because I wanted to relax. Even if I was putting myself right in the line of danger and risking getting caught, I had to do something.

I had to save the world.

CHAPTER TWELVE

I slipped away from the bar easily enough since the Philosophers had their hands full anyway and made my way deeper into the city. If my dancing partner wasn't lying, and if Burne hadn't been full of shit, the Harbingers' base was several miles away.

The city was quiet, and I moved quickly, trying my best not to get lost in the maze of alleys and dark roads. Burne's words echoed through my mind as I took in the closed storefronts and peaceful homes.

The war is beginning!

Not here, it wouldn't. Not if I could help it. My chance at a normal life might have ended, but I could still fight for my family to have one.

I could still hear his voice as I pushed through a gap in the rusty gate of what looked like an abandoned warehouse. Essentially an ugly pale concrete rectangle plopped down in the middle of a parking lot, it reminded me of my brief days of Lego engineering. My imagination conjured a glorious castle. I ended up with a rectangle. A rustic woodland cabin. Rectangle. Impressive city skyscraper. Slightly taller rectangle.

I entered the building through an unmarked door in the back and crouched behind a wall about as inspired as the outside of the building. I waited, the tension building in my stomach as the seconds ticked by. No alarms, no guards coming to arrest me.

The details Burne provided me about the hideout weren't much, but it was enough to assure me as I stood there in the dust and dirt of the forgotten warehouse floor that I'd found my way to it. Or at least close by. But something didn't feel quite right.

Standing next to the wall and not being able to see anything wasn't getting me anywhere. Bracing myself for a situation that could seriously suck if it went wrong, I eased myself further into the room and the sound of voices immediately struck me. I fought the panic rising in me and made for a pile of discarded metal.

From where I hunched behind it, I could barely see two figures. One was dressed in a long red robe that definitely made me think he had bought it at some discount Cults-R-Us store. He stood stone-like in the middle of the room, his face concealed in the darkness of his hood.

The other was a young man with a thick bush of red hair. Instead of a robe, he dressed in jeans and a tattered flannel, but there was no mistaking the pointed ears of a Philosopher. The redhead Philosopher gestured wildly as he spoke while the robed figure stayed eerily steady. Finally, one robed arm moved, a single sharp gesture that shut the young man up.

He nodded, his red hair bobbing, and then he ran off into the shadow of the factory.

Which left only one robed man and me.

I didn't know what to expect here tonight. Burne's blathering made it seem like I'd be coming up against an army, but I could probably take down one weirdo in a robe. I started to move, when a sound behind me made my heart jump into my throat.

I whipped around, grabbed the person behind me, and slammed them up against the wall.

"Sara? Holy hell, it *is* you."

CHAPTER THIRTEEN

The voice clicked in my mind before the face did. Jumbled memories from another lifetime rushed through me. When they finally meshed after a few seconds, I realized I was staring into the shocked, bewildered face of my best friend Alejandra. At least, maybe my best friend. It had been ten years since we'd seen each other, but that was all I had to go with, so I was sticking to it.

"I can't believe it's you," she said.

In that moment, I wasn't really believing it was me, either.

"What are you doing here?" I asked. "How did you find me?"

"I was in the bar." As soon as she said it, the memory of her face among the other patrons resurfaced. It had been so familiar. Now I knew why. "I snuck out after you and followed you here. What the hell is going on? Where have you been?"

Before I had a chance to try to catch her up or figure out what I was going to do to get her out of the serious danger she'd wandered into, a set of huge bay doors opened. My eyes darted to the shadowy corner where the robed figure had been standing, but I couldn't see him anymore. In the time I'd been paying attention to Ally, something had changed. The grinding of metal and roar of an engine announced a truck rolling through the warehouse toward the large open door.

"Oh, shit," I muttered. "I was right."

"What?" Ally asked. "What were you right about? What's going on? Who is that?"

"The Harbingers," I said. "You need to go. Get out of here."

"Who are the Harbingers?" Ally asked.

I made sure the locket was secure around my neck. It didn't have much charge left, but it would have to do.

"Ally, you need to go. Now. Seriously. You need to leave."

I took a step down the short corridor leading into the open warehouse, and she followed.

"Sara, what's going on? What are Harbingers?"

I sighed, trying to find an answer that would get her to shut up. I tried the truth.

"The Harbingers are radicalized followers of Hobbes the Twenty-third. They are essentially a cult who will do his bidding no matter what, which right now means starting a war to bring down the *Pax Philosophia* and go to war with The Near," I told her as fast as I could get the words out of my mouth.

Her large dark eyes blinked.

"I don't know what any of those words meant."

"Yeah and unfortunately now is not the time for a seminar," I told her.

I pulled the switchblade from my pocket.

"What is that thing?" she asked.

"What does it look like?"

"It looks like you're about to join up with the Sharks to fight the Jets," she said, her voice getting higher.

I couldn't help but laugh. "You're not far from the truth. Now please get out of here. I have to stop them. If they get out and I lose them, there's no way I'll find them again," I told her before running toward the truck.

It was almost out of the warehouse, but its slow pace meant I could still catch it. Once I caught it... Well, we'd cross that bridge when we came to it.

Taking Solon's switchblade from my pocket, I aimed it toward the truck and threw it. As if he could sense that shit was about to go down, Splinter scurried out of my pocket and across the floor. I wasn't worried about him. He'd find a crevice where he could hide and pretend the fight wasn't happening, then join up with me again when it was over. It was better that way. Him not being in my pocket meant I didn't have to worry about crushing him while fighting.

The sound of the blade popping the tire and the subsequent flattening was enough to slow the truck's progress. A second later, the driver put it into reverse so it came back into the warehouse before screeching to a halt. I barely had long enough to rush forward and reclaim the blade. The back doors swung open as I backed away. I knew I couldn't hope it would be bungees and electrical cords coming out of there. Farsiders spilled out of the truck.

A lot of Farsiders.

I fought the urge to run as the mob of creatures circled me, each one more gnarly than the last. I had expected a fight, maybe even a bad one. But Burne's fever dream of a rant didn't come close to describing what I'd be up against. This was no trumped-up goblin gang. Hobbes' Harbinger cult outnumbered me at least ten to one.

Solon had always taught me to be careful, to keep my wits about me. Rushing in like this was beyond stupid. But I had no choice. My head whipped from one side and I met eyes with several of them, trying to size up what I'd be fighting. A nasty warthog-looking guy snorted at me, sending spews of slimy green snot all over his face. Another of the creatures, covered in what looked like matted feathers from head to toe and a stench so strong I could smell it over all the others, cackled in a high pitch.

I would lose. I knew it then without a doubt. Every step I took tonight had been a risk, a long shot at best. But here I was at the final stage, and I knew in my bones I couldn't stop them.

That wouldn't stop me from trying.

"So," I said, trying to make my voice sound as casual as possible. "This is like one of those Kung Fu movie fight scenes and you guys are going to come after me one at a time, right?"

A moment of silence greeted my hopeful joke, and I realized their silence was an attempt to scare me. I responded by standing up, no longer in a ready fighting position, and looked down at my nails.

"Well, whoever's first better get on with it. I don't have all day."

A sound like an anvil being struck in a canyon

answered my taunt, and I spun to see a golem step forward. He was hairless, and his skin looked like it was made of cut stone. One whack with his rocky hand and I might not be functional for a few weeks. My hand slid back behind my waist and grasped the blade.

"I'll go," the thing said, pulling his hood off his face to reveal large, round white eyes with a single, lonely black dot in the middle. "I'll make your death quick...and painful."

Pleasant.

He charged at me and I rolled to the right, narrowly avoiding his hands, and sliced at his stomach. The blade barely penetrated his thick skin, and when the golem stopped his momentum, he looked down at where I had swiped him and laughed. The switchblade was a fabulous weapon. Solon made it perfectly balanced so it was easy to throw and was sharp enough to cut through almost anything without dulling. But it was still a switchblade. The edge wouldn't do much damage to this creature's stone-like skin. He charged again, and this time, even with the locket's magic helping me, I wasn't fast enough. His hand grasped my waist and pulled me close to him. I frantically swung my blade at his hands and arms, but they barely made any indentions. A small bit of pus-like red blood bubbled to the surface of one cut, but otherwise it looked like I had marked him with a Sharpie.

He tossed me aside and I flew through the air, rolling until I hit the front wheel of the truck. A thought ran through my mind, and I stumbled to my feet. The golem was preparing to charge me again as I wiped the slow trickle of blood from my nose on my sleeve. I touched the blood on my upper lip with my fingers and then looked down at it, then at him. Then I showed him one particular finger.

The golem ducked low to charge me and I jumped straight up and over his head as he barreled at me. He crashed into the truck and sent the whole rig tumbling sideways before it exploded in a shower of fire and steel. He'd feel that.

The golem was hurt, and I prepared myself to hurt him more when I felt a massive blow to the back of my head. I crumpled to the dirty ground, fighting to maintain consciousness. I turned to look up at my attacker.

A light behind him created a shadow so dark I couldn't make out his features too well, and my vision was blurry from the hit, but there was no mistaking the scar across his face. It wasn't the cool, Bond villain kind of scar. His whole left side from chin to temple was a ragged mess of burned flesh.

I knew immediately who he was.

Spinoza the Eighth. A Philosopher and one mean son of a bitch. Not that I'd had the opportunity to sit down for tea with him or anything. I'd only heard Solon's stories and the mad ramblings of some of my fellow inmates who had found themselves on his bad side.

Turned out, I was right. One of the group behind him called his name and Spinoza held up a hand to silence him. He unbuttoned the top button of his shirt and reached behind him to pull out a long sword. I realized that he must be in charge of the group as they all kept back, letting him advance on me.

I tried to stand, but the locket around my neck was spent and my body along with it.

Spinoza was a few steps away when suddenly there were sirens everywhere. He looked up, and with another authoritative jerk of his arm, he motioned to the Harbingers who all ran to another waiting truck.

Slowly, he raised the sword and pointed it. "Next time." He turned on his heel and ran to the truck. The sound of squealing rubber accompanied them as they jettisoned away.

I should have been grateful to be alive, but all I could think was that they were escaping. After all that, the Harbingers would get away.

That was a serious bummer.

My head rolled to the side, and I caught sight of the redhead wizard staring at me from the shadows. He watched me for only a second, then ran deeper into the warehouse. I felt someone tugging on me, and I wrenched my arm away before realizing it was Ally. She grabbed me again and started pulling me to my feet.

"We need to be gone before the cops get here," I said.

"Sara," she demanded, "who the hell *are* you?"

CHAPTER FOURTEEN

"I'd really love to catch up, but this is not the place," I told Ally. "I kind of kicked a hornet's nest. This place could be swarming with danger." As I spoke the sirens changed in sound, and I hoped that meant they were speeding toward the Harbinger truck and away from me.

"You can't expect me to accept that," Ally said incredulously.

"Yeah, I kinda do."

"It's been ten years, Sara," she insisted. "I thought you were... I didn't know what happened to you. Now you wander into a bar and beat the living snot out of a couple of guys, and I'm supposed to just roll with it? Like—hey, no big deal, but I'm a fucking superhero now?"

"I'm definitely not a superhero," I told her.

"Well, that's reassuring," she said sarcastically.

"Look, I'll tell you everything if you'll come with me out of this place. You don't need to be here," I bargained. Ally gave a weak nod. "Good enough. Come on, Splinter."

"Splinter?" Ally asked, but before I could say anything,

she screamed and jumped back. "Sara, watch out! There's a mutant rodent coming after you!"

I leaned down to scoop up Splinter. He settled onto my palm, and I held him out toward her. She cringed and pulled away from him.

"This is Splinter," I told her.

"You have a name for it?" she asked.

"Of course, I do. He's my friend."

"He's a rat." She looked a little closer. "I think. Whatever he is, he's super gross."

I pulled Splinter close to my chest, pressing my other hand to the side of his head.

"Don't say things like that about him. He's very sensitive."

"I'm sorry." She pressed her hand over her eyes. "I'm apologizing to a creepy-looking rat thing. What is happening right now?" Her hand fell away from her eyes, and she looked at me. "Come on, then. Let's go."

We rushed out of the warehouse and dipped back through the fence. I was starting down the sidewalk when I noticed Ally head the other direction.

"Where are you going?" I asked.

"Well, I don't feel like walking."

"You brought your car?"

"Yeah," she said as if she couldn't fathom anything else. "I'm surprised you didn't notice me behind you. I had to drive slow as hell to keep you in sight."

"I guess I was too focused on the task ahead of me."

We walked up to a sleek green sports car.

"It's unlocked. Keep the rat off the leather."

"Hey, you don't have the station wagon anymore," I pointed out.

"Not for a long time."

It was a sad moment, but I pushed right on past it, opening the door and climbing into the cool grey interior.

"Go ahead," I said when the wheels were rolling and we were getting away from the warehouse at a good clip. "Ask me whatever you want to know."

Ally glanced over at me, then back at the road.

"Where have you been for the last ten years?"

I was a little touched, to be honest. She could have asked about the golem, or that weird bird creature, or Splinter. That's what I would have asked about—the normal-reality-shattering nightmare creatures she witnessed firsthand. But instead, she asked about me.

Ally was a pretty good friend.

"In The Deep," I told her.

"The Deep what? The Deep Shit? The Deep Blue Sea? The Deep Intellectual Thought?" she pushed.

"Well, I mean, kind of The Deep Shit, but it's just The Deep. It's a prison."

"A *prison*?" she asked in disbelief. "What did you do to get shipped off to the hoosegow? And how did nobody know about it?"

"It's not a normal prison. It's a Far prison."

"Like, in Russia?" she asks.

"Like in a different dimension," I told her. She looked at me sideways and I nodded. "I know what I must sound like, but you need to hear me out on this one. Reality is not quite what you think it is. It's a tad complicated and even after ten years, there are parts of it I'm still a little rusty on, so I'll give you the Reader's Digest Abridged version."

"The TLDR version," she said. Now it was my turn to look at her blankly and her eyes widened slightly. "Too Long, Didn't Read? No? You didn't get a lot of internet time in there, did you?"

"None," I told her. "But listen up. Here we go."

We drove through Charleston as I gave Ally the rundown of The Near, The Heights, and The Deep, and what had happened to me in the decade since I sent her drunk ass home to her brother and didn't see her again. She stayed quiet the whole time I spoke and for several seconds after. By that time, we'd been parked behind an apartment building for almost twenty minutes.

"Uh-huh," she finally said.

"That's it?" I asked.

"Just processing," she said. "Letting it all percolate."

"Take your time." I leaned my head back against the headrest.

"So, we have The Near. That's our world. Earth. Humans. Rolling fields. Purple mountains majesty. CPAs. The whole thing," she said after a long silence.

"Yes," I confirmed.

"And then we have what used to be The Far. That's the other world where all the magical creatures and folk live. At least, it was until something, but nobody really knows what, happened and the two realms smashed into each other and dumped everybody from The Far into The Near," she continued.

"Right," I said. "Pan'Rhea. The great collide which

forced all of us together. The dimension that was The Far split into two broken realms, The Deep and The Heights."

"The Heights is a super-pure dimension only special magical people are allowed into, but no little Earthlings like me," she said.

"The more popular term is *Nearlings*," I told her. "Since we all kind of have to share Earth now, that's the accepted differentiation."

"Seriously, I was just getting the hang of political correctness with the species I actually knew existed. Now you're throwing all this at me?" she complained. "All right, so the other part is The Deep, and that's the really, really bad place where they send all the magical folk who misbehave, and that's where you've been for ten years."

"Yes."

"Because you confessed to crimes you didn't commit to save your father," she continued.

"Yes."

She pointed at my lap.

"And that's your rat," she said.

"Splinter," I confirmed.

"Splinter. And you escaped the inescapable jail because you need to stop a cult that wants to end the balance between The Near and The Far, and abolish the laws regulating the cooperation between the two realms." She dragged in a breath after spitting all that out in one go.

"The *Pax Philosophia*. You're catching on really well," I told her.

I had condensed down months of Solon's lessons to me into that one spiel and Ally's absorption of it was impressive.

"It would seem that way, but there are still a lot of questions happening in this area." She swirled her hand around the top of her head. "Let's go inside."

I looked through the windshield.

"Where are we?"

"My house," she told me.

We climbed out of the car.

"You moved? I thought your parents loved that house," I said.

She looked at me strangely.

"They do. That's why they still live there. This is *my* house."

"Oh. Right. You're an adult now."

She nodded.

"So are you. Strange, isn't it?"

I mirrored her nod.

"In a lot of ways."

"Come on," she told me. "Let's go inside."

I hesitated. Running into my old chum hadn't exactly been the plan. I knew the Guild was looking for me, and I had firsthand experience with the methods they were willing to use to catch me. Ten years had gone by and I had never forgotten the sight of that sword hanging over my dad's head.

"Can we stay out here? I'm enjoying the fresh air. It's been a while. Do you have any other questions?" I asked, trying to gloss by the strangeness of wanting to stay outside in the middle of the night.

"What are the Philosophers again?" she asked. "Not old dudes sitting around thinking about thinking?"

I laughed as we started to walk around the block.

"Not exactly. They're wizards. Each of them takes on the name of a great Philosopher from history," I told her. "A group of them, the Guild, kind of hold all the strings. They send their agents to police the Farsiders and oversee the *Pax Philosophia*."

"Did you learn any magic from them?" she asked.

"It doesn't work that way," I told her. "The Philosophers are their own race, their own species. They look human in most ways, but they aren't. They're Farsiders through and through. Although there are a bunch of different disciplines and most of them really only use one or two, the magic they use is specific to their species. It can't be taught to another species."

"Then how did you strengthen yourself for the fight?" Ally asked.

"Dyadology," I explained. "Runecraft, is how most Farsiders refer to it. Making them requires strong magic and specific items from The Far and The Near, but once they're made, anyone they're given to can use them. My teacher, Solon, was a skilled Runescraftsman. He made several of them for me."

"And he was in the prison, too?" she asked.

"Yes," I told her.

"So, these runes. Can they do…anything?"

I smiled. It felt good to talk, felt good to say all this out loud. Sharing it with Ally, with another human, made everything I had gone through feel less crazy.

"Anything is a bit of a stretch but they can do a lot. It's not a discipline that's greatly respected among the Philosophers. Runes require Near items, which means they aren't allowed anywhere near The Heights. Possessing them and using them isn't illegal, *per se,* but according to Solon, there are some shady dyad dealers here on Earth," I said.

"And one of them made you strong?" she asked.

I pulled out my locket and showed it to her. A faint light had reappeared, letting me know that its charge was returning.

"Solon designed it to give me greater strength and some protection. As a human, I've always been at a disadvantage in The Deep. He wanted to make sure I stayed safe," I explained. "That, and he taught me how to throw a mean right hook."

"I saw that right hook. That and some wild ninja moves. You said that guy in the bar you fought was a troll?" Ally sounded like she was piecing it all together but was still wary of the details.

"Yeah," I affirmed. "I didn't go in there looking for him, but once I realized he was there, he had to go. Trolls are not the type you want hanging around, especially when there are vulnerable women involved."

"I guess magic is as good an explanation for what you did as anything else. My working theories were aliens, government conspiracy, or someone had put something in my drink," she told me.

"All good theories. Speaking of which, what were you doing in that shady bar?"

"Well, we need to go backward a little for me to answer that," she said.

"I'm ready for it."

"When you disappeared, your dad told everyone you were kidnapped. He said he saw nothing suspicious happening."

She sounded suspicious, and I knew she was starting to question my father.

"He probably doesn't think he did," I told her. "The Guild wouldn't want him running around talking about a key that opens a door in reality. They would have wiped his memory after taking me. It's what they did to everybody in the bar after I left tonight, too."

"Then I'm glad I slipped out when I did."

I remembered the moment I glimpsed her in the bar and the look that flickered across her eyes. It had been recognition, even if that recognition brought with it total disbelief.

"Me, too," I agreed. "What else? What happened with my father?" I cringed. "You're not going to tell me the two of you have a thing now, right? Like, he wasn't at the bar or anything?"

Ally's face scrunched up so tight it threatened to fully absorb her eyes. Which sounded much more possible after having watched it happen to a fellow prisoner.

"*Ewwww.* Gross. No. Your Dad cooperated as much as he could. They splashed you all over the news. Your kidnapping was a big story all across the nation. For a while there, it seemed like everyone in the world was looking for you. But no leads ever turned up. No clues ever surfaced. There was nothing to go on and the investigations fizzled out. Everyone moved on. But not me."

"Not you?" I asked.

She shook her head.

"Hell, no. You're my best friend, Sara. You always have been. I wasn't about to let you disappear and pretend like everything was normal. Your father had four other little ones to take care of. He couldn't pour himself entirely into looking for you. But I could, so I did. Losing you really messed me up, so I never stopped searching."

"You have no idea how much it means to me to hear you say that."

"I'd do it again in a heartbeat," she insisted. "I better not have to. But I would. As it is, this search brought me all over. I ended up in some weird places and dove into the nitty-gritty of some strange conspiracy theories."

"Did you find anything?"

"Maybe. Did you know that in the years following your disappearance, all sorts of odd things happened all over the world?"

I leaned toward her.

"I know literally nothing about the years following my disappearance."

"Well, they were weird as hell. Unexplainable things were happening all over the place. Tornadoes in New England. Flooding in Nevada. Terrorist attacks in itty-bitty small towns with no apparent motive. Murder sprees that didn't seem to involve a murderer. And everywhere these things were happening, there was the same story. People with only vague recollections of the time leading up to the events. No idea what really happened. But, like with you, people couldn't figure it out so they eventually moved on."

"But you wouldn't?" I asked.

"No way. In fact, I turned it from a hobby into my career. For the last several years, I've been an investigative blogger. I travel all over trying to figure out what the hell is going on. Which brings me back to the theories of alien interference and mass government conspiracy. Not so much on the whole something-in-my-drink thing. That would be a seriously long-acting mickey."

"Then why were you in the bar?" I repeated.

"One of my investigations," she said. "I never would have believed it would have ended up like this." Her eyes brightened. "Wait…if there was a Far where all sorts of magical creatures and whatnot lived, that means things that people here think are myths might not be."

"In a lot of cases," I agreed.

"You have to tell me." She dropped her voice to a whisper and looked side-to-side conspiratorially. "Is Bigfoot real?"

Laughing, I nodded.

"Yes."

"What about mermaids?" she asked, delighted.

"Absolutely. One ended up in The Deep and they had to flood a cell to keep her in. Sometimes they'd let it drain out, and she'd flop around all miserable until they filled it back up."

"Well, that's mean as shit," she commented.

"They're not the best hosts."

"How about vampires?" she continued.

"Them, too," I confirmed.

"I *knew* it," she said. "There are all sorts of forums online dedicated to cryptozoology and mythical beings. I use them for research and to find people to interview all the time. Let me tell you, there are some whacked-out specimens in this world. One crazy in particular, however, might not be so crazy. She constantly talks about living next to a coven. She says they leave at all hours of the night and bring home people she never sees leave. One time, she looked through her window and saw a ton of blood everywhere."

Ally looked surprised when I laughed.

"Vampires aren't really like that," I said. "Only on TV. The real ones are mostly whiny little nerds. From what you're saying, it sounds like the Philosopher's Guild has been having a field day wiping memories over the last few years."

"Do they do that often?" she asked.

I nodded. "The *Pax Philosophia* has very specific laws regarding how people from the two realms can interact. When those rules are broken, the Guild shows up and wipes everybody's memories to keep things quiet. Most people in The Near have no idea about The Far, and the Guild wants to keep it that way. But it seems like the wipes don't always work. Apparently some things sneak through, or people get away without being caught up in the coverup."

"And end up as people raving on blogs and YouTube videos," Ally added.

"What was the investigation that brought you to the bar?" I asked.

"There's been a string of kidnappings the last couple of months," she replied. "It's happening all over the place and there doesn't seem to be any explanation. There's no connection between the victims and none of the incidents have anything in common. Several have happened right around here. Because they can't figure out what they would have to do with each other, the cops say the disappearances aren't linked in any way."

"But you don't buy that," I guessed.

"Of course, I don't. People don't start vaporizing with no explanation. They have to be related in some way. So, I've been investigating and trying to figure it out before more people die," she said solemnly.

That brought my stomach right up into my throat.

"Die?" I managed to force out.

"In the last few months, several women have gone to that bar, disappeared, then shown up dead three days later."

CHAPTER FIFTEEN

That kind of took the zip right out of our happy reunion.

"They just show up dead?" I asked. "Nobody knows what happened to them or who did it?"

"No." Ally shook her head. "Their bodies weren't exactly in the best condition when they found them. There haven't been any leads for the investigators to follow or anything."

"Yeah, I can see why that would be an issue," I said.

"You don't think it could have anything to do with that troll in the bar, do you?" she asked. "It could have been some Farsider monster doing this because of how much they hate The Near."

The idea made her shudder, but unfortunately there weren't a lot of comforting words coming to mind that I could throw her way. All I could do was be honest and take the edge off as best I could.

"Maybe. But not every Farsider is a raging, bloodthirsty monster. I mean, everyone that I've ever met has been a bit of a dick, except for Solon I guess. And he told me not to judge his kind based on those I met in The Deep. According to him, most Farsiders are good folk, nice enough, and want to live their lives in peace. Not all of them love the idea of interacting with Nearlings on a consistent basis, but they aren't seeking out thrill kills because of it. But, like humans, there are a few bad apples. That troll, for example. Definitely won't be making a pie out of him anytime soon. I can't know for sure, but my guess is that he was at that bar for one reason and one reason only, and that was to pick up chicks so he could kill them."

Ally's eyes widened.

"Why would he do that?" she gulped. "Did he want to… rape them?"

I shook my head.

"Probably not. That's not a thing most Farsiders will do. The *Pax Philosophia* is really specific about the interactions between Farsiders and Nearsiders. Remember, the vast majority of Farlings live in The Near. That's why all the laws had to be created. When they were dumped into this realm, measures had to be put into place to control them. One is a strict regulation against any carnal relations between people of the two realms. It's not all that hard, honestly. Most Farsiders think people from The Near are pretty gross. I highly doubt he'd start prowling bars for that purpose," I told her.

"Thank goodness," she breathed. "I mean…hurtful on the whole self-esteem front. But thank goodness."

"He was probably planning on eating their livers," I said.

Ally's face contorted.

"Because that is *so* much better."

I shrugged.

"That's how they roll." I laughed. "That's how they *t—roll.*" Ally wasn't laughing. "Sorry. I haven't been around people in a long time."

"If turning people's livers into tapas is something this troll dude enjoys, do you think it's possible he could be the one who did the other kidnappings?" Ally asked.

I thought about it for a second. "Maybe he's been using that bar as a hunting ground. But you said this has been happening all over, not only at that crappy honky-tonk. No way the troll did that. Much like the unrefrigerated seafood their smell often resembles, trolls don't travel well. They're the type to pick one place they like and hunker down there. Not to say it definitely *wasn't* a troll that did it, but if a bunch of kidnappings happened in different states, it's highly unlikely they were caused by only one troll."

"So, we're talking a band of trolls situation? A crime ring?" she asked.

It was obvious Ally thought she was right on the edge of some huge break in the case she'd been following for so long, and it was getting kind of sad having to discourage her over and over.

"Probably not on that front, too. Trolls aren't friendly. They don't play nice with others. They separate from their mothers as soon as they're old enough to find food and shelter for themselves, and don't go back," I told her.

"I'm guessing there aren't any beautiful troll weddings or anything that happen regularly?" Ally asked.

"That would be a no. Trolls don't do the whole courtship and mate for life thing. From what I hear, it's more a mate and hope they both survive situation. Fortunately, or maybe not depending on how you look at it, getting pregnant isn't hard for trolls."

She nodded.

"Never thought my late-twenties would include a lesson on the reproductive opportunities of trolls, but you know…life's a journey." She sighed and tilted her head slightly. "Speaking of families, are you going to see yours?"

My heart squeezed, and for the first time in years I was happy my time in The Deep had smashed the tendency to cry right out of me. That was not what I needed right then. Besides, it felt like if I let even one tear slip out, it would reduce me to a sniffling puddle of worthlessness and that wasn't a direction I wanted to go at this particular juncture in my life.

"No," I told her.

I carried hope in my heart that my best friend would accept that answer as enough and move on with our conversation. Not so much.

"Why not? Don't you want to see them? They've been looking for you for ten years."

Her sympathy abounded.

"I know that, and it makes me feel terrible to not be able to go see them. To let them know that I'm okay. Of course I want to, but it's too dangerous. I shouldn't even be talking to you. They'll target anyone I get near. The Guild is after me. I didn't exactly leave The Deep on the best terms with the people there, and I still have nine and a good chunk's worth of lifetimes left to serve. These are not nice people and I want to keep them as far away as possible from anyone I care about."

Ally stared at me intently, but she let whatever she was thinking pass.

"What are you going to do?" Ally asked instead.

"Well, as much as I'd like to think the world is my oyster and I can go frolic through the meadows now, that's not realistic. The truth is, I probably don't have a lot of time ahead of me before I get caught, so I need to use it as effectively as possible. And that means keeping the city safe. These dudes are no joke, Ally. They're planning something terrible and if it happens, it will be a disaster. The only problem is, I have absolutely no leads. The only thing I could use from all his ravings was the location of that warehouse."

"I'll help you," she said without hesitation.

I shook my head adamantly, holding up my hands like I was trying to shove the commitment back at her.

"No. Absolutely not. There's no way I can let you do that. It's way too dangerous."

"Charleston is my home, too," she pointed out. "If they pull off their plot, I could get hurt. It's too dangerous for me to *not* get involved. You might not have any leads, but you have me. I've built up some pretty good investigative skills over the last decade."

I stared at her, not wanting to accept the offer, but also knowing there wasn't a ton of choice left to me. With no idea of where to go from there, it limited my plans for what to do next to sitting on the ground and hoping one of the Harbingers wandered by handing out flyers about their evil plan.

Shit.

"All right," I finally said. "You can help me."

Ally grinned.

"Awesome. They won't know what hit them. We'll find these guys and stop whatever they're planning before they have the chance to hurt any innocent people."

"And once we get that under control, I'll figure out how to escape before the Guild catches me and dangles me over the Pit in The Deep for a month," I said.

"I don't know what that means, but it sounds like a good plan," she said.

She offered me her fist and I bumped mine against it. That was it. We'd sealed our partnership for life. Now I needed to figure out how to make that whole "for life" part last more than the next couple of days.

"Trust me, you don't want to know what it means. If for some strange and sadistic reason you do, I'll tell you over tacos sometime." I gasped, my hand going to my chest. "Tacos! I need some."

Ally laughed.

"Still an obsession for you, huh?" she asked.

"I haven't laid lips on a taco in a decade, Alejandra. *A decade*. I was denied a whole plate of them the night they took me to The Deep. You and all three hundred r's you put in your name should have some compassion for that," I told her dramatically.

She laughed again.

"I know that's hard on you. But it's late. I know I need some sleep and I'm sure you could use some, too. Why don't you come to my place?"

We had made it back around the loop, and she was pointing toward her apartment. It was an amazing offer and one I wanted to jump on, but I couldn't bring myself to put her in even more danger. Being near her at all was already a risk. There was no way I was going to potentially lead the Guild to her house.

"Thanks, but I already have a spot. I'll meet up with you tomorrow."

It was a complete lie, but at least it would funnel the Guild away from her if they showed up.

"Are you sure?" she asked suspiciously.

"Absolutely," I confirmed.

Absolutely not.

"All right. Well, if you need anything or change your mind, call me." She pulled out a smooth, flat little device and poked the screen on the front. "What's your... Oh, shit. You probably don't have a cell phone, do you?"

"Nope, didn't have a chance to snag one in the less than five hours I've been out of the pokey." I snatched the device from her hand and stared down at it. "Is this seriously what phones look like now? The words at the top of the device caught my eye. *"There's an iPhone 8 now?"*

"Actually, that's outdated as hell. I haven't been able to afford a new one since I so inconveniently smashed the last four during investigations." She carefully took the phone back.

"It's so sleek."

"You should see some of the other ridiculous stuff they have on the market now."

"I want to see *everything.*"

"We'll get right on that as soon as we get through the first two steps of our mission," she promised.

"Stop the destruction of Charleston and escape the Guild," I recapped.

"Those are the ones. You're positive you don't want to come back to my house? Old-school slumber party?"

She was pulling at my heartstrings, but since I'd prefer all her heartstrings to remain in their current not-snapped-in-half-by-magic condition, I had to decline. She finally relented and gave me a hug.

"I missed you." She must have really meant it. Even in my grimy condition, she didn't flinch as she pulled me close. "I'll see you tomorrow."

The words were insistent, like they held the unspoken parenthesized comment *because you damn well better not get yourself stolen again.*

CHAPTER SIXTEEN

One of the few things Solon didn't teach me during our years of lessons was what to do if I finally *did* manage to break out of The Deep. There were no simulations or role-playing sessions that could guide me through wandering around the city a couple of hours before dawn, completely exhausted, and with zero concept of what to do next.

As I walked along a dark sidewalk a few blocks away from where Ally and I had split up, I contemplated my next move. Whatever it was, it needed to balance my need for sleep and shelter with my need to duck the Guild as much as humanly possible, for as long as humanly possible.

It took me twenty minutes of strolling the street, but I ended up doing what any self-respecting escapee does when they find themselves out in the world for the first time in a decade.

I broke into the first abandoned hotel I found.

It was at the end of an unused avenue, creating a dead end that more appropriately embodied that term than anything else I'd ever seen. Except possibly the Dead End in The Deep, which was an unfortunate nickname thrown around by the guards for the bloody heap of bodies that ended up piled at the end of a hallway during what amounted to a prisoner hunt they held for fun. A tall chain-link fence surrounded the lot, but it might as well have been a welcome mat.

It only took a few seconds for me to find a vulnerable spot in the fence and lift the bottom where it was loosened from the ground. My prison-shrunken frame slipped under easily. Splinter popped his head out of my pocket and looked around like he was surveying the surroundings.

"What do you think, buddy? Think this could be our new digs for tonight?"

He didn't retreat into my pocket while shuddering, so I took that as a good sign and crossed the cracked parking lot over patches of grass and small trees attempting to reclaim the area for nature. The building looked like it had been hunkering in that spot on its own for years. I commiserated with it. Even before I found the front doors, only blocked with two pathetic boards crossed over them, it felt like the hotel was welcoming me. We understood each other. Both a little broken down. Both a little janky. Both still determined to stand after time had done its best to beat the living hell out of us.

It took almost no effort to break the boards out of place. The doors opened, and I slipped through into the abandoned lobby. Enough moonlight and glow from the streetlights outside filtered through the glass doors and large windows to illuminate the silhouette of furniture, clustered in little seating arrangements throughout the space. Small sofas and chairs covered in dust and cobwebs waited for someone to sit on them, with coffee to rest on the table in front. I walked through the damp, musty-smelling room toward the front desk.

"The name's Sara Slick," I said to the empty space behind the desk. "I'll need a room for one." Splinter's sharp little teeth sank into my thigh, and I jumped. "Sorry. A room for two."

I paused for a silent moment to let the fake hotel employee answer.

"You have a vacancy? Awesome. Just down the hall? Sounds perfect. Thanks for your help."

The light from outside was having a harder time getting this far into the space and by the time I reached the first hallway of rooms, it was almost completely dark.

I pulled the locket out from under my shirt and opened it. As soon as it did, a bright blue glow stretched out from it, filling the entire space around me. That was enough to show me the first door along the hallway. It was the typical cheap hotel room door and the distinct imprint of a boot coupled with the hastily patched frame told me someone else had taken a more industrious path toward getting the door open than using a key card. I saw that as encourage-ment. Right before taking aim with a kick, I reconsidered. Key cards required electricity.

This place didn't have any electricity.

I took hold of the knob and easily opened the door. Hot, heavy air washed over me, bringing with it the smell of old carpet, dust, and beds that had been sitting in a stag-nant state of expectation for years. What it didn't smell like was Goblin or Ogre or Troll or blood, and I was excited about all of it. Well, maybe a little blood. But not nearly as much as I was used to.

The light of the rune brought me across the room to the window. I forced one curtain open a few inches. I wanted to throw them all the way open, but it was far more likely someone would notice a wide-open set of curtains in the abandoned hotel than they would a small sliver. It was enough to let me see to move around, and that was all that mattered. I closed the locket and set it carefully on the nightstand. One of the two beds had experienced something major in its life and was teetering at a sharp angle with one corner sitting on the ground. The other looked stable, and I peeled back the gold blanket to slide between sheets that reminded me of slightly sticky sandpaper. The pillow made a crinkling sound when I rested my head on it, but it was the first pillow I'd seen in ten years.

This was heaven.

I expected to fall asleep immediately. My body was exhausted and while I was walking along the sidewalk, it felt like any second I could tumble into a pile on the concrete and stay there for a few days. But now that I was lying in the creepy bed, marveling at the comfort and far lower population of potential bitey-crawly inhabitants, I couldn't get my eyes to shut. My brain had gone into overdrive and nothing would make it calm down. I even stared at the ceiling and counted the cracks in the plaster.

The image of Solon in my mind wouldn't go away. It was his lessons that brought me here. If he hadn't shown up in that holding cell my first night in The Deep, there would be no way I would have made it to see the next morning, much less last ten years. Not to say he was a wise old grandpa I could think back on and remember for his hugs and hard butterscotch candies that seemed to come out of nowhere. Solon was nothing if not hardened, and that translated into his training. It had to. He had to be as intense and forceful a teacher as he could be to make sure I made it. He knew a human had next to no chance of surviving The Deep and took it upon himself to give me the strongest chances possible.

When he could be with me, Solon trained me day and night. He taught me how to survive. How to fight. How to hide. How to think. Everything I thought I knew about life had to change when I got to The Deep, and he didn't baby me through it. There wasn't a No Child Left Behind safety net to sweep me through if I didn't do well with this extension of my education. If I didn't pick up what he was teaching me, it would be No Pieces of the Child Left Behind. That was exactly what I was when he found me. A child. Not anymore. I was so much more, and I was ready to make him proud.

As I reminisced, letting pleasant memories lull me to sleep, I heard something. It was a high-pitched sound, and at first I thought the hotel had betrayed me and was about to collapse around me. I heard it again and realized it was coming from outside. The sharp, desperate cries were from a dog and it sounded like it was being tortured.

My stomach flipped, and I crawled out of bed and hurried to the window. Pushing the curtains open more, I looked down into the parking lot. My eyes swept over the space until I noticed movement. Pushing the curtain all the way open, I saw a group of guys around my age or slightly younger. They were obviously drunk and by the way they'd gathered around, it looked like they were turning tormenting the animal into their late-night entertainment.

I knew I should leave it alone. This dog wasn't my problem, and with the Guild searching for me, I really should keep my head down. That's what Solon would tell me to do. But then again, Solon stuck out his neck for me, so maybe it was more of a do as I say, not as I do kind of thing. The dog yipped again, followed by more raucous laughter.

Not fucking happening.

CHAPTER SEVENTEEN

The laughing band of merry ass-bags were at the back of the building. It would have saved a ton of time if I could pry the window open and fling myself out at them, but the current condition of humans, and hotels being what they were, the windows didn't open. It didn't seem like a practical move to smash through the glass with the nightstand. That likely would have blown my cover, anyway. Instead, I had to go all the way back through the lobby and out the front door.

Once outside, I rushed around the back of the building as fast as I could. I didn't want them to see me before my attack, so I slipped behind an abandoned dumpster to make sure they hadn't noticed.

When it was clear they hadn't, I snuck up within throwing distance and picked up a broken piece of pavement. Taking aim, I chucked it at one of them and had to stifle a laugh when it connected with the back of his head, making him fall over sideways mid-sentence. The other three looked down at him, swaying in their drunkenness before bursting into laughter of their own.

"Hey Mark, can't handle your beer, man?" one of them yelled at his unconscious friend.

He laughed again, and I chucked another rock that grazed his shoulder.

"What the hell?" another one shouted and turned toward me.

Enough games. Now to teach these boys to pick on someone their own size.

Or half their size, but seriously pissed off, not drunk, and trained through hell and back.

I stepped out of the shadows, my hands behind my back. One of the jerks stepped forward aggressively, and I saw the dog behind him. It was certainly hurt, but it was moving. When I looked closer, I saw one of its legs clamped in an old trap. Seeing it on the ground, these three and their now lumpy-headed friend drunkenly kicking it, sent my blood boiling. I'd been that fucking dog. And I'd watched people die that way. There was no way I would let these wastes of space get their rocks off hurting an innocent animal. I stepped forward equally aggressively, and he stopped, his eyes struggling to focus on me.

"Who the hell are you?" he asked.

At least, I was pretty sure that's what he was asking. It had been awhile since I'd been around drunk people and my ability to translate their slurs was rusty.

"I'm Batman," I growled.

I had *always* wanted to say that. The images of me saying it had always come with better clothes and a sexier atmosphere, but I'd take it.

His face contorted like he had smelled a particularly vicious fart.

"But, you're *a girl...*" he said.

Instead of responding, I rushed forward, closing the space between us in a few long strides, and jumped. His eyes bulged, but the beer slowed down his reaction time enough that the kick I sent his way had no resistance when it connected with his jaw. His body flew backward, and I was pretty sure a tooth soared out as I landed where he'd been standing. Even if it didn't, I would totally say it did in all future retellings of the fight. He deserved nothing less than to have to scramble around looking for it.

The locket which enhanced my strength was lying on the nightstand, recharging. I was on my own and outnumbered. But that was fine. My daddy hadn't raised no fool, and Solon hadn't trained no weakling.

"Anybody else?"

The two remaining frat-boy-looking drunks looked at each other for a moment before apparently deciding on their next course of action. A really dumb one. By the time they had gotten a few steps closer, I was already on them. A left fist and a smashed kneecap sent one bro to the ground, crying out in pain, while I continued pummeling the other. He swung a lame fist toward me that I easily ducked before rapping off a couple of jabs to his ribs.

I knelt low and came up, upper-cutting with my elbow to his jaw. His entire body stiffened on impact and he flew backward like Glass Joe in the old *Punch-Out* game. Much like Glass Joe, that was the end of his night. I spun around to see my now tooth-impaired friend shaking his head and struggling to get off all fours. I raced forward and soccer kicked him in the ribs, and he rolled backward, hollering a few slurred curses before either blacking out or giving up and going to sleep.

Turning again, I focused my attention on the only remaining conscious guy. He was still crumpled on the ground, holding his nose with one hand and putting the other up in an effort to ask for mercy. I was about to tell him to get out when I saw the unmistakable ball of spiky hair that was Splinter appearing behind his head.

"Please, I'm sorry, I... what the hell! Oh god, get it off me," he screamed.

His desperation only got louder as Splinter went to work, spiking him with his hair, clawing at him with his annoyingly sharp nails and occasionally biting him with his vampire fangs. One of the other prisoners in The Deep once said my precious little Splinter looked like all the bits and pieces of reject animals the Maker had tossed onto the workshop floor had been glued together to make him. Right now, it looked like not only was that right, but they had also been all the vicious, feisty parts. That really sucked for the drunk dude.

It was amusing as hell for me.

The frat boy was rolling around screaming, surely unable to tell what was attacking him as Splinter darted all over him. Finally, he shook Splinter off and scrambled to his feet to run. The first guy tried to join him in his hurried retreat, but promptly tripped over a trash can and rolled into his friend. The two stumbled and fell into a tangled heap. They got back to their feet, took one look back, and bolted around the corner.

Splinter's claws clicked as he came up beside me. He

looked distinctly proud of himself. I checked the pulse of the guy I had hit with the chunk of asphalt and noted he was still fine. He would have a raging headache when he woke up, but otherwise, he would be okay. Then I turned my attention to the dog. I went to take a step toward it when I heard Splinter behind me make a growling noise. I looked over at him and saw that his bristles were standing on end and he was staring directly at the cowering black form.

"Splinter," I scolded. "What are you doing? It's only a dog."

As soon as the words got all the way out of my mouth, I knew they were total bullshit. Being at a closer proximity to the animal told me it was most certainly not Fido from next door, ready to play catch and bring in the newspaper. This thing was huge and had a wild air about it. It looked like a wolf or possibly a coyote. Either way, it was still an innocent animal that deserved protection. I was going with dog. It made me feel better.

Splinter didn't let up. His body vibrated like he was trying to convince himself he could transform into something and only needed to build up the oomph to do it. His spikes stuck out from him threateningly and he occasionally threw his tiny arms out to the sides to show off his impressive and not at all frightening flippity-flaps.

"Chill the hell out, Splinter. It's not doing anything. Stop being such a baby."

I extended my hand toward the dog and made a soothing sound. This was all bravado and making shit up. The truth is, I had never been good with Nearside animals. Not that I disliked them, but they never seemed like the biggest fans of me. Something about me never gave off the Snow White vibe. While she was off frolicking in the woods with the birds landing on her fingers and the squirrels braiding her hair or some shit, I was flailing around trying to stop the woodpeckers from eating my brain and the mice from infecting me with rabies.

But I was willing to fake it to convince Splinter to stop having a fit and to comfort the wounded animal. It bristled as I got closer, but I had to get it out of the trap. Wedging one foot into the hinge, I wrenched the nasty contraption open. I was afraid the dog's leg was shattered, but it was apparently stronger than it looked. It was in pain, but able to move. Those guys were lucky the dog had wandered into that trap. He would have torn their asses to shreds if the metal jaws weren't incapacitating him.

There was still a chunk of pizza crust in my pocket and I pulled it out to offer the dog. It refused the food and dragged itself a few feet away, staring at my hand the whole time like I held a knife instead of a crust. I felt like it was judging me. After a few more seconds, it pulled itself to its feet and trotted off. I took the hint and scooped Splinter up, then started back toward the door to the hotel. Glancing over my shoulder, I noticed the dog had stopped. It was sitting at a distance, staring at me like it was keeping watch.

The image triggered something in the back of my mind. It was like a faint glimmer of a memory, reminding me of something, but I couldn't quite grasp it. I tried to shake the weird feeling and headed inside.

CHAPTER EIGHTEEN

The next morning brought with it a glorious lesson. Even when the electricity wasn't working in an abandoned hotel, that didn't necessarily mean there would be no running water. Now, the plumbing wasn't running to the point where I'd put my confidence behind it completing a marathon or anything, but when I gave the handle of the bathroom sink an experimental turn, the faucet sputtered and let out a small stream of water. This immediately elicited a little dance of joy and I stripped as fast as I could before throwing myself into the shower.

No electricity meant no heat, but that didn't bother me in the least. Inside the shower the water came down on me with a lack of pressure that made me feel like I was standing under a giant watering can, and from what I saw, it had a slight brown tinge to it. But it was water coming down on me, not dripping from a leaky ceiling or being shot magically by a Philosopher. That was enough for me. I'd been standing under the stream, luxuriating in the feeling of it working its way through the dirt and oil in my hair and along my skin, when I noticed something out of the corner of my eye. It couldn't be. It was too glorious to be true.

Trepidation made my hand shake as I reached for it. Maybe it would disappear as soon as I touched it, and with it the image of everything else and I'd realize this, along with my entire escape, had been a delusion. That was a lot of expectation to put on the shoulders of a tiny bar of hotel-issue soap, wrapped in glossy green paper. My fingers closed around the bar. It was solid. The trepidation turned to delight, and I tore away the paper as fast as I could. Little bits of it fell to the floor of the shower stall and swirled around my feet with the rusty water. It was like confetti for my celebration of impending cleanliness.

One silver lining of not having any heat in a shower was not having to worry about the hot water running out, and I was taking full advantage of it. This was a five-star spa experience for me, and although there were no cucumber slices for my eyes or a plush robe waiting, I felt all sorts of pampered. When my fingers and toes were sufficiently pruney, I got out of the shower and dried off using a towel that smelled only slightly of mildew. The Deep had taught me not to sleep for extended stretches, which meant I still had hours before it was time to meet up with Ally again. This gave me the opportunity to run my rags through the water with a bit of my precious bar of soap and hang them up to dry.

There wasn't much fabric left to my uniform, so by the time I had to leave to meet Ally around noon, they were barely damp. I threw my stolen jacket on over them, tucked

Splinter into his pocket, and headed out. Ally and I met up at a parking lot near her apartment. She grinned at me when I climbed into the car.

"You're looking a little cleaner this morning," she commented. "I mean, not *clean*, but cleaner."

"Hey, I took my first shower in ten years. That should count for something," I told her.

"Ten years, huh? That has to tell you something about that guy in the bar last night," she said.

"Right?" I agreed. "I've been thinking about that. He was all sorts of into me, and that has to be some sort of insight into him. Either he was at a whole new level of desperation I have yet to experience, or I pull off prison sexy really well. I'm leaning toward the new level of desperation."

Ally laughed and started the car.

"Are you ready for our adventure?"

"Champing at the bit. What do you think our first step should be?"

"Don't you worry about it, Slick. I have a plan."

Hearing her call me by my old nickname warmed my heart and took away some of the uncertainty I felt about including her in this epic mess I'd gotten myself into. She might still be in far more danger than I liked to think about, but I'd been through enough training for the both of us, and Ally was feisty. I was fairly certain all that spicy food she constantly talked about her mother eating when she was pregnant with Ally went straight to her personality.

"Great. So, we'll go pick up some weapons and then I was thinking we should try to get more information..." I started, but the way Ally was shaking her head told me my plan and hers weren't meshing.

"I told you I have a plan."

"And it doesn't involve getting weapons to defend us against the scary magical dudes trying to wipe our hometown out of existence?"

"Not exactly. That's like step three of today's agenda. Step two is visiting the thrift store," she told me.

"Why is that before arming ourselves? Don't you think weaponry is important?"

"Yes, I think weaponry is extremely important," she confirmed. "But we'll start with the basics. You've already admitted you won't be able to stop the bad guys if the magical cops catch you first, which means you have to avoid being caught, which means you have to blend in. This look you have going on with the rags and the bloody jacket... it's not exactly inconspicuous."

I pulled the lapels of the jacket closer around me, feeling defensive of my pilfered finery.

"It's what I had available," I told her.

"Yes, but that's not the case anymore. We're going to get you some normal people-looking clothes. But like I said, that's step two," she said slyly.

"What's step one?" I asked nervously.

"Tacos!"

Oh, joy and rapture, happy days are here again.

"Floor it!" I commanded.

Ally wove through the town with a little more lead in her foot than the local police would probably enjoy, but none sprung out of the side streets at us, so the time saved was worth it. We pulled along a curb, and she parked. I didn't know where she was leading me, and my eyes widened when we turned a corner and a parking lot spread in front of me. There were food trucks as far as the eye could see.

"What is this?" I asked in an awed whisper.

"This is a Food Truck Rodeo."

I gasped.

"A whole rodeo of food trucks?"

"Yep. Food trucks are a big thing now. I got very familiar with gatherings like this while traveling around searching for you over the years. I told you I never believed you were gone, that I knew you had to be somewhere. While I went from place to place, the Food Truck Rodeos lured me in. They reminded me so much of you. Roaming around them always made me feel closer to you."

I was still dumbstruck by the majesty of it all.

"It's food trucks everywhere. Ten years in the future is *awesome*. Where are the tacos?"

We started around the large outer ring of food trucks, then circled the center cluster. By the time we got to the end, I was no longer as happy.

"I'm sorry, Slick," she said.

"What kind of self-respecting rodeo lacks tacos?" I asked.

"I'm sorry," Ally repeated. "I was sure there would be a taco truck. There are *always* taco trucks."

"First the bar, then the food trucks. The world doesn't want me to have tacos," I lamented. "I went to a prison no human had ever been to, survived, and escaped although no one had *ever* escaped. I deserve the reward of a taco."

"Yes, you do," Ally comforted me. "You absolutely

deserve the reward of a taco. And we'll keep looking. But for now, be strong. Pick something else."

I looked around at the disappointing non-taco food trucks and one finally caught my eye. The man in the tiny window was shocked when I ordered three cheeseburgers and even more so when I asked for bacon and extra mayonnaise. Our eyes stayed locked firmly on one another, a standoff at the Cheeseburger Corral as he slid the burger-filled basket toward me. He barked a price at me and Ally looked at me expectantly. I shrugged.

"Sorry, left all my cards in The Deep," I said.

The man looked at us strangely, but Ally stepped up to the window.

"It's fine," she said. "I have it."

I found a spot sitting on a curb and dove into my burgers. Ally went off to get herself something to eat and by the time she got back with her pulled pork, I was already most of the way through the second burger.

"This is ridiculously good," I said through a mouthful of bacon and cheese.

"I'm glad you're enjoying it." She settled down beside me to start eating. "Do I even want to know what you ate in The Deep?"

"Hell, no."

An hour later, we'd finished at the rodeo and I was being held hostage in the changing room of the thrift store. Ally stood outside, shouting to hurry up, but nothing hanging from what looked like thirty hangers she had brought in appealed to me.

"Did we have to come to a thrift store?" I asked. "All

these clothes look like they've been sitting here for decades."

"They haven't," Ally insisted. "I noticed tags still on a couple of those things. That's why I brought you to this one."

"Because it frequently carries the never-worn clothing of people who are now retired or dead?" I asked.

She groaned, and I envisioned her rolling her eyes.

"No, because it's a hidden gem I discovered on my many excursions this way. There's a rich neighborhood not too far from here and a lot of them buy clothes, never wear them, get tired of them, and bring them here," she explained.

"So, you're telling me these are contemporary fashions?" I asked suspiciously.

"Yes," she confirmed.

"This half looks like I should be hitchhiking to Woodstock and this half looks like I should be doing cocaine with a hair metal band."

"Both valid descriptions of contemporary trends."

"Well, I'll be damned." I chose an awkward macramé dress. "I was gone so long the world whipped back around until before I was born."

"It happens. Now put something on and let me see."

I wriggled into the dress and stepped out of the dressing room. The immediate burst of laughter that made Ally bend over at the waist was not the most encouraging moment of my day.

"I don't know if 'olive green old woman door hanger' is really the look for me." I swept my hands up and down my sides to display the dress to her.

"That's amazing," she said, still laughing. "I was really hoping that was the first thing you'd put on."

"You did this as a joke and it was mean and I missed you so much. Don't ever leave me again."

"Me leave you?" Ally protested. "Let's try to remember who got siphoned out of reality, here."

"All right. We'll call it equal blame." I stepped back into the dressing room.

"I am not taking partial responsibility for you confessing to crimes you knew nothing about and being thrown in a prison in a different dimension."

"Already in the dressing room. All decisions pre-dressing room are final," I insisted.

She laughed, and I put on another of the outfits, casting the dress into the corner of shame.

"That one looks better," Ally told me when I stepped out.

"You know what?" I said as I tried on my third outfit.

"What's that?" she asked.

"I'm having *fun*. Actual fun, not like the time two other inmates and I were punished by having to clean out the bone pit because it got too full and I tried to teach one of them how to play pick up sticks with all the femurs."

"I'll skip my initial reaction and go straight to 'awwwwwwww.' It's good to hear that. You have a lot of time to make up for and I'll make sure you have plenty of fun doing it."

"Thank you."

An hour later, my love of shopping was resurfacing. It was like cabinets in my brain were opening and little bits of myself that I'd shoved away were coming back out. I wanted to stay in this shop forever, trying on clothes and laughing with my best friend, but I couldn't. Dressed in tight black jeans, a black tank that went perfectly with my jacket, and combat boots, I felt adequately badass as we walked out of the shop.

There was work to do.

CHAPTER NINETEEN

"Ugh," Ally said. "I really wish we didn't have to return to the backdrop for all my future nightmares."

We were creeping down the narrow street toward the warehouse from the night before. I'd made her park a block away so we didn't attract attention, but the futility of that concept was making itself known as we alternately walked, jogged, crouch-scurried, and slunk along the wall of the nearest building. When we reached the large open area between that building and the warehouse, we ran, throwing ourselves inside as fast as we could.

There was no real way of knowing if there were Guild members watching us as we zipped across in full view. Unfortunately, they weren't like rattlesnakes. There was no warning noise before they struck unless they wanted you to be afraid before it happened.

"This is the scene of the crime, Ally. Or at least the scene of planning the crime. This is where we'll find all the information if there's anything available," I told her.

"But they know they got caught," she pointed out. "I

don't think the Harbingers will forget that fight last night anytime soon. If what they're doing is so secret, don't you think they would have moved by now?"

I shook my head as we moved down the hallway toward the main open area of the warehouse.

"I'm sure they did. But this isn't some tiny operation. According to what Solon told me, and Burne's ramblings underscored, Hobbes' cult is complex and constantly doing something. There are too many moving parts for them to disappear without leaving some of those parts behind."

We reached the spot where I'd battled the Harbingers the night before and surveyed the aftermath. It wasn't as bad as I was anticipating.

"It looks like nothing ever happened here," Ally noted. "Are you sure we're in the right place?"

"We're in the right place. They sent a team to sweep up. Hobbes and that lot don't like to be beaten. They'll try to conveniently gloss over anything that might make it look like they aren't absolutely dominant."

"How much do you really know about this Hobbes guy and his followers?"

"Honestly? Not a ton. Solon was able to tell me the basics of what he gleaned from the other prisoners, but he'd been excommunicated for being a traitor and been in The Deep way longer than I was. It limited his access to up-to-date information. We're in kind of a learn-as-we-go situation here. But this is definitely the place. Look at that."

She followed my finger to where I pointed at deep grooves in the floor.

"What are those?"

"Satyr scratches," I told her. "Nature spirits. You know

that whole phrase 'hung like a horse'? Well, the satyr is. He just happens to have the ears and legs to match. But the rest of him is a guy, so it balances out."

"Perfect," Ally sighed while following me deeper into the space.

My feet scraped against something on the ground, and I picked it up.

"They didn't do as good a job cleaning as they should have. See this?" The pebble in my hand was tiny, but I knew exactly what it was. The fact that it was on the ground was probably totally on me. "This is golem dandruff. Likely knocked right off our buddy's head last night."

"That's charming. Have you seen many of those?"

"Golems? No. There was one in The Deep when I'd only been there for a short time, but I never really interacted with him. But Solon taught me everything I needed to know about fighting them."

"I'm sure he would have been proud of you last night," she murmured

I laughed. "He would have boxed my ears for taking a risk like that. But he probably would have done the same thing."

We continued, and I drew a breath, cringing at the stench that hit me.

"Yep, we're definitely in the right place. I know the smell of goblin anywhere."

Ally took an experimental sniff and her eyes squeezed closed in reaction.

"You know, I've never really thought about what a goblin would smell like, but now that I've gotten a lung full of that, I can attest that is exactly what I imagine it would be."

"Yeah, you think this is bad? This is after one has been out of the space for probably hours. Imagine what it would be like stuffed in a tiny room with a couple of them for days."

"That is not something I'll add to my visualization board anytime soon."

"I don't blame you. It's pretty well etched into my brain and I'd really enjoy attaching a sanitizing wipe to a pipe cleaner and scrubbing it clean via my nostril."

"Your nostrils have probably been through enough," she commented. "Let them live."

"I'm sure they appreciate your advocacy."

"Okay, so help me get a few things straight," she started.

"Lay it on me."

"Ogres and trolls are not the same thing."

"They're not the same thing."

"But they're real?"

"They're both real," I confirmed.

"And goblins aren't the same thing as either of those?"

"Right."

"And not the same as a demon," she continued.

"Right," I repeated.

"But also real?"

"Also *very* real," I concluded.

"Just keeping it all straight. Do you think there's, like, an FSL class? Far as a Second Language?"

"There should be. Maybe we can start a distance learning program for that once we get through this."

"Look at us planning out our futures. Saving cities.

Escaping Philosopher posses. Having fun. Eating tacos. Teaching the children. We're good people, Slick."

"I always knew it, Alejandra."

The moment would have best been sealed with an 80s-style movie montage of running through the warehouse and accomplishing all our life goals before leaping into the air for a freeze-frame high five. But before we could do any of that, movement caught my attention. It was exactly like the night before, and I braced myself for the onslaught of Harbingers who would now be prepared for my arrival and ready to smear me across the floor, then top the me-smear with accents of Ally.

My body tensed and I touched Ally's arm to warn her to get ready. We crouched slightly and crept toward where I'd seen the movement. It darted deeper into the shadows while slinking along the wall. I shouldn't have chased it. I shouldn't have pursued the unidentified mass shifting through the darkness.

But I did. I needed answers.

I took off toward whatever it was, and Ally hissed from behind me. I'm sure there were words in the sound, but I didn't hear any of them. She reluctantly chased after me.

"Rethinking your decision to help me, yet?" I asked when she caught up with me.

She shook her head adamantly.

"Not at all. If I can't risk life, limb, and future mental stability for my best friend, who can I risk those things for?"

"That should be etched into a greeting card."

She nodded, but I saw her eyes widen suddenly. I whipped around, and a figure stepped toward me. My hands clenched by my side and if I opened my mouth, he would probably see my heart beating on the back of my tongue. It was a Philosopher. One glance at his pointed ears and glowing eyes confirmed it. I suddenly realized he was the same young man I'd seen flee from the warehouse the night before when I was lying on my back trying not to snap at my joints and fall apart after the fight with the golem.

The realization sent a surge of anger through me. I stepped toward him.

"Who are you?" I demanded.

He stared at me, dumbstruck. But before I had the chance to ask again, two voices echoed throughout the building, voices I recognized. I pushed Ally, and we ran toward a nearby piece of abandoned equipment. After crouching behind it, I looked around the machinery to see where the voices were coming from. Young man had disappeared and now all I could see were the two Guild members wandering into the area.

I knew them immediately and didn't want to tangle with them. A visit from them in The Deep a few years ago had been plenty to keep both of their faces seared in my mind for the rest of my life.

"What's going on?" Ally asked. "Who were those guys?"

"Bentham and Thrash," I told her.

"Where are you?" Bentham called. "We know you're here."

Oh, shit.

"We know you were here last night," Thrasymachus added.

Oh, double shit.

"And we know you've been here many times before, Archimedes," Bentham said.

Oh, triple... Wait. That didn't sound right.

It hit me. These two weren't here in the warehouse looking for me. They were hunting for that other guy.

CHAPTER TWENTY

"That was *who*?" Ally whispered as we ducked behind a wall and crouched down.

"Bentham and Thrasymachus."

"Who are they?"

"Guild agents," I told her. "They came to The Deep to see me once. It was not a pleasant afternoon." A pile of pallets sat next to the wall of the warehouse. I motioned to Ally to follow me, and we wiggled behind it. Footsteps reverberated in the room as someone very large made their way forward. Faintly, I heard a second set of footsteps behind the larger ones, but they both abruptly stopped.

I peeked around the corner in time to see a burst of white light and hear a shout of alarm. Bentham used her magic to pull the young man out from his hiding place.

"Archimedes." Her voice was monotone. "I'm Agent Bentham. This is my associate Agent Thrasymachus. We've come to ask you a few questions. Please do not resist."

The voice was cold and authoritative. There was a pointed take-no-shitness to it which seemed to make it extremely clear that her questions were to be answered truthfully, completely, and immediately.

Thrash's voice held none of the control of his partner.

"I begin at level one, Bentham. Ask before I proceed," he boomed, his voice bouncing off the walls and bypassing the ear to land directly in the brain, like an anvil being struck by Thor's hammer.

"Archimedes, confirm your name," Bentham stated.

"Me? I don't—" Archimedes began before a massive fist came into view, rocking him in the jaw.

Thrash was a mammoth of a man. He wore a long coat and hat with a pair of sunglasses that slipped down his nose. I made out the cold, blue glow of his eyes above the rim. Thrash's fist seemed to pulse as he held it up, and he looked back at Bentham.

"Level two, now. Ask again," he commanded.

Ally gasped as the fist grew by at least ten percent. I clasped my hand over her mouth to shush her as Archimedes got whacked again. This time he bounced off the wall behind him, shook his head, and looked Thrash as directly in the eye as his much shorter stature would allow.

"Damn," Archimedes said. "Is beating on guys like me the only way you can get hard?"

Wow. I sincerely hoped this Archimedes guy had more than that going for him.

Thrash grimaced and looked back at his partner. "I said ask him again, dammit."

Bentham stepped forward. She was dressed like Thrash, the long coat and hat covering most of her body and head, but one ear poked out of the hat, and I saw that it was pointed. She pushed her glasses back up and looked down at a notepad in her hands.

"Archime—" she began as Thrash suddenly hit the man again. "Thrasymachus, you need to at least allow him to respond first."

"Why? So he can tell more jokes? Let him tell jokes with no fucking teeth," Thrasymachus spat.

Archimedes stood from where he'd crumpled against the wall, seemed to swirl something in his mouth, then spit it out, hitting Thrasymachus in the chest.

"Only one, you giant prune. Yeah, I'm Archimedes. Now, why don't you ask your partner here to keep his hands to his damn self?"

"Level three." Thrash emphasized each word. His fist grew bigger still, but Archimedes didn't back down, despite how his eyes kept darting back to it.

"Archimedes, I am here to get a confession. He doesn't have to hurt you any more if you are truthful with us. Do you understand?"

There was almost a hint of compassion in that voice, but it was still emotionally disconnected.

"Archimedes, we know," Bentham began, any warmth I might have imagined in her voice now gone completely, replaced by a nearly robotic certainty of purpose. "We know you have been dealing illegal runes. Where are they?"

"I haven't the faintest idea what you're talking about." Archimedes looked at Thrash again, stoic resistance in his eyes.

Thrash grinned. His fist came around with terrifying speed, and Archimedes slammed against the wall. Before he could slide down it, Thrash grabbed him with his other hand, which had now grown to equal his hitting fist, and kept him upright.

"I can do this all night, Archimedes. In fact, I *want* to do this all night," Thrash sneered.

"Archimedes," Bentham interjected, "the runes. Where are they?"

"Please," Archimedes began, his voice different, some of the bravado gone and replaced with defeat. I knew that tone quite well. "Please, I don't know what you're talking about."

Ally tugged on my elbow, and I turned to her. She was pointing at Archimedes, and then the back of her pants. It took a second to understand what she was trying to tell me. Archimedes was using one hand to fiddle with something behind him. It looked like a pouch, tied to his belt, and two of his fingers were now inside it.

"Level ten," Thrash said.

Bentham looked up at him, and her demeanor changed.

"That is not necessary," she said, but Thrash's hands had already grown impossibly large.

I knew that trick, but only in passing. Thrash was an atomizer, able to use magic to contort his body in a hundred different ways. It wasn't the most elegant use of magic, but it seemed damned effective.

"Level ten. Where are the runes, Archimedes?"

"Up your ass." Archimedes' hand whipped out from behind him.

A red stone flew in the air and landed directly between Thrash and Bentham. It exploded in light and sound and Ally muffled a scream. Thankfully, the sound covered it up, and when my vision returned all the way, Archimedes was running toward where we were, and Bentham was struggling to regain her feet. Thrash was a few feet away, laying on his back and holding his head with a massive hand.

"Archimedes," she shouted, and a burst of a blinding white beam came from her hand.

The magic lassoed Archimedes's legs, and he fell directly in front of the pallet tower, yelping in pain. Our eyes met through the slats for a moment before Thrash was suddenly on top of him. He reached down and pulled the bag off his belt, easily snapping the rope that kept it tied. He tossed it to Bentham, who caught it with her free hand. Her aethermancy magic was still holding Archimedes down, and Thrash took the opportunity to smash one of his heavy fists into the prone man on the ground.

I suddenly felt like my body had locked up. Thrash sent another fist down and my vision grew blurry. I tried to shake it off, but instead of Archimedes and Thrash in front of me, all I saw was my father, being held by those goons who kept hitting him and saying such awful things.

Just like that night, I acted without thinking. This time, I was prepared. I met eyes with Ally, putting my finger over my mouth to tell her to stay quiet. Then I rolled out from behind the pallet and ran toward them.

Thrash's head snapped up as he heard the sound, and as he turned toward me, I buried my fist in the most vulnerable part of his stomach. My locket was at full charge, and he crumpled to his knees, his fists deflating to normal size. I kicked his face as hard as I could, knocking him onto his back.

"You?"

I turned to look at Bentham, her eyes full of recognition, and maybe fear.

"Me."

She wasted no time. Bentham pushed her hands forward and whipped a beam of energy at me. I ducked it and ran in for a close-up, but she was prepared for that. She blocked my kick and responded with a punch to my temple. Even with the locket absorbing some of the attack, I felt a jolt of electricity running through her hands. Aethermancers used that energy to do serious damage, and although I barely got caught at all, it felt like I had a wet hand stuck in an electrical socket. I caught the scent of ozone, and my body felt jittery for a moment. But I had the presence of mind to spin out of the way as she aimed her magic at me full blast.

A large pillar rose in front of me and I leapt toward it, using my legs to run up and backflip behind her. As she turned, I charged her and pushed her against the wall, face-first. A shot to the ribs seemed to affect her, but a now recovered and furious Thrasymachus suddenly grabbed me from behind and tossed me a dozen feet.

Thrash reached his arm back and then swung it forward at me like he was throwing a heavy ball. His arm extended, and his fist took the shape of a hammer. I rolled out of the way, and it crashed into the ground. I crawled backward and avoided another blast of energy from Bentham, this one not trying to lasso me as much as impale me. She was closer now, and I knew that using too many blasts like that was wearing her energy out, but she wouldn't need much. One strong shot, if it caught me full, would easily end my night if it didn't directly end my life.

That's when I saw the sack of runes.

I dove forward and grabbed the bag as I rolled to my feet. After pulling out a marble-shaped rune, I held it high.

Bentham stopped in her tracks and Thrasymachus yelled in frustration. We were in a standoff, and I had no idea what to do next. I didn't have long to form a plan.

Damn it, and now I want tacos even more.

Ally let out her version of a war cry as she came up behind Thrash and swung a lead pipe at his head like she was aiming to win the World Series. The pipe bent at a hard angle, but he didn't move. Bentham barely reacted, only shifted her eyes momentarily to assess the situation, then settled back on me. Thrash stood stock-still before reaching up with one hand and removing the bent pipe from his head. Achingly slowly, he turned toward Ally, who was now backing up, her eyes as big as saucers. She didn't yet understand that with creatures like this, it was all about the element of surprise and finding the soft spots.

"Bentham, think fast," I shouted and tossed the bag in the air.

She reached for it as I threw the marble-looking rune in my hand at Thrash. When it hit the ground, a sound like high-pitched wailing filled the room and everyone went to a knee, covering their ears. It seemed to affect Bentham and Thrash the most, and I used the opportunity to run full-tilt at Thrash and dropkick him in the face. His head smacked against the wall, and he went down all the way.

I reached behind me for my blade, but before I could get it out of my pocket, an explosion of smoke filled the room. I scrambled backward until my back was against the pallets and felt around for Ally. I pulled her close to me, and she buried herself in my back. Whatever wanted to get to my friend would have to go through me, as soon as I could see again.

The smoke slowly cleared, and I heard Archimedes coughing. Thrash's hulking figure and the smaller yet more intimidating figure of Bentham were gone. She must have used one of the runes to beat a hasty retreat. I stood, tentatively looking around to see if they had hidden somewhere. Once satisfied that they'd left, I turned to Ally. She had the bent pipe again and was twirling it around like she was ready to swing and was standing mere feet from Archimedes.

I put up a hand to stop her and knelt on one knee, coming closer to eye level with him as he struggled to a sitting position. The intensity of his pain was obvious as I extended my hand to him.

"Let's try this again. I'm Sara Slick."

CHAPTER TWENTY-ONE

His face going completely white told me Archimedes had heard my name before. Not only had he heard it, but he was one of those who either didn't believe I existed and was only a legend, created to spook Farling children, or was terrified of me and what I could do. Either one was good with me. I was getting used to the power my name had and was enjoying it. It was considerably better than the mocking laughter that had often come from the other inmates and the guards.

"Sara Slick?" he repeated.

All the blood draining from his face made his shock of red hair even bolder as it hung a little too long over his forehead.

"Yep, that's me. Have been my entire life. Well, Sara Slickerman, but I prefer to leave out the whole '—erman' part."

"I can understand that," he said.

My eyes narrowed at him.

"Yeah, coming from a dude called *Archimedes,*" I snapped.

"Fair enough," he responded.

"This is a really heartwarming interaction and I appreciate all the love going on here, but do we have to stay in this particular spot?" Ally asked.

She didn't sound like she was relishing hanging out in the warehouse.

"Something wrong?" Archimedes asked.

He looked over at her like he couldn't possibly imagine what might be bothering her.

"I haven't been part of this whole thing for long." Her hand swirled around in front of us like she was trying to encompass both of us and the circumstances she'd found herself in since discovering me again. "But something I have learned is that these issues aren't isolated. When serious shit goes down, it's safe to bet it will happen again. I'd rather not be here when it does."

"She's right. We should go somewhere we can talk." We started out of the warehouse, and I gestured between the two of them. "Archimedes, Ally. Ally, Archimedes."

"Can I call you Archie?"

"Why would you do that?" he asked.

She looked at him strangely.

"Because...it's shorter than Archimedes?" She wasn't sure what he was asking or why.

"Why does that matter?" he pushed.

"Just go with it, Ally," I said.

"No." She shook her head. "I'm not calling this man Archimedes. That's a fluffy bird in a cartoon about King Arthur. I'm calling him Archie."

I sighed and glanced over at Archimedes.

"Her full name is Alejandra," I offered. "In case you want to throw some of that back at her."

He thought about it for a second, then shook his head.

"No. I like Ally. Or I could call you Al, if you prefer."

Well, this will be fun.

I led the two out of the warehouse and made our way back to Ally's car.

"Where are we going?" she asked.

I considered bringing them back to my place, but since my place was a damp, abandoned hotel without electricity, although it was the big time for me, I couldn't imagine it would be terribly impressive to either Ally or Archimedes. Besides, I didn't want Ally to know I'd rejected her offer of me staying at her home to commit a felony.

"I'm not sure," I admitted. At least it was honest.

"I know a place," Ally offered.

Archimedes and I had a standoff at the door to the passenger seat. I glared at him as I grabbed the handle.

"I'm calling you Archie, too." I ducked into the seat.

Archimedes got in behind me, and Ally drove off. She finally stopped, and we climbed out into a small green park. It was empty except for one man sitting on a bench and a young woman pushing a stroller that looked like it could contain about ten babies.

"Is it safe to talk here?" Ally wanted to know.

Archimedes took a few steps toward the bench where the man was sitting and stared at him intently. For all I knew, he was scouring the man's brain and figuring out who he was. That wasn't a specific magical discipline of which I was familiar, but my education wasn't exactly structured. I could have missed a lesson or two.

"It should be fine," he told her. "But stay vigilant of our surroundings. You don't know who could be listening."

We walked farther across the open green space and sat. Being fully exposed out in the middle of the field made me feel safe. At least this way nobody could sneak up on us without someone noticing.

"I saw you last night." I stared unflinchingly at Archie.

This was not the time to pull punches and tiptoe through the tulips. I wanted to know who the hell this man was and what he had been doing in the warehouse with the Harbingers.

"Where?" he deflected.

"At the rave," I told him. "You were wearing glow sticks on your nipples and sucking on a pacifier. You know what I'm talking about. Don't play dumb with me. I'm not some stupid Guild agent."

"Oh," Ally said. "I was about to be furious you went to your first rave since getting out and didn't invite me."

I resisted the urge to roll my eyes at her.

"Yes, I was at the warehouse," Archie admitted. "I watched your fight. That was an impressive showing."

"Thanks for the support. I noticed you didn't feel compelled to jump in and help or anything," I pointed out.

"You seemed to have a good handle on it by yourself. Besides, you might have noticed I'm not exactly in the best of graces with the Guild. I didn't want to hang around and risk them showing up," he told me.

"I'm shocked," I retorted in my least shocked voice. "You

seemed to make fast friends with Benny and Thrash back there."

"Most of the Philosophers aren't too fond of me," Archie admitted. "But that's only because of my work."

"That has to be one seriously shady side hustle to have them send Thrash after you like that," I pointed out.

Archie shrugged.

"What did you expect? I'm a runes dealer."

"Is it safe for me to assume this isn't a multi-level marketing Farside Mary Kay-type situation?" Ally broke in. "He doesn't pull out, like, a pink suitcase full of runes and convince people to buy them, then sell them to others, too?"

"Not exactly," the Philosopher said.

"No," I told her. "He's on the black market."

Archie looked at me, a hint of surprise in his eyes at my blatant recognition of what he was telling us.

"What I do definitely skirts the *Pax Philosophia*. Runecraft is a form of magic that is highly regulated by the Guild and creating runes to sell to less than savory characters isn't appreciated by those who move in my circles, so to speak. I'm not exactly respected by the other Philosophers, but that doesn't stop them from concerning themselves with what I'm doing at all times."

"Then why do you do it?" Ally wondered.

He looked at her incredulously.

"Because I'm really freaking good at my job. I create powerful, unique runes and I find the right market for them."

"So, you're an honest-dishonest businessman," I stated.

"Why do you say that?" he challenged.

"I told you, I saw you here last night. Not only after the fight, but before. That was you handing something off to the Harbingers, wasn't it? You were selling runes to them. That's treason against the *Pax*. Do you know what they're planning on doing? Do you know what they've already done?"

Archie held up his hands to stop me as my voice started creeping up louder.

"Look, yes, I was selling to the Harbingers, but I want to make something extremely clear. I wasn't doing that because I wanted to or for my benefit. It was purely under duress."

"Under duress?" I questioned him. "It didn't look like you were being pinned down and threatened."

"That's because you missed the being pinned down and threatened portion of my interaction with them. The Harbingers found out what I do and butted in. They decided if anyone could give them a leg up in their efforts, it would be me. They found me and told me in no uncertain terms that either I would help them, or they would feed me to a Minotaur. *A Minotaur.* Have you seen those things? They have cow's teeth! It would have taken forever for one of those to smash me to death."

"Well, isn't that a lovely image," Ally muttered sarcastically.

"It wasn't exactly the most delightful concept for me, either," he snapped back.

"All right, you two. Enough. What did you sell them?" I demanded.

"Weapons," he admitted. "But I also sold them some

runestuff that you can't exactly pick up at the corner market."

"Runestuff?" Ally asked with a sigh.

"It's exactly what it sounds like. It's the materials used in runecrafts."

"Basically, he sold them the D.I.Y. kit so they can make their own runes when the ones he made for them either no longer fulfilled their purpose, ran out of power, or were confiscated," I explained to her.

"What kind of stuff would that be?" she prompted.

"It can be many things, really," he told her. "The most popular items are those that are rarest and hardest to get. They're also illegal. Bones, hair, teeth, skin. Organic materials from Farsiders and Nearsiders. Those make powerful runes, but it's prohibited to sell them. Which makes it profitable for those willing to risk it."

"Selling people's skin?" Ally sounded horrified.

"I mean, I don't generally walk around with a knife and skim slices off people for my customers," he told her.

"Oh, because pre-packaged skin is so much better," she retorted.

"Do you eat the crispy part of fried chicken? What do you think that is?"

"Am I going to have to put the two of you in time out?" I huffed. They both stared back at me, but their eyes flickered at each other like they were waiting for the other one to make the next snide comment. "If the Harbingers and the Guild have your number, why the hell are you sticking around here? Why did you go back to the warehouse today? Isn't that putting yourself in serious danger?"

He shrugged. "I went back to the warehouse to see if there was anything of value left. I'm a businessman, after all." He gave a mirthless laugh. "Sorry if that messed up your plans."

"Well, it seriously did. I'm not here doing business, and I'm certainly not here for fun. You obviously know who I am, which means you know I escaped from The Deep. The Guild's on my ass and I have no idea how long until they roll up and throw me in irons, but in the time I do have, I have to stop the Harbingers from following through with their plan."

"What plan? I assumed they were up to their old nonsense."

"Not this time. I don't know what it is, but it has something to do with Charleston, which happens to be my hometown, and Ally's. So, yes, you screwed up my plans. But I'll give you an opportunity to make it up to me."

"How?" He sounded wary.

"By helping me find the Harbingers."

CHAPTER TWENTY-TWO

"Look," he protested, "I've already pissed these guys off enough. I'm not interested in further poking the bear. And after our little dance with Bentham and Thrasymachus, I'm probably now considered one of your accomplices."

"Perfect. Since The Guild already thinks you're with me, there's no added threat to you helping me. And if you're afraid of the Harbingers, taking them down is the best way forward. So, tell me what you know."

It felt strange, lying on this well-maintained park lawn while discussing our plans to stop the end of the world. But I was having a hell of a lot of fun doing it.

Archie sighed, probably realizing that resistance was futile. I didn't get a nickname like The Heinous Sara Slick by being accommodating.

"I don't know what they're planning, but I know what they need. Since you so elegantly blew up their truck last night, all the runestuff I sold them was destroyed."

"Let me guess. They're not the type to call it a wash and move on."

"Not exactly. They want their hands on materials for their runes and will get it wherever they can. Since they've already tapped me out, they'll probably go see Vincent."

"Who's Vincent?" Ally asked.

"A shady vampire who owns a seedy club not too far from here," Archie explained.

"There are vampires running around owning clubs and interacting with humans all the time? And people don't notice?"

"Did you ever notice when you were in a club owned by a Farsider?" Archie challenged.

"I'd notice if I regularly patronized an establishment owned by a non-human entity," she snapped back.

"That's highly doubtful. You probably wouldn't even recognize that I'm not human if you ran into me. Humans aren't the brightest creatures."

"Zip it," I told them. "What's the name of the club?"

"Reapers."

I stared back at him with a blank expression for a few seconds, waiting for him to laugh and tell me he was joking. He didn't. Son of a bitch.

"Seriously? The vampire named his club Reapers?"

"I said the dude was shady, not that he was poetic or creative. Besides, having a name like that helps with the ulterior motives of his club. The clientele drawn to that type of theme are much more likely to go along with his side business," Archie pointed out.

"What side business?"

"You'll find out when you get there. Have a good time."

He got up to leave, but I jumped to my feet and stood in his way.

"Where do you think you're going?"

"I'm leaving. I gave you all the information you needed to know."

"Oh, no." I shook my head. "You're not going anywhere. If I don't get to lie down in the middle of this field, make a grass angel, and spend the rest of the day staring at the sky and making up what I see in the clouds, you don't get to do what you want, either. You're coming with."

"I don't want to go to Reapers. Vincent and I don't exactly get along."

"Do you seriously think I care? From the way you described him, old Vinny and I won't be the best of chums, either. If something strange happens and we hit it off, then you're free to leave."

Archie rolled his eyes but relented.

"It's still early," Ally pointed out. "Will the club be open at this time of day?"

"Vincent keeps his place open twenty-four seven," Archie told her. "Again, helps with the side hustle."

"I'm really getting tired of you saying that," I informed him.

He shrugged, and we made our way back to Ally's car. She followed his instructions, and we moved deeper into a part of town I probably wouldn't have ventured into before my time in The Deep. I told her to park, and we collected on the sidewalk in front of a stretch of buildings that looked derelict and abandoned.

"It's down that way." Archie gestured partway down the block.

"Let me guess. This is all a part of the appeal?"

"You can say that," he agreed.

We walked until we reached a door that looked about as accessible as the hotel had before I liberated it from the wood. The only thing that set it apart was the relatively fresh-looking etching in the glass that read 'Reapers.' Archie reached around me and pushed the door open. We stepped into a room that made my hotel even more appealing.

The entire place felt like it was crawling. The light was so dim it was hard to see where we were going, and it smelled heavily of smoke, spice, and bodies. The word bodies immediately came to mind rather than people because there were hints of odors laced through the air I knew couldn't be attributed to my kind.

"This is disgusting," Ally choked out.

"What did you expect? Vincent keeps it all in the back."

"What's 'it all'? What exactly does he move through here?" I asked.

"Pretty much anything you can think of. Runes, Farstuff, Nearstuff, drugs, all types of illicit shit. Essentially, if it's illegal to buy or sell, Vincent most likely has it or has a connection, or he can get it for you," Archie told us.

"People?" Ally gulped.

"Now you're catching on." He wove his way through the club to lead us to the back room.

"Vincent sells *people* here?" I asked.

"Not whole people. Not usually, anyway. The humans who come here are drawn to a type of life they don't realize exists. They come here wanting to give themselves over to the darkness and seem edgy. They like a little danger and crave something far more intense than they can get at other clubs. Vincent is happy to comply. He gives them exactly the experience they want, then propositions them to provide runestuff. Every rune needs something from The Far and something from The Near, but some elements are inherently more powerful than others. Since he can source most of the materials from them without killing them, it produces a sustainable, renewable source he can tap into until the humans decide they've had enough of their sacrifice game."

I looked at Ally.

"You didn't get into any of that screwed-up shit while I was gone, right? You didn't grieve yourself into a tizzy and fall off the deep end?"

"Are you asking me if I let a vampire draw blood and regularly chop off bits of my hair and skin? No. Didn't do that."

Archie looked her over. "There would have been good money in it."

Everyone in the club was so wrapped up in their various forms of debauchery they didn't notice us moving across the space. When we got to the back room, Archie propped the door open. It led into a short, tight hallway that fed into the room itself. We stepped inside, and Archie immediately let out a string of creative profanity. The space was empty.

"They already got to him."

"Is there anywhere else we could look? Another storage room? A basement? A dungeon of some sort?" I paused. "There isn't a dungeon here, is there? Because that would be seriously not cool. I need a heads-up before we start getting around things that resemble The Deep. Like a three-count or something."

"It's called a trigger warning," Ally offered.

"It's called a what?"

"A trigger warning," she told me.

"That's a thing now?"

"Yep."

"Perfect," I told her. I turned back to Archie. "So, anything? Anywhere else like that around here?"

"There's one other room, but if they got everything in here, they got to that, too."

"Let's look anyway," I said.

The second room was more cluttered than the first, with nothing interesting in it. Chairs, tables, and various other bits and pieces of discarded bar life were piled in the corners. There was a fireplace along the wall full of ash.

"This is where he keeps some of his rarest items," Archie told us. "They're harder to find here so he's more likely to skate by if there's a raid."

We started digging through the room. No luck. Everything in the space had been touched, shifted, flipped over, and otherwise violated, and we found nothing. We were leaving when a golden-skinned man with piercing eyes came into the room. Massive men on either side of him wore plain black suits and dark sunglasses. They'd clasped their hands in front of them, but they twitched like they were ready to go into action at any second.

"Vincent," Archie said.

It wasn't so much a greeting as an acknowledgement that we weren't in the best position. Vincent drew in a long, dramatic breath and rolled his neck slightly.

"Having a fun treasure hunt, Archimedes?" His eyes moved over to Ally and me. "Who are your friends?"

"They're none of your concern," Archie informed him.

"Now, I don't think that's true. After all, this is my club. That means everything that happens inside is of my concern." His gaze scrolled over Ally. "This one looks particularly tasty. She'd make a nice snack before the stress of the evening rush."

He took a step toward her, but before he could reach out to touch her, I grabbed a nearby chair and aimed for his neck. My swift movement pinned him to the wall, the chair pressing hard against his throat so he couldn't move.

"Keep your filthy fangs to yourself, slime bag," I growled through gritted teeth.

My body was preparing for a fight. Muscles tensed, and I readied myself for a battle.

But it never came.

Instead, Vincent squeezed his eyes closed and squirmed against the wall.

"Don't," he whimpered. "I'll leave her alone."

Ally's laugh helped break the tension. "You weren't kidding. Vampires are nothing like they are on TV."

I pushed the chair harder and smiled. "Nope, not a badass at all. Only a greasy pimple about to be popped."

"Please," he begged. "Please don't kill me."

I saw an opportunity. The coward was at my mercy, and I was ready to take full advantage of it.

"Tell me about the people you made a deal with."

Vincent shook his head.

"I don't know anything about anything."

I leaned into the chair.

"I'm not playing with you. You know what I'm talking about. Tell me about the people who came here and bought your stuff."

"Telling you, I don't know anything about it. They paid, and I delivered."

"What should I do with him, Archie? Ally? Have any ideas? Maybe now is the chance for me to try out a few of the fun things I learned in The Deep."

"Sara, stop," Ally called. "I found something."

I turned to look at Ally, who was pulling a charred piece of paper from the fireplace. But as I did, Vincent's goons made their move.

Fangs bared, they leapt at Ally. But I was quicker. I smashed the chair over the back of Thing One and with the remaining shard of wood in my hand I rammed Thing Two through the chest. He squirmed, then fell to the ground in a pile of thick blood.

A scream filled the room, and I turned to see Thing One burst into flames before disintegrating. Archie stood behind him with a lighter in hand that I could tell was more than a lighter.

"Nice."

He shrugged. "I don't usually enter a vampire's lair unarmed."

"Holy shit," Ally exclaimed. "So vampires really are flammable? And the wooden stake thing is true, too?"

"Everything is flammable with the right rune." Archie put the lighter back in his pocket. "And it's the rare creature who can survive a chunk of wood through the chest."

I checked to make sure Vincent wasn't a threat, but he simply huddled on the floor while whimpering.

"Get the hell out of here, man," I growled. "And if I find that you're taking things from humans without asking, I'll come back."

He nodded, then slid out the door.

"Are you okay?" I asked Ally.

Ally nodded. "Fine. But look at this."

I moved closer to the table she was leaning against.

"What is it?"

"Don't know. Found them half-burned in the fireplace."

She handed me a stack of papers. I looked down at the strange writing and shook my head.

"I'm not entirely sure, but we may have found our lead."

CHAPTER TWENTY-THREE

"We need to figure out what all this means," I said. "I don't understand most of it."

Something small and hard fell on me from the top of a teetering pile of furniture to one side. Impulse ground into me from my years of training made me swipe back at it. Ally grabbed my arm and yanked me out of the way in time for most of the stack to tumble down. This created a domino effect, and we hurried away from it. It felt like the worst Indiana Jones movie ever.

When we were finally out of the room and harm's way, Archie looked at the papers again.

"It looks like it's written in code. I think I can read it, but it will take some figuring out."

"How about we do that somewhere other than here?"

"Why don't we get something to eat?" Ally suggested. "You look like you could use as many good meals as you can get into you. Besides, you've always thought better on a full stomach. It's part of who you are."

It was a casual comment for her, but I felt it in my soul.

Who you are. She knew me, the real me, and little by little, I was finding me again.

"It *is* part of who I am, isn't it? Well, I can't deny the basic elements of myself. Let's eat. I vote tacos."

Ally laughed.

"Is there ever going to be a point in your life when you *don't* vote tacos?"

We started back toward the main part of the club.

"Thanksgiving," I promptly replied.

"Try to tell me you wouldn't accept a turkey taco with a shell made out of stuffing, and gravy instead of salsa," she dared me.

"Okay, I probably would. Because that sounds delicious. You'll have to make me one of those at Thanksgiving." I gasped and grabbed her arm. "Wait." I tried to do some calculations in my head. I knew how many days I had spent in The Deep, but had long since lost track of what that meant in terms of the date. "How far away is that?"

Ally shook her head.

"It's going to be a little while."

"Damn it. The Guild will probably snatch me up before then."

"No, they won't," Archie said as we emerged from the darkened club.

I turned to look at him.

"How would you know that?"

"Because the Harbingers are more likely to kill you first."

"How encouraging. All the more reason to enjoy what meals I can. Ally." I turned to look at her. "Bring me to the tacos."

She pulled out her phone and tapped a few commands into the flat screen. A few seconds later, she nodded.

"Got it. Let's roll."

We piled back into Ally's car and Splinter scrambled out of my pocket onto his favorite spot on the center console. I made a mental note to figure out a way to make him a little bed for it. He deserved some comfort and luxury after everything he'd gone through right alongside me. Maybe when the Guild came for me, I'd leave him behind with Ally so he could live a good life.

The thought made my eyes sting, and I forced myself to concentrate on my excited anticipation as we started toward the promise of tacos.

It wasn't to be.

"What do you mean this place is closed?" I protested. "Didn't your little fancy phone have that piece of information available?"

"It didn't say it was closed." Ally pulled her phone out again and jabbed it angrily. A few seconds later, she let out an exasperated sigh. "Apparently they were shut down last night temporarily due to health code violations."

"To be fair, some of my favorite tacos have come from places that have had their share of run-ins with health codes. What's the alternative?"

"It looks like there's a twenty-four-hour diner across the street," Archie offered. "Maybe they have something good."

The menu at the diner was as disappointing as every other eating establishment I'd visited in the time I'd been out. No tacos. Not even any taco-adjacent food like nachos. I would have settled for a few slices of jalapeño and a sprinkle of cumin on my burger. As it was, I had to settle for what they called a 'gourmet grilled cheese' because it had five different types of cheese and was slathered in garlic butter. It was gooey, greasy, and satisfying, but a far cry from a good taco.

After we'd been eating for a few moments, I wiped my hands off on a napkin, then pulled the papers out and spread them across the table. I gestured at the mess.

"What can we figure out so far?"

"It's an outline for the plan they're working on. I recognize some of this stuff from other Harbinger documents," Archie informed us.

"Whatever it is, it's massive. They must have been working on this for a long time."

It was abundantly clear how much work went into crafting the plans laid out in front of us. Of course, that didn't do us a hell of a lot of good since the vast majority of it was coded or burned and what we could read was so vague it could mean almost anything. It was in a Far language and I recognized a few of the words as ones I'd seen or heard during my time in The Deep. But most of it I couldn't decipher. I scanned the pages over and over and my mind picked up a pattern. I went back to the first page and swept my eyes over it.

I pointed out a shape on the first page. "This symbol is on all the documents. Do you know what it means?"

Archimedes looked at it and nodded, then swallowed his mouthful of French fries.

"It's the symbol for Dyadology."

"That's runecraft, right?" Ally confirmed.

Archie looked at her, impressed. "Right. It's a discipline

of magic, like Thrash's atomism or Bentham's aethermancy. Not many of us practice it, though."

"Why not? Sara can really kick ass with that locket around her neck. Why wouldn't everyone want to do that?"

"That's part of the problem, anyone can use them. The most respected among The Guild don't like the idea of us sharing our magic around. They completely prohibit them in The Heights."

"Nothing that has anything to do with The Near is allowed there." I preempted Ally's next question.

"Runes require something from The Near and something from The Far, as well as specific spells. The fact that it's reliant on items from The Near means it seems pretty shady by magical purists, but they are extremely useful. I've seen Dyads that can do just about everything. That's why they're so heavily regulated by the Guild."

"But that doesn't stop the black market," Ally criticized.

"Do your human laws actually prevent any crime?"

"How long do they last?" Ally ignored him. "Can you use them into perpetuity?"

"It depends on who made it and the quality of the material used. Different runes have different shelf lives depending on what type they are and the skill of the maker, along with the materials. Some of them can only be used once. Others can be used hundreds of times before they're rendered unusable. Others can be utilized in small doses, but then need time to recharge before they're effective again. There are some that can, in theory, be used indefinitely."

"Wow. I may have to rethink that whole selling my skin thing."

Archie looked at her. "It's not only blood and guts. Runes made with biological material like that are often incredibly powerful, but it's not necessary. I've seen amazing Dyads made with pieces of plants and bits of buildings. It's all about the type of magic the maker wants to instill in it and how long they want it to last. The thing is, even when creating powerful runes, Dyadologists don't usually need a large amount of any material. But the Harbingers are different. They bought everything I had available, and asked me to source more. I sold them quite a variety. I don't know what they needed it for. They never explained it. But they wanted a huge amount."

"Maybe they're planning on making a massive rune?" I hazarded a guess. "Is that even a thing?"

"I suppose it could be," Archie agreed. "But I've never heard of something using this amount of materials. I don't know many Philosophers who would take the risk of making something that big. It's too dangerous, too much potential to run afoul of the Guild."

"You said you sold them more than the Farstuff," I pointed out. "What else? What else did they want from you?"

"I told you I sold them a few of the runes I'd already made. It wasn't many of them, but they were effective ones. Mostly weapons. What was really strange is they chose my flashiest weapons over my most powerful."

"They wanted flashy weapons that weren't powerful?" I confirmed.

He nodded.

"Exactly. They didn't want anything like your locket or switchblade, something subtle and small that could be easily overlooked. They wanted things that grabbed attention more than would have a tremendous amount of impact. More bark than bite. That's not my normal style. Can I see your switchblade?"

I took it out of my pocket and handed it over to Archie. While he examined it, I snatched a few french fries from his plate and slipped them into my jacket pocket so Splinter could eat.

"It belonged to Solon."

"This handiwork is better than mine, and that's saying something. Most runes don't last long, even the good ones. The fact that they're made from elements of two different worlds means they're highly unstable. But this blade looks ancient."

He handed it back, obviously impressed by my little weapon.

"I honestly never thought about it. It was something he always had that he taught me to use. I guess he knew it would be mine one day."

I was lost in a sudden wave of reminiscing about Solon when Ally jumped in the booth beside me, nearly making me choke on my milkshake.

"I found something!" she exclaimed.

"A cockroach?"

"No, a zip code."

That was both better and more surprising.

"A zip code? Where?"

She pointed on one of the documents, and I saw a series of numbers.

"It's not just any zip code. I know where this place is."

"You do?" Archie asked.

"I told you about the story I was working on before I found you again, Sara. About the missing people?"

"Yeah, you said there were several of them spread out across a few different locations."

"Right." Ally shook her head. "But the first one happened in a small town in the middle of nowhere in South Carolina called Alton. I read addresses from that small town probably a thousand times. I'd know that zip code anywhere. So, what are the odds that same zip code for that small town would be written here in these documents?"

She and I exchanged glances, then looked at Archie.

"It's a stretch," he cautioned.

"But it's our only lead. I say we follow it."

CHAPTER TWENTY-FOUR

"You two be careful and let me know when you get back," Archie said when we stepped out of the diner.

"What are you talking about?" I asked.

"I need to bow out of this part of our mission."

"You mean you're going to punk out of it," I corrected.

"Are you kidding me?" Ally asked. "You're seriously going to run off?"

"I'm not running anywhere. I'm helping the only way I know how. These Harbingers are well-equipped, and if you're going to stop them, you'll need some weapons. Here." He pulled out a card and handed it to me. "This is where I'll be. Find me when you're done."

"That's fine." I shoved the card into my pocket. "Ally and I can do it ourselves."

"Yeah!" Ally said enthusiastically. She looped her arm somewhat aggressively through mine, and we turned to stomp toward her car. "Are you sure we can do this? Without him?" she muttered at me.

"Of course, we can. I got this far without him, didn't I?"

We got into the car, and she grinned at me.

"Before we go, there's one thing we need to do."

"What's that?"

"You'll see."

I rolled my eyes as I shoved my seat belt into place and slumped back in the seat.

"I'm tired of the riddles and surprises."

Ally laughed and pulled out into the street. We'd been driving for about twenty minutes when I started to recognize things around me. They didn't look exactly like I thought they would, but they were familiar enough to know where I was. We were headed toward Charleston.

"Don't worry," she reassured me after seeing the look on my face. "I'm not bringing you to see your family."

"Good. That would be the worst intervention ever."

A few minutes later, she pulled into a driveway I hadn't seen in a decade. My heart pounded slightly when I looked at the house and noticed all the details that hadn't been there the last time I was here. Flower beds along the front were blooming with flowers where box hedges used to be, and the massive weeping willow that had taken up most of the front corner of the lawn was gone. There were Jones For Congress signs in the yard.

"Nobody's here. My parents are out of town for a few days, so you don't have to worry about anybody seeing you."

"What are we doing here?"

She pulled me around to the back of the house.

"There's something we need to pick up."

"You're kidding me." I grinned when I saw it. "I thought it was gone."

"Never." She climbed out of the car and gave an affectionate pat to the hood of the old station wagon. "I don't drive it regularly anymore, but I couldn't bring myself to get rid of it."

"Does it still run?"

"Sure, it does. My dad takes it out for a spin around the neighborhood every couple of months to make sure it's still functioning. Tinkers around with it on the weekends. It might be in better condition now than it was when we were teenagers."

She reached into the wheel well and pulled out a magnetic key box. She took the key from it and unlocked the driver's door, then leaned across to unlock mine. I jumped in and immediately felt the comforting, familiar surroundings take some tension out of my shoulders. Everything since I escaped felt so strange, but this felt like home.

Ally got in and cranked the engine over.

"Hold on. It gets better."

She reached into the glove compartment and pulled out a CD. After popping it into the portable player she attached to the radio, she hit the play button.

"You still have this CD!" I nearly shouted as the sound of *Panic! At the Disco* filled the car.

"Of course, I do. Do you know how long I stood in line at that merch table waiting to buy this thing? There was no way I was getting rid of it."

I laughed. Ally had bought this CD at the concert the

night I was arrested. The concert I missed. Listening to the song brought me back to that night, but instead of studying and getting arrested, I was at the concert, blissfully unaware of everything I now knew about my world. I was back in a miniskirt, watching Ally dancing with some asshole, and thinking about how we'd never have more fun than we were right then.

As we drove down the road, Splinter worked his way out of my pocket and found a sunny spot on the console between us. He curled his little body up and rested his head on his paws. I'd never seen him quite so content. He was practically purring.

"Where did you get that thing, anyway?"

"His name is Splinter." I affectionately rubbed one fingertip along his bristles. I learned a while ago not to attempt to pet him with a full palm. "Be nice to him."

"I'm sorry, Splinter."

"I told you he found me when I was in The Deep. He needed me as much as I needed him, and we stuck with each other. He's been my companion, and he's looked out for me when I didn't have anyone else."

"He might still be creepy as all get out, but I'm glad you had him when you were there. It makes me feel better to know you weren't always alone."

"Me too."

The track switched and both of us burst into song, our dancing reaching a pitch so fevered the aged station wagon was nearly bouncing like it was on hydraulics. Our sudden enthusiasm didn't amuse Splinter, but he wasn't willing to give up his cushy spot on the console or the patch of sunlight that likely represented the only time in his life he'd been able to sunbathe. So, he dug his sharp little claws into the console, held on for life, and buried his head lower to ride it out.

Several hours later, we were still dancing and singing and making fun of each other for forgetting the lyrics, then making fun of each other even harder for remembering them, when we approached the town of Alton. Ally's face dropped, and I looked through the windshield to see police tape stretched across the road and tied to utility poles on either side. Beyond it, where the town should be, was blackened rubble.

"What happened?" she muttered in a muted, defeated tone.

The road stretched in front of us should have been a quaint small-town main street. One of those places people call downtown as a joke because it has about ten shops, a tiny hotel, and a coffee shop. Instead, it was a wasteland.

"It looks like it burned down. There's a notice."

We got out and walked toward the pole positioned in the middle of the street that displayed a notice on county letterhead.

"A gas main burst," Ally read. She looked out over the town again.

I shuddered.

"Something isn't right."

Ally pulled out her phone and a few seconds later had an article about the town up on her screen.

"It says that they haven't found a clear explanation for it. They're considering it a freak accident. But everyone had to evacuate until further notice."

Her eyes slid over to mine, and I shook my head.

"This wasn't an accident."

She shook her head back.

"No."

"Let's look around. Maybe we can find something that will give us an idea of what really happened."

We skirted around the police barricades and made our way along the side of the town. Or rather, what used to be a town. A barn ahead of us was the only building that had escaped the brunt of the blaze. Parts of it were singed, but it was still standing. That meant there was space inside we could search.

"What do you think?" Ally nodded toward the barn.

"I don't think it's a coincidence it's still mostly standing."

"You think it's another hideout for the Harbingers?"

I nodded.

"What better way to find some privacy than to burn down the entire town?"

"That sounds like some twisted villain logic."

"Well, we're dealing with some twisted villains. Let's go."

We rushed up to the barn and pressed our backs against the side, looking around and listening carefully for any indication that they'd seen us. When all stayed quiet, we crept toward the door. I had the compulsion to toss myself on the ground and roll a few times for the effect.

It seemed like all the most successful spies threw in at least two or three floor rolls per investigation, so maybe there was something about it that made the investigating part more effective. We made it around to the door faster than I anticipated, and I decided to forgo the roll.

"What are we looking for?" Ally asked.

"I'm not sure. I guess we'll figure it out when we find it."

"That's super helpful."

It took both of us to open the large, heavy door to get inside. If there had been a huge stash of Farstuff here, it wasn't anymore. Empty crates cluttered the floor and shelves designed to hold feed and tack supplies were bare.

"Let's look around. There might still be something here."

Ally countered, "It looks like they cleared it out. They must have known we were coming. Maybe the ones from yesterday gave them a heads-up."

"Doesn't matter. There still could be something here. You have to understand, it's like I said. Most Farfolk are fine and go about their lives without causing death and destruction and mayhem to anyone. Not everyone is like that. The ones who aren't and, let's be honest, some who are, have very few good thoughts about the people of The Near. Nearlings are fairly low life forms in their eyes, but their low opinion of us kind of gives us an advantage. It means we get to prove them wrong."

"What do you mean?"

"The Farsiders with that perception of us think that Nearsiders are nowhere near as smart as they are. They wouldn't feel like they needed to be careful about clearing out everything because any Nearling who found it wouldn't be able to recognize it or realize it mattered."

"Like this?"

I looked across the space and saw her holding a grisly-looking needle between two fingers.

"Oh, dear jiminy, what the shit is *that*?"

She shook her head while pressing her lips together like

she didn't trust herself to open her mouth again. I rushed toward her and took the syringe from her as carefully as I could. There was no telling what the strange green and blue swirled substance inside was or what it might do if the tip pricked me. I really didn't want to find out. What I did want was prepare myself for whatever ridiculousness might lurk around this place. My locket had powered back up, and I made sure it was ready to go so I'd have as much strength and speed as possible if the need arose.

"I don't know, but I hope it's not an accessory to these."

Ally picked up a thick chain attached to the wall with a heavy ring. I snatched it from her hand and let it drop to the floor.

"You *have* to stop touching things," I scolded.

"That's what I do, Slick."

"Touch things?"

"Investigate. We need to find out what this place is and what was here, and the only way we'll do that is…"

Her voice trailed off as I added the syringe to a row of them laid out across a slate table. They carried various colors of the liquid, some more filled than others.

"Is what? Finish your thought." She didn't say anything. "Ally?"

I looked up and saw her eyes wide, her expression mesmerized.

"He's so beautiful," she murmured.

That couldn't possibly be good.

"What's going on? Ally!"

Ally didn't move when I shouted her name. I stepped forward, then heard a noise behind me. I froze, some instinct willing my body not to spin around and confront the thing lurking in the shadows.

"Ally, what do you see?"

"An angel," she sighed.

Shit.

CHAPTER TWENTY-FIVE

"That's right," a voice sang behind me in a rich baritone. "Come look upon the face of God."

"Ally, close your eyes!" I shouted. "It's a Malak."

I knew the word meant nothing to her. She didn't know what the creature was or how much danger she was in. I did. The Malak was an angel in the same sense that a flame was a safe place for a moth to land. A Farsider so stunningly beautiful he could capture anyone by making eye contact. But that was where their appeal ended.

"Close your eyes," I told her again in vain.

She didn't respond, and I knew he had her in his trance. I only had one option now, and it wasn't my favorite one. I closed my eyes and yanked off the lightweight shirt I wore over a tank top. I wrapped it around my eyes like a blindfold and turned, fists raised to fight the Malak.

His laughter echoed through the spacious barn, making it hard to home in on him. I heard feet scuffling. Then a fist slammed into my stomach. I lashed out into the surrounding air, finding nothing but laughter.

"That's right," he purred. "Follow the sound of my voice."

"You won't be laughing once I rip your wings off," I muttered, but I knew I was in trouble. How could you fight what you couldn't see?

I heard movement to my left and lunged for it. I got lucky and tackled the Malak to the ground.

We tussled on the floor for a moment, and I tried to grab whatever I could. I felt the opening of the trench coat they always wore and pulled it to me while I swung my head down. The crunch of the Malak's nose as my forehead bust into it was loud in my ear, and I swung wildly at where I figured his face must have been.

But my tackle wasn't enough. The Malak wedged his feet between us and launched me into the air. Strength and speed did diddly-shit to stop me from being flung, and I tried in vain to brace for a landing. The ground hit me hard, harder still because I couldn't see it coming.

As I pushed myself off the hardwood, I heard the sounds of Ally swooning and moved toward her. I felt for her face.

"Sorry, friend," I shouted as I slapped her hard across the cheek.

"Ow," she cried. "What the hell, Slick?"

"You were in a trance." I covered her eyes with my hands. Drawing my face closer to hers until her breath was warm on my skin, I hissed at her in a hoarse whisper,

"Keep your eyes shut and get to the wall."

A sudden thump on my back made me fall forward. Ally's terrified scream told me she was making it to the wall as powerful hands lifted me by the cuff of my jacket and the back of my pants and tossed me into a few hard, wooden crates. I frantically searched the area around me, hoping my sense of touch would trigger a memory to tell me what I felt. My hands clasped a tool. By running my palms and fingertips carefully along it, I felt the handle and long, curved blade of a scythe.

Badass.

I grabbed the scythe and swung up while climbing to my feet. It sliced through nothingness, and I slowly turned, trying to orient myself so I could find the creature. The familiar feeling of Splinter's claws up my back and onto my shoulder emboldened me. He was impervious to the effects of the Malak's gaze.

Be my eyes, little buddy, be my eyes.

A second later, he bit my collarbone. I reacted with a sharp thrash of the scythe. Resistance told me the blade had caught something, and the Malak screamed in pain and frustration. Feeling a little gutsy, I pulled my makeshift blindfold slightly out of the way to hazard a look through mostly closed eyes. The angel stood, holding his face. Blood gushed from between his fingers and by his feet was a soft fleshy mound. It quickly dawned on me that it was his nose. I had removed his nose. That was a fucked up follow-through of the game my uncle used to play with me when I was a little girl.

Then it occurred to me. Swiping the angel's nose meant his face was jacked to hell. Which meant his spell wouldn't work. Awesome. I could use my eyes again.

I straightened while tugging the blindfold off, then

pulled the scythe back like a baseball bat. He raised his head, and we met eyes. He dropped his hands to give me a full view of his face. After a few seconds of staring, he stepped forward, assuming I was entranced. I swung the scythe back around, stopping short of his neck. He nearly fell backward in surprise as I shook my head, smiling.

"Not too pretty now, are you?" My smile fell away. "What are you doing here?"

He moved to crawl away, and I held the scythe higher. "Unless you're ready to meet your cousin, the angel of death, you'll answer my question."

"I was left here to make sure no one came looking around," he said through gritted teeth.

"What is this place?" I demanded. "What was kept here?"

"It doesn't matter." He shook his head. "None of it matters. There's nothing you can do now. Nothing." His voice grew higher as he slipped into a spate of cryptic speech. It reminded me of Burne's apocalyptic and frantic babbling, the words only barely linked together with any sense. "The joyous end of the world is near. There's nothing you can do to stop it, and I'm not afraid. All true followers of Hobbes would gladly die for the cause."

"You better be afraid. And you better start making sense, or I'm going to do more to you than mess up your pretty face."

He laughed, sending droplets of blood through the air to settle on my skin.

"I know who you are, Sara Slick, and I know what you do to my kind."

Before I could ask anything else, he reached forward

and grabbed the blade of the scythe. In one swift movement, he plunged the tip into his stomach, twisted it, and yanked it up. His torso split open, and he gave one final, crazed smile before collapsing to the ground.

CHAPTER TWENTY-SIX

The burned town and bloodied barn were fifteen minutes behind us when Ally finally spoke.

"What happened?"

It was like her brain had decided it was going to come back and needed a recap.

"We found another Harbinger lair, but a Malak guarded it."

"Which is..." she guided.

"The Far version of an angel. Only not the good, harp-playing kind. You got sucked in by their biggest weapon. They're so beautiful they entrance anyone who sees them, which means it's easy for them to capture or kill the people they're after. Unfortunately for them, it also means there aren't many of them."

"Why not?"

"They're pretty entranced by themselves, too. They're so vain it's rare for them to find another they think is good enough for them, so reproduction is extremely limited."

"I guess that's an upside. Why did he..."

She gulped, and I knew what she was thinking. The image of the Malak sliding to the ground while a pool of blood spread around him had seared itself into my memory.

"He's a follower of Hobbes. His deranged loyalty means he would rather die than reveal anything about the cult or what they're going to do. A lot of them want to die for Hobbes."

A surge of frustration rushed up inside me, and I slammed my fists against the dashboard. Ally jumped.

"Oh. Okay. Now we've gotten to angry Sara," she commented.

"I'm sorry. It's just… I need answers. I'm seriously confused. I'm more than a tiny bit pissed off. And I'm working on borrowed time, which means I don't have the wiggle room for any of this shit."

"What are you going to do?"

"I need to talk to a Farling. They'll have more insight. And there's only one person from The Far I know."

Ally sighed.

"Give me the address he gave you. I'll get directions."

I gave her the information Archimedes had provided, and she put it into her phone. She didn't seem delighted about the idea of going to talk to him, but it was becoming increasingly obvious I wasn't going to be able to do this on my own, even with Ally there to help. We needed what Archie knew.

Considering my current living arrangement, I wasn't the person who should be judging other people's houses, but I was surprised when we pulled up to the address the Philosopher had given us. The neighborhood looked like one that had been sitting there for decades, full of comfortable, cozy homes where you would visit your grandmother and eat butterscotch candies.

Archie's house was the one you skipped when you went trick-or-treating. The mostly brick house had windows and trim that used to be painted white but had peeled and faded to blotchy wood. The neighbors on either side must have loved the lawn that looked like a tiny jungle and the assortment of broken, rusted cars I saw cluttering the backyard.

"Is this it?" Ally asked.

"It's the address he gave me."

We sat in the car staring at the house for long enough that the front door popped open and Archie came out. He squinted, then gestured for us to come inside. We got out of the car and walked up a cracked sidewalk that was gradually being reclaimed by nature. The steps leading up to the porch didn't look like they had nearly as much structural integrity as I'd like, and I braced myself to rush up them in case they crumbled. They held, and Archie ushered us into a living room that looked pretty much like the outside of his house.

"This is charming." Ally looked around at the piles of boxes, crates, and unidentifiable junk on the floor and furniture.

"Come with me." Archie didn't give any explanation or apology for his house.

That made me like him more.

He led us on a weaving path through the living room, into an equally cluttered dining room where one small space had been carved out of the mound on the table. A hallway led past two closed bedrooms and a bathroom, then finally to a door. Archie opened it, and we made our way down a rickety wooden staircase into the basement. From my experience in the upper portion of his house, I didn't hold out a tremendous amount of hope for it. I expected floor-to-ceiling boxes and possibly an assortment of new friends for Splinter.

Instead, I walked into something spectacular.

"Wow." I looked around at the elaborate displays, intricate equipment, and containers of various materials. "This is like a steampunk Dexter." I looked over at him. "The smart little science kid one. Not the murderer one."

"Are you sure about that?" Ally held up a glass vial that appeared to contain an eyeball.

"What did I say about touching things?" I snatched it out of her hand and put it back in the wooden stand.

"I don't know these Dexters you speak of, but welcome to my workshop. How was your search?" Archie responded.

As I told him about the town and the barn and the creepy angel, he turned toward a desk and leaned over it, clearly working on something. There was a Bunsen burner, and he adjusted the flame under a beaker. Something sputtered in the container, and he tipped the contents of a test tube into it, changing the color from amber to a dark purple.

"What do you think he meant?" I fretted. "When he said he knew who I was and what I did to his people?"

"You know your name is famous. That shouldn't come as that much of a surprise," Archie reminded me.

"I know, but the other part. It seemed strange. Like he was telling me he knew the truth and other people didn't."

Archie nodded as he dipped a narrow rubber hose into the liquid inside the beaker and fed it into another container. It changed color as it moved through the tube, shifting from the dark purple shade to bright blue to a noxious green as it fell into the next beaker.

"There are a lot of conspiracies about you."

"Why?" I was confused. "I figured they arrested me for murdering a bunch of Farsiders."

The truth was, I didn't know why I was supposedly so heinous or what people said about me. I'd picked up a few bits of information throughout my time in The Deep, and the only conclusion I came to was murder.

"Right." Archimedes gave me my first real confirmation. "But *why*? That's the thing. It's so much of a story. You're part boogeyman and part folk hero. Everyone hates you, but at the same time, there's a huge following of people who are trying to figure you out. None of them could explain it. How could a *human* child commit such horrific murders? And why? Everyone seemed to have ideas about it, but among all the conspiracy theories, one voice stood out. Hobbes."

Ally spoke up. "Who is this Hobbes?"

Archie carefully dropped an arrowhead into the liquid, which had turned darker as it cooled, and gently swirled it around.

"No one knows," he told her. "It's probably not his real name anyway. But he wrote a treatise about how the *Pax Philosophia* is failing Farsiders. Have you heard of *Mein Kampf*? This thing rivals it. Hold on." He set down the container and walked over to a stuffed bookshelf. His fingertips ran across the spines of the books for a few seconds, then grabbed one and offered it to me. "Here."

"You have a copy?"

"I'm well-read. It's all about how The Near is taking more and more, committing greater and greater atrocities against Farlings. Hobbes rails against it and says The Guild's covering it up. You know his prime piece of evidence?"

"What?" I didn't need to ask. I figured I already knew the answer.

"You. In that book, he calls on all Farsiders to rise against the evil Nearsiders before being brought to nothing. He wants to bring down the *Pax Philosophia* and wage war on the humans."

Ally noted, "That Malak was completely obsessed. He eviscerated himself in honor of Hobbes. Why would anyone be so devoted to a raving lunatic?"

"That's the thing." Archie went back to his rune. "His followers may be raving, but Hobbes isn't. He makes some fair points."

"Oh, fantastic," I snapped.

"It's true. You might be innocent, but every day we hear about Nearlings brutally killing Farsiders," Archie continued.

"It goes both ways," Ally jumped in. "I've been investigating for years since Sara disappeared and I've found out some seriously strange stuff. Of course, I didn't know about all this before we found each other again, but now that I do, it makes sense. All these odd stories I've been chasing about humans dying in bizarre ways. It was all The Far."

Archie nodded.

"I've heard about those things, too. No one is going to say Farfolk haven't done their fair share to The Near. The Farsiders are getting restless. Everyone is saying the *Pax Philosophia* is starting to crumble. The Philosopher's peace is fragile now. Hobbes's cult is preparing to give it the final blow."

My mind churned, piecing it all together. Realization settled in, sending a wave of chills down my spine.

"That's why they bought all the runes. This is what they're preparing for. They're going to create a spectacle."

"Why would they want to do that?" Ally asked.

"The *Pax* is based on secrecy, right? What better way to destroy it than to reveal the existence of Farsiders to the human world? Then there would be no choice but to go to war." I shivered. "They want to do this and do it with a bang."

"And Charleston is Ground Zero," Ally agreed.

CHAPTER TWENTY-SEVEN

"So now what? Ally asked. We know the Harbingers are planning some grand entrance, but we don't know where. How do we stop them?" Ally asked.

"There isn't much else we can do today," Archie pointed out. "It's getting late, and both of you look exhausted. I think the best thing to do would be for everyone to get some sleep and come back to this early tomorrow and see what we can do."

"We don't have time for that," I shouted. "They could initiate their plan at any moment."

"I think we have more time than you believe," he stated, his face turned toward his desk.

"Explain."

He faced me and sighed like he was lecturing a bunch of preschoolers. "Whatever their plan is, it involves a rune, right? A big one. That'll take time to make."

"That…" I let my argument trail off. "That makes sense."

I thought about the almost ten years it took for Solon to finish the lense.

"How much time?" Ally pressed him for answers.

Archie cocked his head. "Honestly, I don't know. Probably more than twenty-four hours, which thanks to Slick they haven't had yet. I say you sleep, then we hit this thing fresh tomorrow."

I wanted to argue with him, to tell him we needed to keep going, but he was right about me being exhausted. It wasn't only my body that was tired from my lack of sleep and everything I'd gone through in the last few days. My mind felt drained, and I knew it needed some time to recharge before I'd be good for anything. Ally and I said goodbye to Archie and got back in the station wagon. I had her bring me to a spot a few blocks away from the hotel and drop me off.

I still didn't want her to know where I was staying. Especially after our encounters with the Harbingers, I knew every minute I was near her increased the danger she faced. Merely going by her house would be like sketching a target on it. I wouldn't do that to her. She deserved to have at least one space that was relatively safe, even if I knew in the back of my mind either the Guild or the Harbingers would eventually trace her there. Hopefully, I would stay a step ahead.

Once the station wagon disappeared around the corner, I hurried through an alley and down the street to the hotel. Breaking with his usual protocol, Splinter tried channeling his inner parrot and perched on my shoulder. It was his angry chattering and digging of his sharp little claws into my skin that alerted me to the shadowy form in front of the door. I took a few steps closer and realized it was the dog from the night before.

He sat outside the door like he was on guard, his head swinging slowly back and forth to scan the parking lot. His eyes locked on me, and he got to his feet. Splinter kept up the fussing, and I could only imagine all the nasty things he was saying to the dog. I reached up and grabbed him, then shoved him into my pocket.

"Hey there," I said to the dog. "It's good to see you up and about. You feeling better?"

He looked back at me and his head dipped, almost like he was nodding. Oh, hell. It was finally happening. I had officially lost my ever-loving mind.

Whether I'd lost it or not, the dog seemed to understand what I said and looked at the door like he was asking to come in. Considering the sun had set and he was probably waiting for the crew of drunk dude-bros to come back and finish him off, I could understand. I opened the door and nodded toward the lobby beyond.

"You're welcome to come in with us."

He trotted inside and I used the glow of my locket to lead the way to my room. I had spent the last decade of my life living in darkness, knowing that the light illuminated me as much as the surrounding threats. But here, out in the world, using it felt luxurious and a little indulgent. Maybe I'd even put it on my nightstand for a night light. That beat the hell out of the bioluminescent eyes of the cellmate I had for six months in The Deep, especially since he spent those six months hovering over me while I slept.

Imaginary housekeeping hadn't come, so the bed was still a mess. That didn't stop the dog from jumping up onto it and settling down. Usually I'd push him away and reclaim the spot, but he'd been through a lot. Besides, there was a perfectly good chair waiting for me to plop down into. Which I did and promptly fell asleep.

My mind immediately filled with the image of a dark hooded figure hovering in front of me. I didn't know who it was but had the distinct impression this was Hobbes. My fingertips tingled with anger and I launched toward him, but before I could grab him, he dissolved and nothing was there but a swirl of colors. It looked like I was stuck in a spiral of red and purple light. It reminded me of when I was fifteen and the guards pushed me through the door in reality to bring me to The Deep. The colors were brighter and more defined, but the sense of disconnection and panic was still there. I ran. Maybe if I went fast enough, I'd be able to escape it.

It didn't work. No matter how hard I ran or how fast I tried to force myself, the colors followed me. I looked back over my shoulder to see if Hobbes was chasing me, but there was nothing. When I faced forward, he was there. I skidded to a stop, my heart pounding in my chest as stress made my body shake and my vision blur. His hand reached out to me, and I fought the compulsion to recoil. Instead, I grabbed his hand and yanked him toward me so I could reach up and push the hood away and reveal his face.

The hood dropped back and the sound of Splinter chattering rose around me. It was so loud it drowned out the sound of my breath. The end of the world was coming. It was pressing down around me. I hadn't been able to stop it. But Hobbes was there in front of me, and I had removed his hood. Everyone would know who he was now. I turned my attention back to him and saw the cloak had disappeared.

A steady dim blue replaced the swirling colors. And there was no longer a hooded figure standing in front of me, but a massive man. A massive and very naked man hovering over me with a knife. He drew closer and Splinter got louder, his little voice sharper and higher-pitched. It occurred to me that he could see the man, too. He must've come with me to confront the end of the world. The naked man moved closer, and something struck me.

I couldn't smell him. After all the years spent in prison and learning exactly how to identify different species only by their smell in long periods of absolute darkness, I'd become very attached to my olfactory abilities. It wasn't exactly a superpower, but it was enough to give me the reassurance that he wasn't actually there. I was dreaming. Why I was dreaming of a huge naked man with a knife coming at me was something for me to analyze on another day. Now was the time to wake up.

Come on, Slick. Wake up. Wake up. Pantsless McStabby won't be there anymore.

Finally, my eyelids popped up. *Shit.* It wasn't a dream.

The part about Hobbes and running through the portal to escape the end of time had all been in my head, but the naked man wielding a blade certainly wasn't. He was all muscles, rugged face, and long dark hair, and he really was standing over me. Splinter was doing his best to give him hell from his perch on the nightstand where he crouched on the edge, his bristles up like spikes as he prepared to attack, all the while screaming bloody murder. I reached for my switchblade, but it wasn't there. My eyes locked back on the man and I realized my knife wasn't in my

ST BRANTON

pocket because he was holding it. He was threatening me with my damn blade.

This was *so* not how I envisioned my first time in a room with a naked man. Family Life classes freshman year did nothing to prepare me for this.

Worried thoughts flowed through me, and I looked around the room for the dog. He was nowhere to be seen. Splinter made his angry sound again, and the worry faded into shock as it occurred to me what I was looking at.

"You're a werewolf."

"Not exactly," he replied in a growling voice. "I'm a Loup."

"A what?"

It was hard to pay attention to him while also not acknowledging the fact that he was dangling in the breeze.

"A Loup," he repeated. "Essentially the opposite of what Nearsiders think of as a werewolf."

That struck a chord in my memory, but again, focusing was difficult.

"Listen, before you go on, would you mind grabbing a sheet and throwing it around you? Kind of a toga situation?"

He did as I asked. When he was almost presentable, he continued,

"What you think of a werewolf is a human who occasionally changes into a wolf. My kind are wolves who turn into humans only when the full moon is at its peak."

Now that he was at least symbolically presentable, I seemed to remember Solon saying something about the Loup.

"I've heard legends about that, but I always assumed they were myths."

"No."

Wow. Talkative.

Splinter took a flying leap from the nightstand and landed in my lap, pushing back against me while still facing off against the man. I couldn't tell if it was a position meant to be protective of me or if he was too afraid to turn his back. I held his tiny paw between my thumb and finger to comfort him.

"This is Splinter," I told the man. "What's your name? What do I call you?"

He shook his head.

"We don't name ourselves."

"Okay. Well, I have to call you something, so I'll stick with Dog."

"If that amuses your little human brain, fine."

"Why are you here, Dog?"

His new title didn't delight him, but I was getting a feel for it. I figured if he wanted to stand there with my blade still pointed right at my face, then I got to call him what I wanted.

"You must tell me the truth," he said firmly. "The absolute truth, do you understand?"

"The truth about what?"

"Anything I ask of you. My inborn abilities mean I will know if you're lying and as soon as I know you are, I will kill you without hesitation."

"Wow. That's the thanks I get for saving your furry ass from the guys last night?"

"I'd gladly give my life a dozen times if it meant finding

the truth. I need to know, will you give it or should I kill you now?"

I thought about trying to talk tough or make a joke and try to attack him while he was distracted. But something about the seriousness in his voice and the steadiness with which he held Solon's blade made me want to play it straight.

"I'll tell the truth."

He looked at me with those dark eyes, like he was assessing my soul. I must have passed his test because he didn't stab me.

"The deeds for which they imprisoned you, your heinous crimes against my kind, did you do them?"

He crouched slightly while inching closer to me and I knew it was so he could sense me. Like I had tried to when his presence in my hotel room had crossed over into my dream, he was smelling me. All the legends of the Loup I'd heard included the warning that these creatures could literally sniff out lies. If I said one word that wasn't true, he would know instantly.

Fortunately, there was no reason for me to lie about that.

"No."

The answer satisfied him enough to lower the blade, but before he could say anything else, a loud sound cracked through the silence and the door to my room smashed open.

CHAPTER TWENTY-EIGHT

The door burst open and I moved. I leapt from the chair, scrambling for a wall to put my back to. A series of guys streamed through the door. All of them carried some type of melee weapon, some with chains, bats, or pipes. It looked like an old fighting game had spat out a series of generic bad guys at me. At that point, it wouldn't have surprised me. The Guild controlled everything else. Why shouldn't they have the ability to sic video games on me?

It only took a second to realize these weren't henchmen sent by The Guild. One man stood out from the rest of them, leering at me with a toothless grin. It was one of the guys who had been beating on Dog when I saved him before, and it looked like he'd shored up his reserves before coming for me again. His buddies—both the guys from last night and new ones, a dozen of them total—filled the room before anyone made a move. I looked at Dog, hoping that he was on my side in all this.

Before I could meet his gaze, he'd already charged forward. His speed was impressive, and he ripped right into a couple of the men before they reacted. Fists flew as the men got their bearings, and some aimed their weapons at the blurrily fast mass of a man that was tearing through them without mercy. It was only appropriate. He was dishing back everything they'd given him. I grabbed my locket while everyone was distracted. The room turned dark, and I felt its power flowing through me.

I'd faced these men without the rune before. I was looking forward to seeing how I could hurt them with it.

I jumped forward, using my momentum to springboard off my hands and dive feet-first into two of them. I regained my feet in time to jump a chain swinging at knee-height. It hit another of the charging guys instead and wrapped around his legs, sending him barreling toward me. I dodged out of his way and he tumbled into a guy that had gotten behind Dog and was brandishing a knife. They fell into a nightstand and it exploded into shards of cheap, shattered wood.

It wasn't a very large arena.

I turned my attention to Chain Man and saw he'd whipped it behind him like some kind of inner-city Indiana Jones. I spun in a tight circle and snapped my leg out, catching his jaw with my heel, then turned my attention to two other goons holding baseball bats and coming for me. I ducked and one missed me, smashing another of his buddies in the teeth, and I hit the other in the back of the knees to take him off his feet. He crumpled, and I uppercut him hard in the throat. After spinning into him, I grabbed the bat out of his unprotesting hands and golf-swung at the back of his head. He went down in a pitiful heap and I blocked the first bat guy's swing with mine.

A second swing from Bat Guy was similarly blocked, and I thrust forward to headbutt him while we were in close quarters. Unfortunately, I missed, and smashed my head into the wall. Bat Guy hit me hard in the ribs with his weapon and I stumbled backward. Tripping over the mattress that had now gone askew in the mayhem, I landed on my ass hard, near the radiator, then looked up and saw him charging me now, bat in the air and ready to crack my skull.

Before he could reach me, Dog was on him and whaling away with punches. He beat the man senseless in a matter of seconds. I stood, adrenaline now kicking in and helping me ignore what would have been a broken rib if not for the locket. I flung the bat at the man now charging me, and it caught him in a sweet spot on the nose. He slammed backward onto the floor. Figuring I was pretty good at this chucking-stuff-at-bad-guys thing, I grabbed the lamp next to me and winged it at a guy across the room. Less luck this time, since it crashed against the wall and landed lamely in the corner.

I turned to one of the remaining standing men and noted that he'd been beaten up pretty good. Dog had finished with Bat Guy and was standing beside me, his breath not even labored, but his sheet-toga covered in other people's blood. I looked back at the three remaining men who had come into the room and realized they were three of the guys from before. The ones who had beaten on Dog outside the hotel. Payback would be sweet.

After grabbing a now-ownerless chain, I whipped it at one of the men as he tried to run for the door. It caught him around the neck and yanked him to the ground.

Another of the men tried going for the window, but Dog headed him off at the pass, shoulder-blocked him into a wall, then gave him a few shots to the stomach that seemed to remove his will to fight.

The last of the three hadn't moved, frozen in place with his hands out to the sides like he was trying to surf an invisible wave here in the hotel room. His eyes darted between me and Dog and then back to the door where his buddy was still being choked by the chain and the window where his other friend laid crumpled against the wall, blood spluttering out of his mouth through heavy breaths.

"Okay, now, wait a minute..." he began, and I saw movement behind him.

Splinter crawled around his midsection and without warning, sank his teeth into the man's stomach. "Not again," he screamed and reached for Splinter, who had already moved and was now biting him at random as he zoomed all over his body. The man screamed in pain with every bite and kept reaching around himself as he smacked his body in a lame attempt to hit Splinter. I slowly approached him, and by his lack of reaction, guessed that he didn't see me coming. I reared back with my fist and aimed, waiting for his jaw to be in the exact right position. When it was, I let fly.

When I connected, his lights went out. His knees bent and he dropped to them when his brain stopped sending signals that they should stay stiff. Gravity held him upright for a moment before he fell back on his ass, then sideways, his head smacking into the corner of the TV stand with a sickening thump. Splinter, extremely pleased with himself, hopped off his back and onto my leg, then scurried up until he found his pocket.

That seemed to be enough for the crew. They scooped up their wounded and rushed out of the hotel room with even more urgency than they'd come in. Dog stayed on alert, his hand wrapped tightly around my switchblade and ready to continue the fight until the last one disappeared into the hallway. As their voices faded, his hand fell to his side and he seemed to shrink. His expression collapsed, and he dropped to sit on the end of the bed. He was obviously upset, but I didn't know what to say.

"Well, there's another one for the record books," he muttered.

"What do you mean?"

"My people see the full moon as a curse. You know how everyone says the full moon brings out the crazy in people? More crimes are committed, more babies are born, strange things seem to happen? For us, the full moon means shifting, and that's not something we ever look forward to. Especially me."

"Why do you say that?"

"My kind has always preferred to stay wolves. We like to live in the wild, away from human interference. But ten years ago, my pack was all brutally murdered. I was the only survivor, and I was determined to find the killer. The trail led me to your house."

The memory from the night before struck me again, and I realized what it was.

"It was you. That night. I was trying to get into the side door. I looked into the backyard, and I saw a dog. That was you."

"Yes, but I hadn't gotten there in time. The Philosophers Guild got there first. When I saw that, I assumed you were the one who murdered my pack. But after watching your actions this week, I had my doubts."

The revelation took my breath away. My lungs burned and my chest ached, but I felt like I couldn't drag in any air. His words burrowed into my brain, stinging and slicing until I was in tatters. No one had ever told me what the supposedly heinous crimes were that justified endless lifetimes in The Deep. The guards laughed when I asked, and the new prisoners that Solon and I had interrogated all had a different story about the notorious Sara Slick. I kidnapped a member of the Guild. I burned down a goblin orphanage. I made a deal with the devil. The ambiguity had kept me going. I could come up with whatever I wanted to justify what was being done to me. But nothing my mind conjured was ever as horrible as what I just heard. It proved there had been no mistake about the brutality of the crimes. Someone had done something unimaginably horrific. It just wasn't me.

"I have no idea why the Philosophers Guild said my family had anything to do with the crimes," I told him when I got hold of myself.

"There was evidence that your father was the one who did it. A lot of evidence. The signs were all over the place. The scent of my people's blood was all over the house. Tracks leading away from their bodies matched your father's car and there was mud on his tires. It was enough to make me confident your father was the Nearling killer I had been hunting. But then you confessed. I couldn't imagine anyone would do something like that if it wasn't true."

"But it wasn't," I insisted. "I only confessed to save my father. They were threatening to take him away and I couldn't let my siblings be without him. But I didn't do anything. And neither did he."

"I know that now," Dog reassured me. "And for what it's worth, I'm sorry for what you must have gone through. You paid for another person's crime."

Even in the dark room, I saw the pain on his face. He handed Solon's blade back to me, then started to leave.

"I'm sorry for your family."

He looked at me over his shoulder and gave a slight nod.

"Not nearly as sorry as the true killer will be when I catch up with him."

CHAPTER TWENTY-NINE

Despite how exhausted I had been when I got back to the hotel two hours earlier, I was still awake. Now that Dog had left, I'd reclaimed the bed and was lying in it, staring at the ceiling again. It was a familiar situation. Splinter was curled up against my side, snoring like a little drunk. Every so often, his bristles would perk up and I could only imagine he was dreaming of his epic heroics. I couldn't get what Dog told me out of my mind.

"Why would the evidence point to my family?" I muttered.

Splinter was wholly unaffected. He kept right on snoring and flipping his little feet around like he was running up the guy again. The thing was, I'd never considered that there was anything that might suggest my family had anything to do with the crimes against The Far. I always assumed the Guild had made a terrible mistake. But now that I knew Dog had made the same mistake, it didn't feel as random or as accidental.

After another forty-five minutes of tossing and flopping around, I decided it was futile to keep trying to sleep. I opened the locket and grabbed Hobbes's book. It only took flipping through the first few pages for my mouth to fall open. Archie was right about me being the prime piece of evidence. I was everywhere in there. My name was splattered across those pages like I was the main character.

Hobbes was terrified of me and wanted everyone who read the book to be, as well. I could attest to its effectiveness. I was reading it and becoming a little terrified of myself. One thing was glaringly obvious as I read through the manifesto. Without me, there was no revolution. All the vehement desire to bring down the *Pax Philosophia* so they could wipe out the Nearlings came right down to me.

I read further and had to laugh.

"You know who this reminds me of?" I asked Splinter. He let out a snuffling sound, and I poked him in the belly hard enough to wake him up. He blinked at me, but I chose to take that as rapt attention and fascination with what I had to say. "This sounds like Solon. I mean, the content is more on the *I hate Sara Slick* side than he'd go, but the tone is like his. Straightforward. No nonsense. That air of everyone should have a basic knowledge of this absurdly complex concept only a select few really know." I laughed again and looked over at Splinter to make sure he was still awake.

"You know, in the early days, he assumed I'd never be strong enough to take on the Farside threats I'd have to face in The Deep. He knew there was no way I'd ever be able to protect myself or fight back against them, so he focused his teaching on showing me how to outsmart them instead. There was this one guy who gave me all sorts of trouble. He was my first experience with a troll. This dude was always picking on me. Anytime Solon wasn't around, he'd threaten to hurt me or eat me or whatever else came to his mind that day. I wanted Solon to get rid of him for me, but he wouldn't. Instead, he said he would teach me how to get back at him without ever having to throw a punch. Considering I had exactly no skills at the time, that was for the best. I thought that meant he would kick his ass for me, but no. He wanted to show me how to outsmart him. He taught me the valuable lesson that the enemy of your enemy can be your friend.

"At his direction, I stole some food from another prisoner. This was a new guy, a vicious cyclops. Solon told me to tell him that the troll had done it and was coming after him. Of course, this new cyclops was still fresh off the streets and hadn't been as ground down by The Deep as most of the others. I wished Solon and I had some popcorn that night while we watched the new guy kick the shit out of the troll who had been threatening me."

I laughed again, but the sound suddenly died in my throat. It hit me.

What if Hobbes framed me?

My family didn't know anything about what had been The Far before the day the Philosophers Guild showed up. It didn't make sense that there was so much evidence tying my father to the murders. We had to have been the patsy. Maybe it was because Hobbes had set it up that way. He had created the entire thing *so* he could have a villain to rally against and achieve his goal.

It didn't matter that he was threatening my city. He had already ruined my life.

CHAPTER THIRTY

Staying in my hotel room for the rest of the night was a study in the limits of my patience. I knew Ally needed sleep and Archie had probably stayed up doing his mad scientist thing for a while after we left, so he'd need to crash for at least a few hours if I wanted him to be any help. That meant I couldn't leave right then and start pursuing my new theory. Splinter had long since gone back to sleep and I bored myself into a few winks by counting his bristles. It wasn't as soft and fluffy as counting sheep, but it worked.

After an hour or two of forced sleep, I was awake again and still had plenty of night to push through. Another shower took up some time and freshened me up some, then came pacing around the room while I waited for my hair to dry. That was swiftly followed by making a list of things I would need during my time out of The Deep. So far it included real shampoo, a toothbrush, and deodorant.

I might as well spend what little freedom I had left smelling well.

For the next hour, I practiced planking on various surfaces of the room and made a mental note to ask Ally when I saw her if that was still a thing. I'd resorted to jumping on the bed in what I would later refer to as dexterity exercises when the sun finally started coming up. That was good enough for me. I changed clothes and headed out. I walked toward Archie's house and had gotten a few blocks away when I heard a car horn behind me. Ally pulled up beside me and tilted her head down to gaze through the window.

"Want a ride, hot stuff?"

I opened the door and slipped into the passenger seat.

"I know you're teasing me, but that's the first time someone's propositioned me in a long time, and it feels pretty good."

She grinned at me.

"I'll throw more at you any time. Just let me know."

I shrugged.

"It's better when it's spontaneous."

Archie was leaning out of his door again when we got to the house, and I started wondering if there was a tracker chip situation going on. I hoped he would tell me if he was going to implant me with something so he knew where I was all the time, but I'd learned not to underestimate the Philosophers.

"It took you long enough," he said as we walked up the sidewalk to him.

His voice was sharp and bitter, putting on full display that he wasn't thrilled I'd roped him into our save the world scheme.

"Are you tracking me?"

"What do you mean?"

I shook my head. "Never mind. Good morning."

"Come on. I have breakfast going." He ushered us into the house.

Ally and I exchanged glances.

"Breakfast?" we whispered.

We walked into the house, and I breathed in the smell of the fabled breakfast. I could detect eggs, sausage, and potatoes, and my mouth watered. There was nowhere in the house for us to sit, but that didn't matter. I'd perch on top of one of the leaning towers of random stuff if I needed to. It had been way too long since I'd had a breakfast like that, and I wanted all of it.

It turned out I didn't have to perch. Instead, Archie shoved loaded plates and oversized mugs of heavily creamed coffee into our hands and urged us back down into his basement workshop. I wasn't the biggest fan of eating near some of those vessels and vials, but chose a spot as far away from his equipment as I could and tucked into the breakfast anyway. Archie set his plate right on the counter next to the Bunsen burner and shoved a whole link of sausage into his mouth.

"I love human food," he mumbled through the bite.

It would seem like a glimpse of humanity from him, if he was human to begin with.

"Me, too," I agreed.

We ate in silence for a few seconds before I washed down a massive bite of potatoes with my coffee and turned to him.

"I read the book. You're right, Hobbes has a serious thing about me."

"That's putting it mildly."

"Something occurred to me while I was reading it. It doesn't make sense that there was so much evidence against my family. We had nothing to do with Farsiders or the division between the realms before the Guild showed up at our house. That means somebody went to extremes to make it look like my father was the one who committed all those murders."

"Yes," he said, like he was guiding me to my next conclusion.

"So, why us?" I asked. "Why my father? He never did anything wrong to anyone, so why would someone choose him to be the scapegoat for something like this? And what really pushes me over the edge...all the evidence pointed specifically to my father."

"So?" Ally prompted.

"Obviously, somebody was doing their best to frame him for these murders, but when I confessed, nobody said anything about it. They went right along with it like that was what happened. This makes me think they were looking for a human to blame for something. And that got me thinking. Hobbes has clearly been against the *Pax Philosophia* for a long time. Much longer than people have thought I was a brutal murderer. But nobody took him seriously. He needed something to be his battle cry. He needed a 'Remember the Alamo' moment."

"So, you're saying that you're the Alamo?" Ally clarified.

"Those murders are. What if Hobbes created this whole thing so his raging against the Pax got some traction and he could get support for it? He didn't care who Farsiders were against, as long as there was a human they could vilify. It ended up being me."

"They framed you as a sacrifice to the cause," Archie stated.

I nodded.

Ally looked at us. "What do we do? Ally asked. Can we go to the Philosophers Guild and explain everything to them?"

Archie shook his head vehemently.

"No. As soon as you got anywhere near them, they would arrest Sara. Even if you convinced them that she didn't commit those murders, she escaped from The Deep and has committed other crimes now. And then, if they were willing to show understanding and mercy because they believe you, there's no guarantee the Guild could stop Hobbes and his cult. The Philosophers Guild is essentially good for cleaning up carnage, not preventing it. You can't involve them unless it's the absolute last resort."

I agreed. "So, it's on us to stop them. How are we going to do it?"

"I spent the night working it over. We already know they're building a massive rune for whatever they're planning. Whatever it is, they'll need a ton of Nearstuff to do it. Not only the type of stuff that's lying around everywhere. That won't make the type of rune they want. They need the illicit stuff, the type that will create an instrument of evil," Archie informed us.

"The rune version of a weapon of mass destruction," Ally summarized.

Archie nodded.

"What I offered got toasted by you." He pointed at me,

and I took a small bow. "And if they want to do something as big as we think, it'll take a lot more than what they could have gotten from Vincent."

"The kidnappings," I blurted in sudden realization. "That's probably where the victims ended up. Ally, you told me that some bodies were in bad shape, and some never showed up at all. The ones who are gone must have ended up with the Harbingers."

"Is there any way we can find them?" She gave us a hopeful look. "Maybe we can save them."

Archie shook his head.

"There's no point in being hopeful about that. If the Harbingers kidnapped them, they're dead by now and turned into supplies. Blood, hair, bone. They'll end up being used to make runes."

Ally shuddered, and I glared at the Philosopher.

"That was diplomatic."

"What's the point of sugarcoating it?" he snapped. "Hope is a delusion we can't rely on. There's no happy ending in this thing, not for them, anyway. They wouldn't kidnap people for fun. By now, they've harvested those people and there's nothing we can do to help them. We need to turn our energy to what we can do."

"And what's that?"

Ally's voice trembled, and I knew she'd held out hope for those victims. All the time she'd devoted to searching for them and finding out what happened had crashed down around her.

"Stop them," Archie told her. "We can't undo the damage the Harbingers have done, but we can ruin their plan. All we have to do is find their stash and torch it. At least then we'll avoid the real devastation, and avenge your kidnapping victims as well. They'll still be gone, but their blood will only have been spilled, not used to spill more."

Ally's eyes widened, and her head snapped to me.

"The old woman."

"What old woman?"

I used the tip of my finger to shove another piece of sausage into my mouth and placed a chunk of potato into the eager pink hands that popped up out of my pocket. Splinter pulled it inside, and I heard his happy little sounds as he dove into the treat. I probably should have paused in stuffing myself during the solemn moment, but like Archie said, they weren't coming back. Letting my breakfast get cold didn't seem like a meaningful tribute to them.

"Remember when we were first talking about The Far and I asked you about vampires because I interviewed that old woman? She said she was positive there was a coven of vampires living next door," Ally reminded me.

"Oh, right. The one who stalked her neighbors from her window and noticed they only came and went at night."

"I notice you conveniently skipped over the whole blood thing."

"What blood thing?" Archie's curiosity piqued.

"She looked through their window one night and saw blood everywhere. She didn't really go into any detail, only said that she saw a lot of blood." Ally jumped down from the stool where she was sitting. "It's probably nothing, but it's worth checking out."

"All right." I finished my meal. "Take me to it."

Archie dismissed it. "It's a waste of time. Odds are, this

old human is merely bored. I need you to gather me some supplies."

"Good. Then I'll go."

"No." I shook my head. "Not on your own, Ally. No way."

"I'm on my own all the time, Slick. It's what I do, remember? This is like any other investigation."

"Except this time, you aren't hoping to find people so you can write a report. You're hoping to sop up what's left with a sponge and save the world. Slightly different motivations," I pointed out.

"Not the world." She grinned. "Not the whole one, anyway."

It was the same thing I'd said about myself, which meant I couldn't very well fight her over it. I'd dragged her into this, but now that she was in it, nothing would stop Ally from pursuing it. Damn my best friend and her motivation.

"What are you going to do if you come face-to-face with the Harbingers? It's not like you're prepared to fight."

"Here. Take this with you."

Archie held out a small golden ring with a brilliant red color woven throughout.

Ally took it. "It's lovely. What is it?"

Archie blushed a little. I didn't know Philosophers could do that.

"It's a rune. A distress beacon. If you end up in trouble, spin it clockwise three times and it will let us know."

Ally and I looked at each other, then back at Archie. He must have worked on that ring all night.

"Thanks. And I'll be fine, Slick." Ally gave me a tight hug. "I always am."

"The second you think something might be wrong, use the rune," I warned her.

"I will." She looked at Archie. "Don't let anything happen to her while I'm not here."

"I'd prefer if nothing happened while you were here," I retorted.

She shot me another reassuring smile and rushed up the steps. It was obvious she thought she was on some sort of trail and didn't want to lose it.

"Speaking of runes," Archie said when she was gone. "I think it's time for you to have an upgrade."

"What do you mean?"

"Like I said, odds are we won't be able to find them. But they want to make a spectacle, right? So they'll show their heads sooner or later. And when they do, you need to be prepared with a little spectacle of your own."

I smiled. "What exactly did you have in mind?"

CHAPTER THIRTY-ONE

When Archie told me I would get a new weapon, I assumed I would take a journey. I envisioned traveling deep into the woods to find a kindly tree to grant me access to a cave that would test my courage and the purity of my heart before allowing me to the inner sanctum where I'd find a silver sword. Which would have really sucked because my heart wasn't that pure these days.

Fortunately, it wasn't that complicated. All I needed to do was gather supplies from some of Archie's less-than-reputable colleagues. They weren't the types to revel in all the pomp, circumstance, and mystery. A giant-ass abandoned grocery store near the edge of town was good enough for them.

Archie gave me the most disturbing grocery list I'd ever seen and sent me on my way, promising to let me know if he heard anything from Ally. I grumbled to myself for most of the walk to the sketchy part of town, pissed that I didn't get a more dramatic entrance than being on foot. Considering I had only gotten my learner's permit when I ended up in The Deep and they didn't provide me with behind-the-wheel driving education during my time there, it wasn't like I had many other options anyway. It simply felt like there should be more than strolling along the cracked sidewalks, listening to the birds and wondering if powdered bone came in sacks or tubes.

When I arrived at the abandoned grocery store, I noticed something seemed off. Archie had sent me here and instructed me to go in the back, making it seem like that was the only way to stay out of sight. But as I got to the overgrown parking lot, I noticed there were several cars in the front and it seemed like something was going down. Some instinct urged me to check the place out first, so I looked around the building until I found a ladder and hopped up onto the bottom rung.

I climbed quickly and reached the roof without much effort. There were a series of skylights at the top of the building, and I made my way toward them. Lights were visible from inside against the gloom of cloud cover that had settled into place since I left Archie's house, and I knelt to look. Discarded advertisements and rusted-out shelves were scattered everywhere, and I saw a cyclops—scratch that, three of them—moving boxes around. One was at least seven feet tall and had shoulders like a brick wall. Almost half his size was a goblin with a clipboard barking orders like she was playing Farstuff roadshow.

It seemed normal enough, as normal as a warehouse for dealing in illicit goods would be, and I was about to climb back down when I noticed something else. In the corner, huddled together with tied hands and duct-taped mouths was a small group of humans.

Shit.

That was probably also normal for a place like this.

Archie had warned me that his colleagues could be a little rough around the edges, but I had expected some lewd comments or maybe tough bartering, not trafficking in humans.

One of the humans, a man, must have pissed the goblin off because she stepped over and paint-brushed the man with the back of her hand. I winced as she did it again, this time harder. Spit flew as she screamed at him. The other humans—a couple of men, a couple of women, and a few of them looking pretty young—were clearly terrified, but an old man stuck in the middle of the group stood and tried to get between the goblin and the man she was abusing.

She turned on him almost immediately. She punched and kicked, even after he fell to the floor and curled up in the fetal position. Then she pulled a bowie knife from her belt and sat on the old man's chest.

Bile rose in my throat. Whether these humans were slaves or snacks or goods, they didn't deserve terror or torture at the hands of some asshole goblin. I had to get in there and stop them, and it needed to be fast. I looked around and found a cinder block laying near the skylight. I hefted it above my head, took careful aim, and dropped it straight down. Not exactly elegant, but effective. It crashed through the skylight and landed on the head of one of the cyclops. I barely caught sight of him slumping over before I darted toward the ladder again. After placing my hands and the insteps of my feet along the sides of it, I slid to the bottom in seconds and jumped off to the ground.

I dashed for the front door and found a window

missing its glass and the board that was supposed to block it off hanging open. I climbed in and made my way to a display shelf. I ducked and watched as several more goblins, obviously middle management, huddled around the cyclops that had fallen while staring up at the skylight. The cyclops workers, not having been told their job was to be altered, continued to move Farstuff into their piles with robotic efficiency. They weren't that bright, but they were damn strong. And there were three of them, which would make this much more difficult.

There were five goblins that I could count, and I had a direct shot at them if I went to the right, around a large shelf, and could mostly avoid the cyclops workers. I waited until one of them had moved far down the long room and drew on my locket.

I darted forward, jumped through the air and kicked a large display toward the huddled goblins. A muffled cry greeted the shelf landing on a few of them, but a couple got out of the way. I dove on top of one and laced a shot to its jaw with my heel. The surprise attack worked since he had no defense, and his eyes were full of visible confusion.

I spun to punch another one right between the eyes. As he stumbled back, he fell onto another goblin who was trying to get up from the shelf falling on him and tangled them both in a mess of arms and snotty noses. A goblin hit me from behind and tackled me to the ground, and we rolled until I was on top of him, raining down fists into his mushy, slimy face. While bouncing to the balls of my feet, I sensed two of them running at me from either direction and I backflipped out of the way, letting them run headlong into one another. Both had been running with knives drawn and stabbed the other.

That left two goblins, and they were regaining their bearings after crawling out from under the shelf. Turning, I saw a cyclops walk right by me, taking no note of the surrounding chaos, and continuing to do its assigned job. Honestly, the dude deserved a raise.

The behemoth looked even bigger in person, and a shiver ran through me at the thought of having to fight not one, but three. I needed to deal with the goblins before they changed their orders.

I grabbed a long metal pole from among the ruined displays around me and spun it over my head a few times. As the first goblin opened his mouth to scream a command, I flung the pole at him. He saw it coming and ducked, but it flew over his head and impaled itself in the head of the goblin behind him. The first goblin stood, looked back at her fallen brethren, and pointed at me.

"Kill that girl," she screamed at the top of her lungs.

"Okay," I said as three single eyes on three giants turned their attention toward me. "Before we get down to business, I have to know. What do I call you? Cyclopses? Cyclopsi? Because that would be hilarious. Cyclopsi. Get it? Because of the...eye. Cyclops...eye... No?"

Not only did they not appreciate my humor, they were advancing at an alarming speed for beings so big. I scrambled backward and wound up with my back against a freezer door. I tested the handle and it opened easily. A wave of inspiration hit me after diving inside, and I hoped my impromptu freezer plan worked. The long-abandoned meat hooks still hung from the ceiling of the freezer and I grabbed one, preparing myself. Cyclopses have one known weakness to go along with their super strength, singular efficiency of purpose, and incredible stamina.

I flung the meat hook as the first one came through the door, and it went directly on target, stabbing into the giant's lone eye. He flailed backward, and I grabbed a second hook. As the second one came through, I repeated the motion and again struck gold. Okay, so there was another weakness. They were as dumb as rocks. I grabbed a third meat hook and waited for the last of them. As the door opened, I took my shot and flung it at him.

He blinked.

Well, shit.

Acting quickly, I rolled forward, through his legs and out the door while it was still open. I popped up and heard him grunt in surprise as I slammed the door shut. The door locked with a click, and I breathed a small sigh of relief. It wouldn't hold him for long, but there was no handle on the inside. The only ways out were to be let out, or to beat the door down. The sounds of the cyclops banging against the door told me that he was going with the second option and my time was limited.

I looked around for the goblin but didn't see her anywhere. I rushed forward, untied the prisoners, and ushered them toward the door. They ran quickly and quietly, not wanting to attract the attention of any more bad guys who might be hanging around. My eyes fell on the Farstuff in the room and I ran to it. I grabbed whatever I could reach and ran like hell for the front exit, boxes of mermaid scales and a roll of dragon skin crushed in my arms.

As I got within a few yards of the window I had climbed through, I saw the last goblin heading the same direction. I let her get to the window before I dove at her, tackling her through the opening and ramming my elbow into her face repeatedly as soon as we stopped rolling. Right before she went unconscious, I heard the freezer door finally give way. Picking up the Farstuff I had dropped, I turned and ran, heading away from the building and back to safety as fast as possible.

CHAPTER THIRTY-TWO

"That sucked," I muttered to myself as I made my way back from the grocery store. "That was worse than Great-Aunt Melba the year she forgot the yams until the Tuesday before Thanksgiving and went ape-shit on the man trying to hoard them all."

The fight left me feeling like I screwed my insides in too hard. When Archie told me he was sending me to see his colleagues, it lulled me into complacency. Not that he was the warmest and fuzziest of people I'd met in my life, but with all his raving against the evils of the Harbingers and Hobbes, I expected the people he kept company with to be at least a little less than insanely violent. It didn't occur to me that I'd walk in on them being as horrible to humans as the people we were supposedly trying to stand up against.

Splinter squeaked and ran up to sit on my shoulder for a comforting cuddle.

"That sucks, too," I said. "Not you. The fact that humans can't protect themselves against wicked Farsiders. It's not because Nearsiders are weak. I mean, look at me. It's that they're ignorant. Literally. That word is thrown around a lot, but this time it's true. The humans are truly ignorant about what's going on around them. They don't know about the different realms, or the issues with Farsiders who hate humans so much. There's no way for them to defend themselves because they don't know what they're defending themselves against.

"Maybe Hobbes is right," I said to Splinter as he made his way back into my pocket. He made an appalled chittering sound. "No, hear me out. Maybe the *Pax Philosophia* is a terrible law. It means the people of The Near have no idea what's going on and The Far have all the power. Look around you. Where is the Philosopher's Guild? According to the *Pax*, they're supposed to be protecting the Nearlings as much as they protect Farfolk. But all they seem to do is clean up the mess afterward. That's not an effective system."

I was so lost in thought that I didn't realize I'd wandered out of the shady part of town and back into the more populated area. It didn't occur to me to pay attention until I nearly ran into someone walking down the middle of the sidewalk. After pulling all the supplies I gathered closer to me for fear the person would see the odd assortment of items I was carrying, I looked up at them. A few choice words had made their way up my throat, but they died in my mouth before I said them. My eyes had locked onto the face of the girl shuffling her way around me, a face that made my heart fall into my stomach.

It was my little sister, Mia.

Well, little might not be accurate. She was my height,

her head bowed and focused on a phone in her hands like the one Ally was always consulting. Her cheeks had lost the little girl chubbiness from the last time I saw her, yet I instantly knew it was her. I would recognize that face anywhere.

She looked up at me from her phone and gave a little apologetic grin.

"Sorry."

She moved right past me, and I realized she hadn't recognized me. She had no idea who I was. I knew that was a good thing, that now wasn't the time to have a tearful family reunion and try to explain everything that happened in the last decade, but it still cut through me. Mia had only been six the night they took me away. In the back of my mind, I still saw her sleepy little head sticking out from her bedroom and staring toward the steps, trying to make sense of the shouting and chaos coming from below. I quieted her and told her to go back to bed. That was the last she saw of me, and now I wondered what she thought happened after that moment.

I should have headed back to Archie's house to give him the supplies that were the point of me leaving in the first place. But I didn't. It was the truth when I told Ally I didn't have any intention of going to see my family because it would be too hard. But my family had wandered into my path, and I couldn't ignore her. This was my little sister, the youngest of my siblings, and to see her so grown up created too much curiosity and draw to ignore. I waited a few seconds until Mia was far enough ahead of me, then fell into step behind her.

There was a stretch of time when I was in The Deep

that I tried to imagine what my family was doing. I'd sit in the corner of my cell, pretending I was curled up in my father's recliner, and pretend their daily life was playing out in front of me. I never got to involve myself in it, but I would try to envision each of my siblings in the ways they might have grown and changed as the years passed. I'd put them in various situations and watch the imaginary versions of them live out their lives in my mind. After a while, it became too difficult to picture how they might have changed and what it would be like for them to face the challenges of life. Eventually, they dropped out of my daydreams until it was only me pretending to sit in my father's chair alone.

Now I didn't have to imagine what Mia looked like. She was right there in front of me, and I saw all the ways she'd changed. Angles and high cheekbones had taken over her face, and heavy makeup reminded me she was a teenager. It hit me that she was a year older than I'd been the night they arrested me. Despite all the makeup and tight clothes, she still looked so young. It made the years I'd lost with her, and the years I'd lost with myself, feel even heavier.

We walked along until we reached a stretch of small shops and restaurants. I recognized it as being fairly close to Archie's house. Mia looked up from her phone and grinned when two other girls walked out of a coffee shop and rushed toward her to gather her in excited hugs. I remembered hugs like that. Ally and I used to exchange them after not seeing each other for a few hours, feeling like it had been so long.

It was harder to watch her subtly now that we were in a public area, but I wasn't quite willing to relinquish my proximity to my little sister yet. She looked happy and healthy. The years had treated her well, and she had obviously grown up adjusted and secure. Even dealing with my disappearance, she was living a good life.

I hovered around the display window at a nearby boutique for a few more minutes and watched her out of the corner of my eye. She and the other two girls giggled and talked, then disappeared into the shop. I walked away, wishing I could go up to her, if only to look into her eyes again. As I put the shop behind me, I felt solidified in my convictions. The *Pax* was for the best. I was glad Mia could grow up shielded from the awful truth. Those few minutes made me feel more committed than I ever had been and clarified exactly what I had to do—stop these assholes from pulling off whatever attack they were planning.

If they wanted to take down The Near, they were going to have to get through the heinous Sara Slick first.

CHAPTER THIRTY-THREE

I pounded on the door when I got back to Archie's place, then kicked it a few times for good measure. He came to the door glaring, at me.

"What is wrong with you?" he asked as I pushed past him into the house.

"You didn't tell me I would be walking in on a party."

"A party?" He was confused.

"Yeah." I stalked toward the basement. "A let's-beat-the-living-shit-out-of-the-humans party. Do you think they went with e-vites for that? The engraving would probably be *really* expensive."

"Sorry. I did tell you they were less than reputable."

"Well, I got your stuff." I dropped everything onto a table in the workshop. "Your colleagues are a little dented, but I'm sure you took out a proper insurance policy on them, so I wouldn't worry about it too much."

"What did you do to them?"

"Nothing anywhere near as bad as they were doing to their human pets."

He dropped it there, which was a good decision on his part.

"I haven't heard anything from Ally yet," he informed me.

"Good."

"Let's see what you got and we'll get started on your new rune."

I swept a hand over the pile of Farstuff to display it to him.

"This is what I managed to snag. I got the 'they were being jerks' discount."

"Does that mean you stole it?"

"You catch on fast. What do you think? Is it what you need?"

He examined the various containers and objects I had brought, occasionally grunting and murmuring to himself. There was a point when I decided he was doing it for dramatic effect and had already long since decided whether he had what he needed. Finally, he nodded.

"There's some good stuff here. But it's not everything I'll need."

"What else?"

"This is the Farstuff part of the equation. I'll need to send you to procure the Nearstuff."

"What did you have in mind?"

"There's a guy not too far from here who usually has some Nearling teeth available to buy."

Gross. Tooth Fairy, my ass. All this time, it's a creepy Far dude snatching teeth from unsuspecting people.

"A human tooth would help you make the weapon?"

"There are other things that would probably work, but the tooth would give it the power I'm looking for."

I shoved a pile of papers off a chair and sat with a sharp thud. After grabbing the arms tightly, I tilted my head back.

"Go for it." I opened my mouth.

"What?"

"I don't need to go shopping again. We don't have the time for me to jaunt off on another excursion. Take your pick." I assumed the dental position again.

"Sara, you can't be serious. I'm not going to simply pry a tooth out of your mouth while you're sitting here in my workshop."

The dismissive note in his voice brought back a rush of anger I'd pushed down after leaving the prison. I straightened my head and looked directly at Archie.

"For two months in The Deep, I couldn't talk because a guard used a stick wrapped in steel wool like a pipe cleaner to scrub my throat after I spoke to him. If you look at my back, you'll see places where they peeled pieces of my skin away to see if it was easier to do after steaming me for an hour. Spoilers, it is, but I wouldn't recommend it. I fought a giantess, a goblin, and a scary-ass chewed bubble gum spider my first night in prison. I'm not afraid of you pulling a tooth. I have plenty of them."

The Philosopher stared at me for a few seconds, then seemed to come to terms with my decision. He walked over to a cabinet and pulled out a small glass bottle that looked like it might have been sitting on the shelf since Prohibition.

"Drink this." He shoved it into my hand. "It'll help."

"You should know that according to Near laws, it's a

serious offense to offer alcohol to minors...which would be applicable to this situation if I wasn't twenty-five years old. Damn. That hit me hard. Am I getting old?"

I punctuated my deflated question with a swig from the bottle. It burned going down, but immediately a sense of warmth flooded through my body, making my arms and legs feel heavy. He reached up onto a pegboard and took down a pair of pliers. My hands tightened around the ends of the chair arms as he approached.

"Are you sure you want to do this?"

I tossed my head back.

"Lay it on me. Or...out of me." I opened my mouth.

Everything in me told me to close my eyes, but I wouldn't. There had been too many times when I squeezed my eyes shut, hoping to block out the world or whatever threat was coming my way. It was the grown-up equivalent of a little child covering their eyes when the thunder came because they thought it would protect them, only it really wasn't all that grown up. I wasn't doing it this time. I was done letting other people push me around and tell me what to do, and offering up control in situations because it was intimidating. I was facing whatever was coming for me on my terms now.

Archie stood over me and looked down into my mouth. His eyes flickered up to mine, and I stared back at him without flinching. Whatever he'd given me to drink made me feel like someone was holding my body down, and I realized that's what he meant. It would help *him* because I wouldn't be able to move.

The pliers moved into my mouth, and I tasted the metal on my tongue. The sharpness flowed down my throat as the tool clamped down on either side of a molar. Archie hesitated.

"Do it," I growled over the pliers.

Without another second of hesitation, he yanked.

My tooth wrenched from my jawbone, and blood filled my mouth. Archie stumbled away from me and I sat up, catching the blood in my palm. He ran a towel under the faucet of a sink attached to one wall and pressed it to my mouth.

"You are hardcore, Slick."

I made my way upstairs to the bathroom to clean up and rinse my mouth. After plugging the new hole in my gums with toilet paper, I headed back down to the workshop and discovered Archie hard at work. He rushed around adding things to his equipment and manipulating various bits of the Farstuff. I watched him for a few moments before settling back into the chair.

"Why are you helping me? You know who I am and what everyone says about me."

"Charleston is my town, too." He didn't look up from his work. "I might live on the outskirts, but I consider this my home. I don't want anything to happen to it. Or to me, frankly. I'd really prefer not to get hurt because of Hobbes's cult. Don't mistake me. I'm not part of your quest and I won't stick my neck out for you."

"I get it. You have to look out for yourself and do what's needed to survive. I can understand that."

Archie straightened and looked at me.

"Don't take it personally. It's the way it's always had to be for me. In this world, I'm not accepted by either side. I have to go through life on my own."

"Maybe it won't always have to be that way. Maybe someday there'll be peace and you'll be able to live your life the way you want to. You may not feel like you fit in anywhere now, and that both sides reject you. But with a major change in the way things work, you never know. You could be a Rune Philosopher out in the open, not in hiding anymore."

"It's easy to dream about that, but I can't really believe it. Not yet."

"You know, if the end of the entire damn world rains down on us, you might wish you had stuck your head out…if only a little," I added.

Before Archie could say anything, a stone on a nearby table glowed and emitted a deep, throbbing sound.

"It's Ally." He rushed over to the stone and scooped it up. "She's activated her distress beacon."

"Where?" I shouted, already grabbing Splinter off the stool where he sat nibbling breakfast leftovers. I shoved him into the pocket of my leather jacket and started toward the stairs.

"Take this with you," Archie called. He tossed the stone to me, and I caught it. "It will guide you to her."

I looped the stone's leather strap around my palm before running up the stairs and out of the house.

CHAPTER THIRTY-FOUR

Following the rune Archie gave me felt like playing a messed up, high-stakes game of Hot and Cold. The stone changed temperature against my skin as I ran, guiding me with searing shocks of heat and icy blasts of cold while continuing to occasionally make the throbbing sound. I wished I could talk to Ally, to hear her voice and find out what was happening.

Fear pumped adrenaline through me and kept me running, following the directions of the rune until I reached a different part of town. It was an older neighborhood, like Archie's, and the quiet that should have seemed peaceful was eerie and unnerving.

Night had set in during my race to find Ally, and the deeper the shadows around the houses got, the more afraid I felt for her. Finally, the rune brought me to a nice, well-maintained home in the middle of the block. A bright white glow emanated from the stone on my palm.

"I'll take that as a 'tag, you're it,'" I muttered to it.

I crept around the side of the house and tried all the

windows. They were closed and locked, and nothing seemed strange or out of place. It was a simple cookie-cutter house. *That might be harboring Far terrorists. No big thing.* I checked the rune again, and it sent up another blinding white glow. Yup, she was here. Now I had to figure out where. It was only a one-story house, which meant there weren't many places to hide her.

A tinkle of glass crunched under my foot, and I stopped cold. It was small, and looked like it was a dark green color, like the kind that beer bottles came in. My eyes followed the side of the house and saw what looked like an odd door on the back of the building. It was wooden, and small, small enough that a normal-sized person would have to bend halfway over to get inside, and there was a padlock on the outside. Nothing says *suspicious* like someone padlocking a door on their house.

After creeping over to it as silently as possible, I looked at the tracker again. If she was here, she was only feet away from me now. But the house seemed silent in the darkening night, and this door looked like it was only for a crawlspace.

I steeled myself and drew on my locket's power. I channeled all the strength the rune gave me and pulled hard on the padlock. The whole damn handle ripped off. So much for the quiet approach. I yanked the door open and stared into the darkness. My eyes took a moment to adjust. What they saw when they did made my stomach drop.

The crawl space was huge, dropping several feet below the ground level, and creating a large basement with a dirt floor. Shelves lined the wall and were filled with oil cans and canned food from ages gone by. Boxes were in piles in various places on wooden pallets, and chains with shackles at the end hung from the walls.

Ally and several other humans were chained up, beaten and bloodied, and several had visible puncture wounds on their necks, dried blood caking their collars and fronts of their shirts. I drew a deep breath and jumped inside, prepared to meet an onslaught of the living dead, but nothing happened.

Ally's head slowly rose, and she turned toward the sound, her eyes opening wide and muffled sounds coming from her handkerchief-gagged mouth. I darted over to her and assessed her damage. She was bruised and had a deep gash above her right eye, but otherwise seemed fine. Dirty, but fine.

"Mmph-umm-umm phumph," came the voice from behind the fabric.

"What are you trying to say, Ally? Let me get this hanky out of the way." I pulled the gag away from her mouth.

"Behind you!" she gasped as soon as the fabric was gone.

I turned and saw a creature unfolding itself to a full height of roughly six feet. His body was hairless and he was thin as a bone except for a large paunch of a stomach. He looked vaguely human, except for the giant gaping hole where his face should have been. I saw a ring of teeth and nearly yacked.

I didn't have time to think, so I charged the human-leech hybrid and pushed hard on its chest, and didn't stop until we hit the wall. Its deceptively strong arms pushed me back, and I fell onto a pallet covered in decades of dust. A shard of wood broke free, and I grabbed it as the creature jumped down on top of me. I pulled the sharp piece in front of me and aimed at its chest. It landed on the makeshift stake, and blood exploded from it. It covered me, the wall, Ally, and everything within several feet. It was the grossest thing I had ever seen.

I spat its blood out of my mouth as I pushed the thing off me. When it hit the ground, a new round of blood shot from it, straight up in the air like a fountain. I looked at Ally, who was now absolutely drenched and looked like she was about to throw up.

"Are Gushers still a thing?" I thought of the raspberry-flavored treats that used to rule my lunchbox.

"Yes," she managed.

"I'm never eating them again."

"Oh, God, that's the worst freaking thing I have ever seen in my life," she said as I rushed over to her and undid the shackle holding her to the wall. "He was like a swollen tick somebody stomped on."

Several of the other prisoners were coming to, and a few were frantically gesturing to be the next ones unhooked. Ally worked on the person next to her as I moved across the room to help another. Once everyone was free, and had run screaming through the crawl space door, I looked around the room. Three small, rickety steps led to a door to the inside of the house.

"Are there others?" I kept my voice low. I didn't know why I was almost whispering. If something was up there, it would have heard the people running outside.

"Not like that." She gestured to the dead creature. "They wore robes like the other Harbingers, but they brought that thing down here to drain us," she shuddered before continuing, "of blood."

"Yeah, thanks. I'm pretty clear on the whole draining part. What are they doing?"

"They were making runes, I think, but then they would let that thing feed off us when they got what they wanted."

"Did it get you?" I checked her neck for signs of puncture wounds.

"No, but it was about to. Right before you came, they pointed me out as the next one."

I didn't have much time to contemplate our luck, because the door to the inside of the house creaked open. Instinctively, I pulled Ally behind me and took a fighting stance.

"Ally, get in the car," I called to her over my shoulder.

"What about you?" she yelled back, already on her way out the door.

"I have business to take care of," I said, mostly to myself. Ally was already out of the door and I heard her feet pounding across the yard to where she'd parked her car. That was fine. I knew it sounded badass.

Three figures stood in the shadow of the door and looked down at me. They wore robes, like Ally said, but their heads and arms were green and scaly and they hissed at me.

Freaking lizard men.

There was mild hesitation in the way they stood there, so I kicked the feet of the creature that had attacked me.

"I killed your leech thingie. I'm Sara Slick, and I'm not here to fuck around. Let's go, already." I gestured for them to come at me.

One of them took the invitation. He shot toward me, his speed catching me a little by surprise. I backed up a step, then pushed off the wall and leapt over him, my back scraping the roof of the basement, and landed behind him. As he turned, I grabbed his head in a headlock and flung him over my hip, smashing him into the ground. I felt his neck snap as I twisted with my arms, and his body went still. I stood and saw the other two circling me, one brandishing what looked like a small pipe and the other a short blade.

I reached behind me for my switchblade and pulled it out as the knife-wielder stabbed at me. I dodged it and smashed an elbow into his face. While ducking, I ground my heel into his toes and swung my blade upward. My foot kept him from avoiding me as I sliced all the way up his chest, and he fell in a crumpled heap in front of me.

Before I could get my bearings, the pipe guy hit me hard in the back. I stumbled forward and hit the wall where they'd shackled Ally. Even with my locket protecting me, that one hurt. I grabbed a chain in my hands and waited until I thought he was behind me, then lifted it. I caught the pipe in the chain and pulled to the side, snapping it out of his grip. He fell forward with the momentum and I jumped, then kicked sideways and contacted his right temple. It was enough to send him headfirst into the wall without being able to protect himself. A solid thud accompanied the meeting and he slid down, unconscious.

I scrambled out of the basement and ran across the yard toward the street.

"Sara!" Ally's voice beckoned me from the darkness.

I looked around and caught sight of her waving at me from in front of her station wagon, parked a few houses down. I ran toward her and we jumped into the car.

"You okay?"

"I will be. When I first got down there, I saw them taking the blood they had drained and putting it in bags. Like a freaking hospital blood bank. The old lady I interviewed must have seen them piling those bags in the yard to be transported."

"Holy shit," I muttered.

"That's only the beginning." Ally started the car and skidded out onto the street to drive toward Archie's house. "I know what their plan is. And it's about to happen. Now!"

CHAPTER THIRTY-FIVE

I learned an important life lesson that night.

A few months with a learner's permit and ten years of not practicing does not a good driver make.

Unfortunately, there wasn't another choice. Ally's adrenaline wore out a couple of blocks away from where she had been held and she could no longer drive. So I took over the wheel. It involved a lot of lurching, screeching, decided recklessness, and a mailbox casualty, but we finally made it back to base.

I pulled up in front of Archie's at an angle that would piss off some neighbors and ran around the passenger side of the car to scoop Ally out. She could walk, but barely, and I had to support her as I brought her up to the house.

Archie opened the door and reached out to wrap his arm around her waist and help me bring her down to the basement.

"Certainly took you long enough," he commented.

"Oh, I'm sorry. Did it take me too long to kill a couple of lizard men, squash their weird walking leech, and rescue my best friend? If I'd known we were going to be late for high tea, I would have gone a little faster."

"And the driving," Ally groaned as we lowered her onto a cot in one corner. "Oh, the driving."

"You drove?" Archie asked incredulously.

"Sort of," Ally muttered while curling up on her side.

"I operated a motor vehicle to the extent that I got us back here," I corrected. "Both our asses are still alive and we won't end up the visual aid for a public service announcement aimed at teens on prom night. I'll take that as a personal victory."

Archie seemed to think for a few seconds, as if debating whether he was going to continue to pursue that line of conversation, then decided against it. He looked down at Ally and started examining her injuries. She was pretty banged up and my stomach turned each time he moved aside a piece of clothing or she shifted and revealed another bruise. I ran upstairs to the kitchen and dug through all the cabinets until I confirmed he didn't have any plastic bags. A drawer offered me dish towels and I took one, filling it with ice from the freezer before rushing it back down to her.

It seemed fairly futile to give her only one ice pack, but if we were to ice all the bruises and cuts, we'd have to submerge her in the bathtub and that didn't seem like a good choice.

"What happened? What did you see?" Archie prompted her.

"I went back to a neighborhood where I had interviewed a woman a while back. I was looking into kidnappings and murders and ended up having a long conversation with her. She told me she thought the people next door were vampires because of their nocturnal behaviors and seeing a lot of blood. It seemed like a decent lead for our current situation."

"That's an understatement. They've set up shop in a little house in a neighborhood closer to the center of Charleston. The humans they kidnapped had been half drained of blood and they were getting started on Ally. But, as you can see, she put up a fight." I looked down at her while running my hand back through her hair. "I'm proud of you."

"I learned from the best, Slick," she said with a painful smile.

I shook my head.

"No, *I* learned from the best. But I'm glad you were able to learn from me."

She laughed.

"Don't sell yourself short. You're a badass."

"This is a beautiful moment, but can we wrap it up? Ally needs to rest."

Archie had gone over to his cabinet and was gathering bottles. Some he deposited on his work counter and others he brought over to Ally. After piling them up on a small table beside the cot, he went to another cabinet and gathered another armful of items.

"There's no time for that," she groaned.

"What did you hear?"

"They were talking about a gathering of humans. They said it would be huge, that most of Charleston would be there. I didn't catch where it was, but they said that's where it's all going to happen. Harbingers will be there with that

Spinoza asshole at the lead, and they're going to reveal the existence of Farlings to the human world in what they said was a spectacular fashion. And they said there would be enough blood spilt to drown the world."

"Wow, that sounds really *unspectacular*." The thought of Spinoza standing over me with a sword made a chill roll down my spine. "We need to figure out where they'll be and how to stop them."

"And fast," Archie added. "With the Farstuff they bought from the vampire and that much human blood available to them, they'll be able to do something incredibly powerful. Start working on her injuries. I'll keep going with this rune."

"Start working on her? I don't know what any of this stuff is."

"Read the labels," Archie instructed.

I picked up one bottle and saw it had careful instructions, like medication from a human pharmacy.

"Oh, convenient."

I went to work cleaning up her wounds and wrapping them in bandages with various ointments. I offered her gulps from a few of the bottles and watched her grimace as the concoctions inside took effect.

"You'll want to sleep while you can," Archie told her. "I have a feeling this showdown won't be a stroll in the park."

Ally complied, closing her eyes and falling asleep within moments. I couldn't help thinking at least one of those bottles aided that along. It wasn't that easy for me. Adrenaline, anger, and determination coursed through me, keeping me on my feet pacing through the basement.

Splinter climbed out of my pocket and ran over to

where my abandoned breakfast plate still sat. I wasn't too worried about him nibbling on the leftover potatoes and bits of sausage. He'd survived plenty of meals in The Deep that had their first glimpse of existence weeks before ending up on the floor of my cell. A few hours wasn't going to hurt him.

Archie kept working, but I could only force myself into a few minutes of fitful dozing before I was back up on my feet.

"Could you stop pacing? You're making me nervous."

"Maybe if it wasn't so quiet down here, it wouldn't bother you so much."

He responded by rummaging in a drawer and pulling out a remote. Pressing the power button brought to life a TV I hadn't noticed bolted into the wall above his workstation. He tossed the remote to me. Growing up with four siblings and my programming-opinionated father made this moment feel immensely powerful. I could dance through the channels with abandon. And I did.

And recognized absolutely nothing.

"What is all this?" I flicked another channel. "Why is *Friends* on? That was over…"

"Fifteen years ago," Archie filled in.

"Shit. It's an oldie. I don't know any of this stuff. Where are all the good shows? *Glee?*"

"No longer gleeful."

"*The Good Wife?*"

"Not sure how good she was, but people stopped caring about four years ago."

"*Parks and Recreation?*" I was getting increasingly distressed by the demise of all entertainment I knew.

"It seems 2015 was a bad year for your shows."

"How do you know all this, anyway? I don't see you as the type to finish up your day of selling people's skin and toenail clippings, pop a bowl of popcorn, and watch the Primetime lineup."

"You're right. I'm much more of an ice cream sundae man. But I, like most Farsiders, function pretty normally in The Near. I have guilty TV pleasures like everyone else."

"I don't think I need to hear about…"

"*Golden Girls.*"

"And there it is."

I changed the channel again in a final bid to settle on something from my era. The news filled the screen, telling me we'd gotten through the night and it was early in the morning.

"The rally will draw in crowds possibly reaching tens of thousands. Candidate Jones is expected to discuss the details of her platform, including controversial social reform measures. Support from the national level is adding to the interest and is expected to test the limits of the space and security."

The voice coming from the TV made me stop in my tracks. My eyes lowered to Archie, and he stared back with the same knowing expression in his.

"Oh, shit," I muttered.

"Preparations are already well underway at Folly Beach County Park since onlookers will begin arriving at the rally within the hour. Those interested in attending are advised…"

I didn't care what else the newscaster had to say. She'd told me plenty.

"That's where they'll be," I said to Archie. "They're going to take over the rally."

"So we go to the rally and stop them," Ally said from her cot. "I'm feeling political today."

"Look who's awake." I grinned. "Are you feeling better?"

"Stiff and sore, but better than I would have anticipated after getting into a rumble with lizard people. I'm ready to take these mofos down."

"We'll discuss your use of the term 'mofos' later, but for right now, we have to decide how we'll handle this."

"Let me know what I'm looking for and we'll divide and conquer."

I shook my head.

"It won't be that easy. They blend in, remember? And I'm sure the Harbingers who will be there today have been practicing hard to hone their human-faking game. They'll be next to impossible to spot in the crowd. Especially with that many people around. We won't know who they are until they reveal themselves. But once they do, they're on live TV. All hell will break loose in front of a national audience."

"Then what are we supposed to do?"

I started pacing again. "It looks like I have two choices. Either I can try to stop the broadcast and eliminate the live TV element of it, which will effectively ruin the Harbinger's plan of revealing magic and the realms to The Near but won't save the lives of innocent people. Or I can wait until they reveal themselves, kick their asses, and save the people, but end up helping fulfill their plan of revealing their existence to the world."

"So, good options all around."

"Essentially." The different scenarios tumbled through my mind for a few moments as I tried to decide which was better. By the time I'd gone over them a few dozen times each, I knew there was really only one choice. It sucked. But it was the only one. "I know what I have to do."

"I'm still working on your new weapon. It might take me a little while to get it right." He made a frustrated growling sound. "If I had some troll hair, it would make the process a lot faster."

My ears perked up.

"Troll hair?"

"Yeah. It's one of the more potent Farstuff materials for a weapon like this. I don't have any right now."

"Why didn't you say something?" I shimmied out of my jacket and flipped it around in my hands until I found the patch of troll scalp still clinging to the leather, a gift from that creep I had beaten up on my first night back in town. "There you go."

"Yes!" Archie exclaimed. "Now we're rolling. I'll have this ready in no time."

I looked at Ally and saw her face scrunched.

"You've been hanging around me with chunks of troll stuck to you?"

I shrugged. "It happens."

CHAPTER THIRTY-SIX

"They weren't kidding when they mentioned limited parking," I said as we joined the flow of people heading toward the rally.

"There are so many people." Ally's voice was tight with the anxiety of knowing what that meant.

If there were this many people still heading into the park for the rally, the number already there would be staggering. Whoever arranged the rally had chosen an interesting place for it. Folly Beach County Park was a peninsula jutting out from Charleston. Water surrounded its long, narrow shape on three sides. Security had set up massive entrance gates to block people from simply passing through into the rally. They meant it as a measure to keep the political figures safe and control the crowds. They didn't realize they were trapping thousands of people on the strip of land.

Watching the group funnel through the admission gate and onto the beach was like watching a herd of cattle being brought to slaughter. We moved as fast as we could toward the entrance. The sooner we could get into the rally, the better chance we had of shutting this thing down before it turned into the disaster the Harbingers hoped it would be. We finally pushed our way through the crowd to get close enough to see the entrance gate and my stomach dropped.

"They're checking IDs," I said to Ally.

"What?"

"The security guards at the entrance gate. They're checking people's IDs before they let them inside. It's probably because of the politicians. The news did say there had been some grumblings from protesters considering showing up to the rally today."

"Probably not the kind they were thinking," Archie commented.

I grabbed each of them by the arm and pulled them out of the way so we could talk without risk of being trampled by the impending masses.

"What are we going to do?" I asked. "I don't have any ID and I really doubt dear Archimedes over here does, either."

"Actually, I do."

"You have a Near ID?"

"Of course." He rummaged in his pocket and pulled out a card. "How do you think I blend in when I'm doing things like getting a house and paying bills?"

"You have a Near ID?" I repeated, trying to wrap my head around an ID with his weird glowing eyes and *Archimedes* across the front. He handed the card to me and I looked down at it. "Steven." I looked up at him. "Steven, why aren't your eyes glowing in this picture?"

"Really painful contacts. Not something I want to do again."

"What are we going to do about me? There's no way they'll let someone in without an ID. I can't exactly pretend to be the press."

My eyes slid over to Ally, and she shook her head.

"Don't get your hopes up. I'm not officially press. I'm like press-adjacent. That doesn't get me access to anything. We'll have to come up with another way to get you inside."

She reached into her pocket and pulled out her phone.

"What are you doing now? You use that thing for everything."

"Everybody does, Slick. They're essentially part of human DNA now. I'm checking Instagram."

"I know you had certain feelings about your sister dating that old guy with kids, but I don't think that's a nice thing to call her."

Ally's eyes lifted over the top of her phone to stare at me.

"I don't." She flipped the phone around to show me a series of pictures. "Instagram. I'm checking to see if anyone I know is already in there posting pictures. They might have caught something that could give us an idea of how to sneak you in."

"That's brilliant," Archie complimented.

Ally looked at him with pursed lips.

"It would be more of a compliment if you didn't sound so stunned about it."

He shrugged, not willing to relent to anything. After a few seconds of scrolling, Ally jumped a little like she'd noticed something and turned the phone back to me.

"What am I looking at?"

She swiped her fingers across the screen, drawing the image up closer to zero in on the barricades around the edges of the peninsula.

"The security doesn't look as serious around the edges," she pointed out. "It's only those flimsy orange mesh fence things. You could slip under one of those and get in without them noticing."

"Are you suggesting I go jump in the water somewhere, swim up to the side of the peninsula, and wiggle under the fence?" I asked.

Ally's mouth opened, then closed as she turned the phone back toward herself.

"It was a suggestion," she muttered.

I looked back toward the entrance gate and watched the security guards checking IDs. The crowd had been funneled into three lines, but the concept of being single-file had never caught on. Instead, they were smashed up together, trying to force their way through like Black Friday at the electronics store. Progress stopped when a man didn't produce a card and got into an argument with the security guard about the unconstitutionality of compulsory identification. An idea popped into my mind.

"I have a better one."

"What are you going to do?"

"Come with me. Get your cards ready."

We joined the crowd again and I willingly smooshed myself into the middle, wedging myself between people so we were all bouncing against each other as we made our way toward the entrance. The woman in front of me reached into her pocket and pulled out her ID. Now was my chance. I slung myself forward, ramming into her and the two people beside her, then whipped around to shout angrily at the crowd that hadn't done anything. I made an apologetic face at her.

"People are crazy," she commented.

"You're telling me." I slipped her newly snatched ID into my pocket.

I slunk back so I was with Archie and Ally again, positioning them on either side of me. The woman got to the security guard and realized she was no longer holding her card. She started searching frantically and the crowd built up behind her. I pushed Ally toward the guard standing in the middle and stood behind her, so I'd be forced between her and the woman without an ID. She showed her card and I flashed the stolen card. The guard asked to see it more clearly, but Archie caught on and pushed up behind me to offer his ID. Within a few seconds, I popped out of the crush of people and into the rally.

"That was risky," Ally said when they met up with me a few moments later.

"But it worked. And that's one potential victim we don't have to worry about. Now to convince all these other people to leave."

Archie looked around.

"Good luck with that. These people are either here to cheer on the local lady wanting to revolutionize the office with her brilliant new ideas or protest the neighborhood chick who will screw everything up because she doesn't know what she's talking about. Either way, they aren't going anywhere."

"The stage is set up toward the end of the park. I have a feeling that's where the Harbingers will go."

"Why wouldn't they try to get right in the middle of the crowd? That's where they'd be able to accomplish the most damage the fastest." Ally looked confused.

"It's not about the death toll," I pointed out. "They're here for the attention, for the shock value. Blood and guts are a pleasant bonus. Remember, their whole goal is to take down the *Pax Philosophia*, and that starts with revealing The Far to The Near. If they can get on stage, they'll be the center of attention. Everyone in this crowd will look at them, and that's exactly what they want. Once they've done their big reveal and it's been seen by everyone here and everyone tuning in on their TVs around the world, then they can have their fun. The war will have begun, and they can start the massacre."

Ally looked toward the stage, the weight of our task written on her face. "Well, shit."

"I'm going up there. I'll get as close to the stage as I can and start looking for anyone I think might be a Harbinger. You two try to get people to leave. Do whatever it takes. We need to thin the crowd as much as we can. They might get trigger-happy and want to turn the crowd itself into part of their demonstration."

We split off, and I ran toward the very edge of the peninsula. The picture Ally had showed me gave me the idea of following the bright orange fence around the edge to get to the stage with as little resistance as possible. The farther I went, the more my stomach sank. Pretty soon it would be flopping around in my feet.

The park was huge, and the crowd filled nearly all the

space. With more people flooding in, soon the park would reach total capacity. Not only did that mean more lives to snuff out, but less chance for escape. The more people who came, the harder it would be for any of them to run when the devastation started. If I couldn't stop this plan from happening, it would be a bloodbath. Dozens of cameras positioned throughout the park only made it worse. They were primed and ready to suck in every second of the horror to come and blast it out to all the households, computers, phones, and lord only knew what else that would tune in to listen to the future of politics.

I made my way along the edge of the peninsula, ducking around people and occasionally yelling at them to leave as I tried to force my way to the stage. It was visible in the distance, and as I got to within a few dozen yards of it, a group ascended the stairs.

Oh, fuck.

If their tight formation and slow, methodical movements didn't give them away, the robes did. The Harbingers had taken the stage. Something was about to go down and I didn't think it would be a tap dance and kick line.

There really wasn't any choice left. I hadn't been able to get the crowd out of the park or stop the cameras from rolling, and the Harbingers were already in place, ready to get their plan underway. There was only one thing left for me to do and it wasn't what I'd ever wanted.

But this wasn't about me.

I stepped closer to the fence, reached into my pocket, and pulled out a key. The ornate metal felt heavy in my hand. It still carried the same intimidating presence as the night the Guild showed up at my house and used it to tear me away from everything. At the same time, it held the same sense of redemption as the night I stole it from the warden to escape from The Deep. It might mean offering myself into the hands of The Guild, but it would save lives.

I drew a final breath and shoved it into the keyhole in reality, turned it, and walked away.

CHAPTER THIRTY-SEVEN

As soon as the Harbingers walked out on the stage, their tight formation spread out and they formed a line that stretched nearly end to end. They each removed their robes and set them aside. They looked human, but they weren't fooling me. It only meant they were using powerful runes to conceal their actual identities. I knew exactly who they were, and my eyes focused in on Spinoza in the middle. His mouth curled up in a nasty smile and I knew this would be bad.

Trying to blend in was no longer either a priority or an option. All that mattered now was minimizing the destruction until the Guild could get there. There was no turning back now. I had used the key, and that was as good as an engraved invitation. Guild Agents would track it and swarm down on this place. As final as it felt, it was exactly what needed to happen. It was entirely possible I was in the last moments of my stolen time in The Near, and I would use them to save as many lives as I possibly could.

Not caring who they were, I started pushing people toward the gate at the end of the peninsula.

"You need to leave. Everybody, get out. Everybody needs to leave the park, now!"

It didn't really surprise me when nobody listened to me or did what I was telling them to. They probably saw me as another raving protester trying to get my way in the political sphere by bullying others. I didn't pause to convince any of them. I kept moving through the crowd, forcing my way closer to the stage while demanding as many people as I could get my hands on to leave. It didn't matter. The cruel yet charismatic Philosopher standing in front of them had already stolen their attention.

He took a step closer to the edge of the stage and lifted his arms toward the sky. Two of the other figures held something large and draped in a tarp between them. They carried it up to Spinoza and set it on the floor in front of him.

"What's that?" somebody in the crowd asked. "What's going on?"

"What the hell is he doing?" somebody else shouted.

"Does anybody know who that is? Is he another candidate?"

The whispers and questions were moving through the crowd at breakneck speed, and I looked up to see all the cameras closely focused on what was happening on the stage. He hadn't said a word, but Spinoza had them all under his spell. Every single person in the park was looking at him, trying to figure out who he was and what he was doing. Nobody seemed to care that nobody knew and that each of his actions was more ominous than the last. He sucked them in, their fascination and morbid curiosity stronger than their instincts to protect themselves.

"Don't look at it," I shouted to everyone who could hear me. "Don't watch him. Get out of the park."

It was useless. Their eyes were drawn to what the Harbinger was doing and no amount of trying to convince them would stop them. I looked up at the stage again. Spinoza grabbed the top of the tarp and whisked it away dramatically, revealing a statue.

"What the hell is that?" somebody asked.

"Is that a...person?"

The statue transfixed everyone in the crowd as they tried to figure out what the hell it was and what it represented. But I knew exactly what it was. This was the rune the Harbingers had been crafting with all the materials that they had bought from Archie and stolen from the others. Something that big would have dire consequences, and it seemed like they weren't slowing down their plan at all.

Spinoza reached behind him with one hand, and another of the Harbingers walked up to him. He had been holding onto his robe since taking it off and now dropped the fabric to reveal a large black urn in his hands. Spinoza held it for a few seconds, increasing the tension and anticipation throughout the crowd. He wanted to completely monopolize the thoughts of every person in the park. The more dramatic he could make it, the less they would focus on anything else. That meant he could reveal himself to a captive audience while also further lessening their ability to escape.

Finally, he opened the urn and tipped it over the top of

the statue. A thick cascade of blood poured out and flowed over the rune. Gasps rippled through the crowd. A few people tried to make their way back toward the entrance gate, but the others were so tightly held by what was happening on stage, they wouldn't move out of the way. I heard some of the onlookers questioning if this was performance art, a demonstration to illustrate the brutality allowed by current politicians.

I wished that was all it was. I wished it wasn't more accurately a glimpse of the bloodshed to come.

I tried pushing my way through the crowd, but it was no use. They were packed like sardines in the middle of the fairway, and I realized pretty quickly my best bet was to keep moving around the edge. Snaking back to the side, I followed the fence until I entered a heavily wooded area that filled in the sides and behind the staging area. I peered through the growth to see how far I had come in my impromptu hike when a massive figure stepped out from behind one thick tree.

I heard Spinoza ranting on stage, his words sounding awfully similar to the writings of Hobbes and the way the Malak spoke right before he carved himself up like a turkey. He was reaching a fever pitch, and the massive figure in front of me squared its shoulders and smiled. He was disguised, but I knew who it was. I had met him before. It was the golem. He took a step toward me, and I reached behind me for my new weapon.

The golem opened his hand, showing a rune of his own. It was a jagged stone that looked almost like he had chipped it off himself, but the teeth embedded in it ended that theory. He activated it by running the pad of his thumb across two of the teeth and the stone seemed to emit a strange light. He touched the rune to a stick he held in his other hand, and it transformed instantly into a heavy-looking spiked club. He tossed the rune into his pocket and the club from hand to hand, showing the lightness of it. He did all this while he made a series of what I assumed were supposed to be menacing faces. Instead, it looked like he had a terrible case of constipation.

Before I could activate my rune, he charged at me while swinging his club wildly. I dodged around him and tried to tackle him from behind. Instead of going down, he shook me hard and sent me flying into another tree. I hit it so hard it temporarily knocked the wind out of me. My locket thrummed against my chest. I coughed and rolled out of the way in time for him to miss a swing with his club, sticking the spikes into the trunk and sending leaves cascading down on both of us.

With a grunt, he pushed his foot against the tree until he wiggled the club loose. By then, I'd already pulled out the rune Archie crafted for me. It looked like little more than the cut-off handle of a broom, but I knew there was more to it than that. It was time for some fireworks. I cracked it in half like a glow stick, activating it in time to turn and show it to the golem. He hesitated at the sight. The rune had created its own beam of red light, but instead of morphing an already existing item, it created one out of thin air. Suddenly, there was a long chain going from the rune through my clenched other hand and down to the ground, where a massive flaming cannonball hung.

It felt light, not entirely weightless, but like I had a tennis ball on a string. I wound it once to get the feel of it, then swung it with more force. The golem watched, mesmerized, as I spun it over my head, the yellow flames dancing off the ball, unperturbed by the wind. I swung it at him, aiming as best I could for his midsection, but the golem instinctively batted it away with his club, sending the ball careening back at me. I ducked and it hit the tree behind me, setting a few leaves aflame and burying itself in the ground. I pulled it out and noted that the flame was still burning as bright as ever when I felt the golem behind me. I leapt forward to roll out of the way, but the club still caught me in the leg, and as I hit the ground, I felt hot, wet blood running down my thigh.

Not even my locket could save me from all damage.

I gritted my teeth through the pain, and stood, applying as little pressure to the leg as I could, and pulled the ball of flame closer to me. Swinging a smaller, tighter arc this time, I locked eyes with the golem. He juked toward me, then fell back, tempting me to swing and miss at him, but I held on and kept the ball in a tight rotation. Beyond the woods, I heard the rally getting more chaotic and intense. Whatever Spinoza planned to try, it would be soon. I had to rid myself of this golem once and for all, and I had to do it now.

Taking a risk that wasn't at all calculated, although I planned to say it was later if I got out of this, I flung the ball at the golem with as much force as I could muster. He made contact again, but this time his club shattered into a million pieces.

Score one point for Archimedes.

I pulled on the chain, guiding the momentum of the golem's attack back around. He grabbed another stick, using his rune to turn it into another weapon, some kind of long axe. But he never got a chance to use it. My weapon swung around like a meteor and there was a sickening thud as the mace crashed into his skull.

He fell to his knees, gripping the axe handle with one hand. He turned halfway toward me, and I could see it hadn't only made a dent, it had caved in one side of his face. And the caved-in side was also on fire. His eyes glazed as he looked into mine. One hand went up to pat the flames in a futile attempt to stop them, then he dropped face-first into the fallen leaves and let out a long, final breath.

As the golem exhaled the last of the air in his stony lungs, I heard a ripple in the crowd, and peered through the trees. Spinoza and the Harbingers with him had removed their disguises. Spinoza was screaming into the mic almost completely unintelligibly, but I made out one word clearly.

"...die!"

CHAPTER THIRTY-EIGHT

That was never something you wanted to hear at a political rally. Especially a political rally taken over by a cult wanting to bring about the end of the world.

While running through the edge of the woods to get closer to the stage, I came to a full stop for a moment as my brain absolutely refused to comprehend what it saw on the other side of the fairway. People were fleeing from the direction of the water, only making the chaos of the crowd worse. Behind them, marching up the bank and into the grass were...pirates? Ghosts? Both?

The water around the peninsula, usually serene and full of children playing and fishermen looking to catch something to brag about, had emptied. What looked like a ship was drifting close to the beach, but there was something wrong with it. Rather than being made of darkened wood or metal, it was hazy and translucent enough for me to see the waves and sunlight beyond it. The men stomping up onto the sand and coming toward the rally with swords held high above their heads shared the general aesthetic.

Freaking ghost pirates. Any hopes of subtlety had gone all to hell.

Splinter ran up to my shoulder and nuzzled my face before leaping to the ground and running away.

Save yourself, little buddy. If I don't get out of this, take over the sewer and become King.

I activated the rune again and felt the chain materialize in my hand. Spinoza and the Harbingers were still on the stage, the mad Philosopher shouting instructions at them. I knew I had to get to him before he wiped everyone out, including me, but the ghost pirates would make that a little more difficult. They were already swarming the park, becoming more solid as they walked, algae-hardened cutlasses swiping at whoever was slow enough to not get out of the way. A security guard tried to fight one off. His fists crashed into the skull and knocked off the bottom part of the jaw, but did nothing to stop its advance. Two more jumped in the air and the three of them tackled the guard to the ground, ruthlessly slashing at him with their rusted blades.

A crowd had formed near the gate's exit, and the pirates were making their advance. I took off for the middle of the two groups, preparing my new rune by swinging it in long, slow loops. One ghost had beaten me to the middle and I flung the chain, the ball sizzling through the air toward the skeletal buccaneer. It crashed into the back of its head and it disintegrated into dust, the rest of the body falling apart in pieces and crumbling into the ground.

Spinning to face the advancing horde, I swung the ball in a long circle. It crashed through several of them, breaking through ribs, legs and arms and turning the skeletons into piles of flaming ash. One had advanced without being hit and was too close now, leaping through the air at me. I pulled out my switchblade and met his cutlass in mid-air. He swung again, thrashing at me, and I parried as best I could. I was terrified and out of my element, and in a sheer panic about reaching Spinoza before he caused any more damage, and yet, somewhere in the back of my mind a little voice was absolutely geeking out. I was currently sword-fighting a freaking pirate skeleton. If I lived through this, I would tell every single person I ever met about the time I beat up ghost pirates.

Maybe I could sell the rights to Johnny Depp.

Thankfully, my geeking out didn't interrupt my survival skills when a second pirate showed up behind me and I instinctively elbowed it in the jaw. While I figured it wouldn't feel pain, it would at least move its attention away from the huddled mass of screaming humans and toward me. I spun and slashed at it, slicing through its center with my blade, and spinning back to the first one. I had pulled the chain of my new rune, and the ball had come back to me. When I yanked it up, the flaming ball split the ghost in two from the crotch upward. It disintegrated into dust and I swung the ball around, taking out a few more pirates along the way.

I was cutting a path through them, swinging the flaming cannonball and the switchblade in alternating swipes. I locked my eyes on Spinoza, and he slowly turned toward me, meeting my gaze. Instantly, a pall came over his face, and he began barking frantic orders at the Harbingers. They were building something on the stage, something massive and powerful, and I knew that whatever it was, I wouldn't live to see it used twice.

A scream from behind me broke my attention, and I saw a second wave of pirates had gotten past me on the sides. They were advancing closer to the humans, who were stampeding at the gates and creating a wall of unmoving mass. I looked back at Spinoza, then spun to the pirates while swinging the ball again.

Flames streamed from it as the ball soared through the air, and it crashed into several ghosts when they were mere feet from the humans. The flame expanded and seemed to take a life of its own, and I realized it was dancing along the pirates as I moved my eyes over them. Where there once was a secondary unit of ghostly pirates was now only smoke and ash.

I turned and locked eyes with Spinoza again and grinned. He wasn't ready yet, and I had wiped out most of the forces he had hoped would distract and terrify people while he built his weapon. A line of the ghost pirates remained standing guard in front of the stage, and I pulled the chain so the cannonball was close to my hand. It surged with energy and the ball of fire blazed painlessly over my arm. An idea struck me, and I ran closer to the stage. The pirates circled me, and I smiled inside. I was getting the hang of this fighting-in-large-groups thing.

CHAPTER THIRTY-NINE

I needed to get to Spinoza and take him out, but the odds weren't exactly in my favor. The Harbingers had no interest in an even close-to-equally matched fight. They wanted to fight dirty, but I'd prepared for battle. The Guild was on its way and there was nothing these Harbingers or their ghost brigade could do to me that was anywhere near what was possible in The Deep. I wouldn't hold anything back.

I jumped and crashed down with the cannonball like I was dunking the world's hottest basketball. It crushed through the pirate I hit and I landed on one knee while pulling the chain up and out, then spinning it in a circle. The pirates who had surrounded me closed in, and I took out a dozen or so of them in one swoop. One broke through the ranks and got in close quarters and I kicked high, sending it flying behind me. I spun the chain around over my head once, then launched it at an oncoming pirate. The flame buzzed as it burned through the air and spread as the ball buried itself in the figure, sending it backward into two others.

But even with my new weapon, the numbers were against me. Something hard and boney crashed into my head and I fell forward. I rolled onto my back as a pirate landed on top of me, chomping at me with a mouth that was missing several of its teeth and smelled like a drawer full of dirty gym socks. I grabbed its arm in one hand as it tried to skewer me with its cutlass. With my switchblade in my other hand, I stabbed again and again at his shoulder until his arm ripped from his body. The hand and cutlass came off in my grip and the pirate lost balance, falling onto me.

"Sorry, not on the first date." I kicked him off, then brought the sword down in the center of his skull.

I stood and looked around at what remained of the pirates, trying to find Spinoza. He was no longer near the podium and had positioned himself behind the weapon they were building. It looked like a demented satellite dish, and was aimed at the rune statue. Spinoza was fiddling with something behind it and I knew my time had basically run out. Whatever they'd designed that thing to do, he would activate it in a few moments and all of my awesome pirate fighting stories would be heard by no one.

Three of the pirates charged me. I ducked, allowing them to crash into each other. I spun the chain and wrapped it around all three of their necks before yanking it backward. Their heads popped off and the cannonball soared behind me, blowing a hole through one of them and burying itself into another.

There were only a few left now. I pulled the chain, yanking the ball close to me as I stalked toward the stage. The fight with the minions was over, whether they liked it or not, and I would get to Spinoza now. One of the pirates came at me from my left, and I stabbed through its skull without looking. I held the ball close to my hand, and as a screaming pirate approached to my right, I shot-put it toward him, exploding his face in a ball of flame, then yanked the chain to get the ball back to me.

I put the switchblade back in my pocket. Two more pirates charged me from directly in front and I grabbed the chain with both hands, winging it at their legs. It wrapped around them, and I continued walking to the stage. As I approached the fallen, tangled pirates, I stomped on their heads, crushing them to dust below my heel. The locket had plenty of power left, and I began to all-out run toward the stage, yanking the chain behind me. The ball soared to me as if summoned and hovered above my hand until I clasped the chain right below it. The fire sparked and grew higher, and I jumped onto the stage. Spinoza's face was a mixture of terror and surprise, and a wall of Harbingers closed in to protect him.

The Harbingers charged me, and I began throwing fists. The cannonball flew from my hand and crashed into the podium, exploding it into a thousand pieces. It had barely missed a nasty-looking ogre. As I reached to pull it back, another hit me hard in the back. I flew to the edge of the stage, and as I stood, I realized that I had lost my grip on it. I searched around for it, but it had gotten lost in the chaos. My rune was missing.

I didn't have time to worry about that yet since there were various Harbingers bearing down on me. I rolled to my side and pulled out my trusty switchblade. Time to go old-school. I swept my leg out and tripped a tall satyr, sending her headfirst off the stage and into a tangle of chairs and teleprompting equipment. Getting to my knees, I slashed a goblin at waist height and spilled his guts everywhere. He fell to the floor of the stage, holding his insides close as he screamed in pain.

Shooting up as fast as I could, I brought the top of my head into contact with the nose of another ogre who had gotten within striking distance. The crunch of his nose filled my ears as I grabbed his shirt and pulled him forward into my knee. I smashed his ribs twice before grabbing the back of his head and ramming my knee into his face. He went down in a heap and I spun to gain momentum to kick him behind the ear, sending him into the sleepy realm of a dreaming ogre. A dreaming ogre who would feel like his brain was full of bees when he woke up.

There was no time to feel good about my situation, though, as the stage filled with more Harbingers. Some were trolls, some were weirdly human-looking, others were rare creatures I had only heard about, and there was even an evil squid-looking thing lumbering around in the back of the group. They outnumbered me—by a lot—and I couldn't find my mace. I scanned as quickly as I could and thought I saw something flash on the ground, several feet away. There were a couple of bad guys in the way, but since that was my only chance, I had to take the attack to them.

I drove my shoulder into a disturbingly spongy chest and turned to punch another in the jaw. Spinning back to the other side, I kicked forward like I was trying to break down a door and crushed a few ribs of another Harbinger.

The first one, a creature that looked like amphibious evolution in reverse, grabbed my shoulders and tried to ram his head into mine. I moved it to the side and tried to grab him in a submission hold, but slimy skin that would be far more comfortable in a lagoon somewhere made it impossible to grip him effectively. As he surged forward again and crashed his forehead into my neck, I made a decision I knew my taste buds would regret as long as I lived. I bit down on his ear and ripped it off his body. The frogman screamed and released me to hold his ear, and I used the opportunity to uppercut him in the jaw and send him to the ground.

Mike Tyson would be so proud.

I knelt to grab the cannonball, but as my fingers reached it, a kick to my stomach made my entire body lock up and fall over. Fists rained down on and around me as I tried to cover up with one arm and reach for the rune with the other. I felt the tip of it in one hand and was about to pull it to me when I saw the flash of a blade in the goblin's hand on top of me. I narrowly avoided it by rolling away from the rune, and I bucked him completely off by smashing my fist into his side as hard as I could.

As I scrambled to my feet, I shook off another one that was trying to grab me by my arms and elbowed another in the nose that ran toward me. I was being pulled away from the cannonball and I tried desperately to make it back when I saw it rise, held by one of the Harbingers.

"No," I yelled as he smashed it to the ground, then

brought a heavy mallet to it, shattering it into thousands of tiny pieces.

A fist connected with my jaw from somewhere in the melee around me and I felt my knees go weak. My locket worked overtime, but I felt its power waning. As I stumbled backward, a kick landed on my hip and I flew across the stage, sputtering to a stop near the edge.

There were too many of them, and they were too strong, and I was now without a weapon that could stop them. There was no way I could stop Spinoza or his doomsday device without it. All I could hope now was that I would go down fighting, and that my death would be quick and heroic.

At least I got to fight some ghost pirates.

Suddenly, I thought I heard my name being called behind me. Assuming it was the desperate plea of my brain, trying to cue up the old life-flashing-before-your-eyes moment, I ignored it on general principle. I had no desire to see a home movie that mainly comprised me and Splinter hanging out in some dank prison cells. Then I heard it again, and I recognized the voice. It was Archie.

I turned as best I could to see him leaping onto the stage, something I could only assume was another of his runes in his hand. Either that or he had come to the fight armed with a pink and green Super Ball, and I really didn't want to think that was the case.

Behind him, Ally hopped up too, one ball in each of her hands. Archie charged into the Harbingers while activating his rune, which seemed to turn his fists purple as they grew three times their normal size. *Nice homage to Thrash. Way to channel past traumas for productive use.* He swung inexpertly at the Harbingers, flailing at them and contacting shoulders, thighs and the occasional chest, but it was enough to get them to fall back on that side. Ally activated the two runes she had, and suddenly she had hands made of pure fire. She pushed one hand out and a small fireball shot from it, hitting one Harbinger with enough force to knock her down, and lighting her shirt on fire. She frantically patted it until it went out, then scurried back to gain her bearings.

The two of them were absolutely stupid for coming to my rescue, and I loved them for it. There was no way they could beat these guys with the runes they had, but it had given me a moment to catch my breath, gain my bearings and get to my feet. While rubbing away the blood that trickled from my mouth, I looked over at Ally, who was firing fireballs at random and giggling like a drunken madman.

"Are you sure you should be playing with fire?" I yelled over the sounds of the chaos while pulling the switchblade from my back pocket.

"Are you sure you should be standing there yakking while I save the world?" she yelled back before dissolving into another fit of laughter as she shot out more fireballs. "Magic is amazing."

I flicked open my switchblade and charged forward, hope and love for my best friend suddenly filling me with a strength I didn't know I had left. I tore through the Harbingers in my way, slashing and cutting anything that moved, and sawing a path to the wizard Spinoza. One last Harbinger stood before me, a cyclops who was holding a piece of the giant rune in place. I jumped on his back and rammed the blade into his eye, sending him crashing to the ground. I jumped off before he hit and rolled to a stop in front of Spinoza. Standing up, I locked eyes with him again.

He turned on his heel and ran.

CHAPTER FORTY

"We're too late!" Archie called. "The spell has already begun."

"What spell? What's the spell?"

"The pirate army was a distraction. It's time for the real show. He didn't want this to be a quick reveal. He's not going for a press conference effect. The ghosts put down the foundation of terror. His spell starts Phase 2."

"Let me guess, Phase 2 doesn't revolve around rainbows and sunshine."

"What happens when blood gets into the ocean?"

"Sharks come."

"That was a lot of blood he poured on that rune," Archie pointed out.

"Are you telling me sharks will come up out of the water?"

"In a way. They're ripping open a hole between worlds. They're staging a breakout in The Deep."

I staggered at the weight of his words. The Deep, the home of every hell imaginable, unleashed upon The Near.

You could say goodbye to Charleston and most of the eastern seaboard. And also home to Hobbes' most devoted and demonic followers. Forget an opening salvo, Spinoza and his goons were trying to win the war before it began.

"Tell me how to stop it."

"I don't know—"

"Tell me how, dammit. There must be a way."

Archie turned back toward the doomsday rune.

"Maybe if you kill Spinoza, it will weaken the spell enough for me to break it, but I can't be sure."

"You keep your ass here," I shouted over my shoulder as I turned to run. "Do what you can to stop this thing."

"What about you?" he cried.

"I'm going hunting."

I chased in the direction Spinoza had run, hopping over fallen Harbingers and pushing through the chaos of equipment set up for the rally. I'd cleared a chair at my feet and rounded the corner of the stage, heading toward the crowd, when an ogre blocked my path by shoving me into the stage wall and jumping down on top of me.

I tried to block his fists, but he got a couple of shots in before I could grab his arm as it crashed down toward my face. I snapped my hips to quickly change position, and his fist shoved down into the grass. Flipping backward, I held onto his wrist and tucked his arm between my legs while thrusting my hips up and falling backward. I felt his shoulder snap as I hit the ground, and I rolled off, determined not to let him slow me down any further.

Ahead of me, I saw Spinoza had turned back to watch. He must have been hopeful the surprise ogre attack would stop me because the look on his face when I stood was one of shock and defeat. There were no more Harbingers between us now, and he had nowhere left to run but toward the crowd of humans still stampeding to get out of the park. He looked around frantically, and I followed his gaze.

The destruction around us was incredible. Ghost pirates were still scattered among the humans, wreaking havoc wherever they went. Several of the humans had taken the chance to fight back, but without weapons, many of them were only delaying the inevitable. Harbingers were still fighting Ally and Archie on the stage, and many had siphoned off and were heading toward Spinoza and me. The endgame for their plan was here and killing me was the only chance they had at realizing it. Humans were fighting each other at the gate, pushing and screaming to get out while they still could. Some had taken to the woods, where Harbingers lay in wait, and there were sounds of fighting and slaughter coming from that direction too.

All around me was the chaos this war would bring, the suffering that the battles would cause, and the destruction of the normalcy that would never again be. I thought of my family, and how I had tried to protect them from this realm, and this war, and knew that Spinoza, even if his weapon hadn't worked, had already levied the first shot. If The Near was going to survive this, I had to play my part.

And that meant ending Spinoza.

I brushed my thumb over my blade while taking a moment to channel Solon, then threw the blade sidearm. It spun through the air and buried itself in the soft place where Spinoza's neck met his shoulder. He dropped to his knees as I heard footsteps pounding behind me.

The Harbingers' reinforcements had arrived, and while I saw Ally and Archie chasing them toward me, they would reach me first. I readied myself for the fight, and as the first wave of them came, kicked and punched and screamed, no weapons but the locket and the skills Solon had imparted to me. I locked arms with an elf—evil woodfolk, not the Keebler kind. He and I tumbled to the ground and threw fists at each other. I had given up on defense, wanting nothing more than to hurt these things threatening my home.

He pulled a long, curved copper blade, but I wrenched it from his hand and shoved it deep into his throat.

"Go back to whatever twisted-ass spooky forest you came from," I snapped at him.

Greenish blood spewed out at me as I severed an artery, and I stood to catch a satyr as he dove at me. I lifted my foot to plant the heel in his face as he went vertical, and the impact knocked me back a step, forcing me to fall to protect myself.

As I stood, the satyr whose face I had rearranged did as well. He pulled his arms back in a complicated motion I could only assume was some sort of Far karate stance and let out a war cry that sounded more like a 1950s housewife seeing a mouse scurry across a kitchen. Combined with his distinctly goat-like characteristics, it broke some of the tension and I laughed at him. This did little to endear me to him.

As he was about to run toward me, his body went stock-still and his eyes widened. Very slowly, he tipped over, falling directly on top of the unfortunate elf who was now missing a large section of his throat. As he fell, I saw Ally standing behind him, her hands positioned like a character from *Street Fighter* and smoke coming from her fingers. I looked down at the Karate Goat again and saw that he had a singed hole in his back the size of a basketball hoop.

"I didn't want to yell 'hadouken' and let him know I was behind him. But you saw it, right?" Ally was positively beaming, and she winked at me as she stood more fully.

"Ken or Ryu?"

"Ken. Always Ken. Geez, it's like you don't even know me."

Suddenly, she spun and shot another fireball at an oncoming goblin that was sneaking up on me from the side. Archie appeared beside her and used his giant purple Hulk hands to whack another that was sneaking up on Ally. It looked like we made a decent team. Archie nodded at me, and I turned my attention back to Spinoza. Ally and Archie could keep my back clear. I trusted them to do that. But Spinoza was all for me.

As I stepped toward him, Spinoza laughed, slowly at first, then louder as I got close. By the time I was within a few feet he was cackling, his head thrown back and his mouth wide, like he was trying to force his laughter as far into the sky as he could. But the sound was garbled and choked from the hole in his neck. His arms were limp by his sides, and blood soaked his chest. His suit was muddied and full of sand from falling down in the fairway. I cocked my head to one side in confusion. What the hell was he laughing at?

"Spinoza, it's over. This whole war, it's over. Tell me where Hobbes is and I'll kill you quickly."

The laughter continued unabated. Either he hadn't heard me, or he didn't care. It got so forceful that he coughed violently, unable to control both the laughter and the cough. After a few moments, it died down, and I tried again.

"Spinoza, it's over. Tell me wh—" I began.

"Nothing is over. Nothing will be over until The Near is destroyed. Hobbes has foretold it, and it will be true. Sara Slick, you will watch it all fall," he forced through the bubbling blood in his throat.

I pulled my switchblade out of him angrily, prepared to use it again, to end this man now before he babbled any further, but his eyes locked onto mine and all joviality seemed to cease. Resentment and condescension replaced it in his voice.

"You can't kill me, Sara Slick. Not if you want to know the truth. I know who you are."

"What truth?" My heart beat faster. He could be lying to save his skin. He could be using this opportunity to distract me so he could survive another day, then try to murder me again tomorrow.

"What truth?" I demanded.

The smile returned to his lips and he rocked back on his heels. Ally and Archie now joined me at my back, and I turned to survey the field. The Harbingers that were still alive had ceased fighting and were kneeling toward Spinoza. Something was happening. Something big.

"What. Truth." My voice came out almost as a whisper,

but anger and frustration filled every syllable. "Tell me or die, right now."

"I know the truth about Hobbes. And you. And I know why you were framed."

The words collided into me like I had been hit with a mountain of bricks. The son of a bitch knew I didn't do it. A cruel choice lay at my feet. Time was ticking on the spell he'd cast with the enormous bloody rune. It wouldn't be long before The Deep cracked open and flooded the park with resentful, tormented creatures ready to destroy. The only way to stop it was to kill him. I was choosing between saving thousands of lives and finally knowing why ten years of my life had been taken from me.

And he knew it.

"If you kill me, you will never know," his voice came out like a serpent, and his head fell back again.

The laughter that came from him this time was deeper and richer, the sound of someone who believes they have won. The laugh of someone who knows more than their enemy. The laugh of a victor.

Too bad he was wrong.

I pulled him close and looked into his eyes, wanting to make sure he heard me clearly.

"I don't need you," I said through gritted teeth. "Do you understand me? I don't need you. I know who I am. *I* am the heinous Sara Slick."

I grabbed his shirt with one hand and lifted him from the ground as my blade sank smoothly into the soft place below his chest. I pulled it up with a sharp motion, slicing anything that got in my way. He smiled through the blood pouring over his lips and down the front of his shirt.

"It doesn't matter," he croaked out. "I've fulfilled my mission. The world knows about us now. The *Pax* dies here today."

"The only thing dying here today is you." I gave the blade an extra plunge for good measure. "I called the Philosopher's Guild before you started. They're probably already here cleaning up your mess." I leaned down closer, my face only inches from his. "You died for nothing."

I wrenched my blade from his chest and let Spinoza's body collapse at my feet.

CHAPTER FORTY-ONE

After wiping the blood off my switchblade, I turned and looked for Ally and Archie. They had disappeared back into the chaos. People were running in every direction, some screaming and crying, others walking aimlessly, their minds incapable of processing what they'd experienced. The number of people crushed into the park didn't seem to have decreased, and when I looked back toward the entrance gates, I saw why.

The gates were firmly closed and when the few people who wandered up to them tugged on them, they didn't move. As soon as they yanked, people I recognized as agents of the Guild stepped in front of them and wiped their memories, then slid them through the gates and released them into the world beyond. I didn't know what was going through their minds now that they were essentially waking up wandering away from the park with no concept of what brought them there. But as long as it wasn't thoughts of the statue covered with blood or the battle I'd fought, it was fine.

Sometimes a little forgetting is good medicine.

I finally found Archie and Ally in the center of a cluster of people. They seemed to be trying to block the view of something on the ground. As I rushed up to them, I realized it didn't matter how close I got, I still couldn't identify the somewhat mushy mound between them. Ally noticed me and reached for me. I took her hands and she pulled me in for a tight hug.

"Are you all right?" I asked.

"I'm fine. Are you?"

"Perfect. Archie?"

"Living the dream." He looked around and occasionally shifted his position to further block what was on the ground.

I decided I wasn't going to ask. There was literally no answer he could give me that would make the situation any better. I heard a familiar squeaking sound and looked down at my feet. Splinter was running around, weaving in and out in a figure-eight position and chattering happily. It was like he was telling me about the whole battle from his perspective. Relief rushed through me. As much as I liked the idea of him living out his life as the revered and pampered King of the Sewer, I would much rather him be with me.

"Splinter! I'm glad nobody stepped on you."

He bared his teeth and stretched out his weird little arm flaps like he was sharing war stories with me. I reached down and scooped him up, giving him a little cuddle before putting him into my pocket and patting him. Hopefully, there were still a few crumbs in the bottom that he could snack on while he took his much-deserved break.

"Did you do what you had to do?" Archie asked.

I nodded.

"Spinoza is gone. Before I killed him, he told me he knew why I was framed."

"The Harbingers know you didn't do it."

"Seems that way."

Before the conversation could continue, I looked up and saw Bentham coming toward me, flanked by several other members of the Guild. They were fighting their way through the crowd at an alarming rate.

"Shit."

"What the hell are they doing here?" Archie asked.

Ally glanced around. "Who? Ally asked. What's going on?"

"It's the Philosophers Guild," I told her as I grabbed their arms and led them away. "I kind of called them here."

"Why would you do that?" Archie was horrified. "You know what they'll do."

"Yes." I spoke firmly. "They'll wipe the memories of all these humans so they don't have to remember what they saw. By now, I'm sure they blocked the broadcast so no one else could see what happened. They'll preserve the *Pax*."

"And they'll take you back to The Deep," Archie said.

"That's a risk I had to take. Walk faster."

I turned back, and Bentham's eyes met mine.

Double shit.

"Run," Ally ordered. "Now."

I nodded, then looked around for escape. At this point, getting through the gates wasn't an option. All I could do was scramble over one of the security fences and hope I made it out. I turned around and looked at Archie and Ally one last time.

"Ally, do you remember your first kiss?" I shouted as I ran.

"Yes?" She looked back, obviously confused by my sudden need for nostalgia.

"Remember the tree and meet me at the end of the street. Outside the city limits."

Without waiting for a response, I took off running as fast as I could. It wasn't fast enough. I had made it to the edge of the crowd and was starting for the orange security fence when something hit me from behind and I stumbled. I got to my feet with my back against a support beam for a disabled camera. Bentham stepped close to me.

"We meet again. I have to admit, Sara Slick, I didn't think I would find you alive."

"You have to let me go."

"Oh, do I? You're a fugitive. You escaped from The Deep and you still have quite a bit of your sentence to serve. From what I see, I have no choice but to arrest you."

"I am innocent. Everything people thought I did, all the crimes that got me sentenced to The Deep. I didn't do any of them. The Harbingers know that. They framed me. Or at least Hobbes did. You're coming after the wrong guy."

"It's not my job to determine your innocence. It's only my job to bring you in."

I felt Splinter leave my pocket and watched out of the corner of my eye as he approached the Philosopher.

"Don't you care that I didn't do what everyone says I did? Doesn't it mean anything that my family was framed for horrible crimes and I spent ten years of my life serving in a prison where no human has ever gone, much less survived, while the real villain is out running around causing shit like this?"

"The Guild didn't send me to find out if you had done wrong and to clear you if you didn't. My job is to catch you."

"You need a better job."

Splinter scrambled up the back of her leg and disappeared.

"I am very good at what I do. If I weren't, you wouldn't be so concerned right now."

"You won't stop me. I'll prove my innocence."

"It will be very hard for you to do that once I throw you back into The Deep."

I felt Splinter crawl back into my pocket and I reached in. His tiny little rat hands offered me something, and I felt a smooth orb clutched in them. My heart swelled. I knew I loved that little bugger, and I had never been more grateful for him than I was in that moment.

"You'll have to catch me first."

I withdrew the marble from my pocket and threw it hard onto the ground at my feet. The massive bang made the ground shudder and the smoke billowed up around me, concealing everything. I ducked into the thickest part of the smoke and ran through it, trusting my instincts to bring me away from the Philosophers and into the depths of the trees. I forced myself through them, reached the fence, and scrambled over it.

I was out. I was safe. At least for now.

CHAPTER FORTY-TWO

Getting out of the park didn't stop the desperation in my escape. I kept running, pushing past everyone who had gotten through the crowds and out of the rally, going as fast as I could until I was away from it all. My pace barely slowed until the energy in my locket gave out. I felt like my lungs were going to explode. I dropped to a jog, then to a speed-walk so I could drag in as much oxygen as possible. When I felt like I had gotten some control over myself, I started running again. This time, I didn't slow until I was nearly at the hotel.

The parking lot was empty, but I flicked my eyes around it, delving into the shadowy corners and overgrown spots to make sure no one else was there. Part of me expected to see the crew that attacked Dog and me coming back for another round, but the other part of me said even they wouldn't be that stupid. We put them through the wringer, and it would probably take them more than a couple of days to recover enough to want more.

I debated the benefits of going into my room and staying outside the building. I wanted to get my stuff packed and be on my way as soon as I could and definitely didn't want to be out in the open in case the Guild happened by. At the same time, going into the hotel would make it much harder for Ally and Archie to find me. That kept me pacing back and forth at the entrance as I mentally reviewed my clue to Ally. I hoped she could figure it out and wasn't at this moment standing under the magnolia tree in the backyard of her childhood home rather than coming to the end of Magnolia Street.

After what felt like far too long, I heard footsteps pounding on the pavement coming toward me and saw Archie and Ally duck through the broken section of the fence. I ran toward them, and we met in the middle of the parking lot.

"Oh my gosh, you made it, Slick." Ally gathered me into a tight hug. "I was so scared."

"I wasn't exactly tiptoeing through daisies myself. Come on. Come with me."

"What is this place?" Archie looked around skeptically. "Where are we going?"

I brought them through the front entrance of the hotel and spread my arms at my sides.

"Welcome to my humble abode. Well, what used to be."

"What are you talking about?" Ally sounded confused.

I led them through the lobby and down the hall to my room.

"I have to leave. The Philosophers Guild knows where I am now. I have to keep moving."

"This is where you've been staying? You chose a creepy-ass abandoned hotel over staying with me? I have to admit that I'm a little offended, Slick."

"It was better this way. Staying here meant the Guild wouldn't target you if they showed up. They wouldn't be able to invade and destroy your home if they didn't know where it was or that it had anything to do with me. Besides, compared to where I've spent the last ten years, this is Club Med. If I had taken you up on your invitation to stay at your place, I might never have left."

She grinned.

"That might not have been such a bad thing."

I shoved my clothes into a satchel I'd gotten at the thrift store, added my trusty bar of hotel soap, and tossed it all over my shoulder.

"I have to go."

"We've been discussing that." Archie stepped into my path so I couldn't get to the door.

"What do you mean you've been discussing it? You know as well as I do, I have to leave. The Philosophers Guild saw me. I faced off against Bentham. The only reason I got away is because my brilliant Splinter stole one of her exploding marbles. They're probably already tracking me."

"Which is exactly why you can't go by yourself," Archie insisted.

"What are you talking about?"

"We want to help," Ally told me.

I shook my head and tried to dip around Archie to get to the door.

"Absolutely not."

Archie shifted, forcing me to step back.

"Hobbes and his cult won't stop. Which means the world is in danger. As long as the Philosophers Guild are failing at their job, the world needs a badass protecting it."

"And that badass will need a top-notch investigator," Ally pointed out.

"And weapons maker," Archie added.

"It's too dangerous," I started, but Ally stepped close to me and stopped me.

She was holding her phone again, and she held it up so I could see the image on it. It was my family.

"Look at this. This is why you're doing this. You're doing it for them."

My hands trembled as I took the phone from her and sat on the end of the bed to keep staring at it.

"My dad has gray hair," I murmured, touching my fingertips to the picture and the silver streaks through the once-dark hair at his temples.

"He's ten years older. But he still hosts a cookout every Fourth of July and challenges all the neighborhood kids to a hula hoop contest. He still makes the best lemonade in the world. He's still an amazing father to your siblings."

I choked back tears.

"Look at them. I barely recognize them."

My eyes fell on Mia, but I didn't mention I'd already seen her. I wanted to keep those moments for myself.

"They had to grow up without you, but they're strong. They're smart and they're talented and funny. You know, Violet graduated college this year. Top of her class. She wrote your name on her cap."

"You're really going for all the heartstrings, aren't you?"

"Sometimes you have to pull out the big guns."

"And maybe one more big gun," Archie added.

I hadn't realized he'd left the room until I heard him come in again. He walked up and into the sliver of sunlight coming through the curtains, and I saw it. Gripped in his hand, held out to me in offering, was a sight so beautiful it made my breath catch in my chest.

"Tacos!" I gushed.

I grabbed the bag and pulled it toward me, opening it and closing my eyes as I breathed deeply, filling my lungs with the delicious scent.

"It's only Taco Bell," Archie advised.

"But... They're tacos."

"Can we at least eat outside?" Ally shifted. "The atmosphere is getting to me a little."

I didn't want to leave the security of the room but was willing to up my risk a little for the promise of tacos. We laughed and moved around to the back of the hotel so we wouldn't be visible from the street. As we sat on the pavement, each of us grabbed a taco out of the bag. I inhaled the first one, offering Splinter the pieces of shell and lettuce that crumbled down into my lap, but slowed down for the second. It was so glorious, I almost felt like I was in a trance. It took Archie's jaded voice to snap me out of it.

"These suck."

"What do you mean?" I finished my third taco and started on my fourth. "They're delicious."

"No, they aren't. They're Taco Bell. They aren't authentic at all."

"Authentic?"

"Yeah. There are much better tacos out there."
My eyes snapped to him, my expression serious.
"Show me," I demanded.

EPILOGUE

The door to the hidden chamber had barely closed before the robed figure let out an angry growl.

"I'm sorry, but Spinoza's plan failed. You planned everything so carefully. I can't believe the fool messed it up."

"It's not to worry, Aldrich," Hobbes said in a calm, even voice. "The crack is thinning, even now. There are plenty of those inspired by my words, powerful allies that we can call upon."

"I don't know." Aldrich shook his head as he paced back and forth across the stone room.

"Do you doubt me?"

Aldrich froze.

"Of course not."

Hobbes smiled, assuaged by the declaration.

"Good. Because it's time for us to move forward. This Sara Slick has served her usefulness. It's time to bury her once and for all."

The End

A dead body. A strange cult. A terrified people.
Sounds like the perfect place for the Heinous Sara Slick.
Continue the adventures in *Kill the Wild!*

Oh hey!

The book's done, but before you leave I just wanted to take a second to share an important message:

THANK YOU. THANK YOU. THANK YOU!

Ahem. I mean, ya know...thanks.

You've just finished *Escape the Deep*, book one of *The Heinous Crimes of Sara Slick*, a series we've been working on for a while now, and I couldn't be happier that you decided to pick it up. I absolutely love Slick. Not just her grit and determination, or her badass left hook, but the thing that I like the best is her positive attitude in light of all the crap that goes on in her world. She's determined to enjoy the life she's got, no matter what.

A lesson I sorely need sometimes.

I guess I should introduce myself, I'm Lee, one half of the writing team that makes up ST Branton (my other half, Chris Raymond, will introduce himself in the next book). If you followed us here from one of our other series (maybe *Forgotten Gods* or *The Rise of Magic* or *Steel City*

Heroes), then you already know the drill (and a special thanks for sticking with us), but if you're new, I just wanted to extend a special welcome to this world.

Chris and I have been writing together for almost five years now, and we're just warming up. And the thing that sustains our writing career is the fact that you all keep reading. So maybe take a second and head on over to Amazon to let us know what you think.

And if you liked the book, you should come talk to us over at our Facebook page. Sara Slick has three more books slated for release this summer, and that's the best place to get news and updates about the series (and ya know, a good place to say hi).

Oh, and one last favor you could do for us: tell your friends! Word of mouth trumps any other form of advertising. So spread the world!

Just don't break the *Pax Philosophica* to do it.

Lee

PS: Want to hear more from us? Sign up for our newsletter and also receive a FREE copy of *The Devil's Due*, our fast and fun thriller:

https://www.subscribepage.com/chris_and_lee

Sign up for Chris and Lee's newsletter for updates, new releases, and promotions. When you join the community, you'll get a FREE copy of their fast, fun thriller, *The Devil's Due:* https://www.subscribepage.com/chris_and_lee

Want more snarky heroines? Well, Chris and Lee also have an urban fantasy series about the mythic gods return to earth in their series with ST Branton, *Forgotten Gods.* The tagline is: *The gods are real, and they're assholes.* And it couldn't be closer to the truth. This series is fun, fast, exciting, and a little irreverent.

Vampires, werewolves, and all manner of monstrous creatures serve the unknown powers of old, but the story centers on the humans who make the heroic choice to fight them. Join Vic and her crew as they attempt to save earth from the gods who want it back. You won't forget, Forgotten Gods.

Oh, and… it is an 8 book omnibus almost always on sale for silly cheap!

While you're at it, we really thing you should try the new and improved *Steel City Heroes*:

A mad scientist fighting the laws of man and nature.

A demon-monster of mythical proportions.

A corporate conspiracy that goes back more than a century.

The Steel City is in desperate need of a hero.

Happy Reading!!

Steel City Heroes Saga

Catalyst
Buy Catalyst

Corrosion
Buy Corrosion

Crucible
Coming Soon

Casting
Coming Soon

Jack Carson Stories

The Devil's Due
Buy The Devil's Due

The Devil's Wager
Buy The Devil's Wager

The Rise of Magic
* With Michael Anderle *

Restriction (01)